江苏省高校哲学社会科学基金项目(批准号:07SJD750028)

Possibility of Transcending:
Chaucer as an Intellectual

超越的可能：作为知识分子的乔叟

丁建宁　著

图书在版编目(CIP)数据

超越的可能:作为知识分子的乔叟/丁建宁著. —北京:北京大学出版社,2010.11
(文学论丛)
ISBN 978-7-301-18058-7

Ⅰ. 超… Ⅱ. 丁… Ⅲ. 乔叟,G.(约1340～1400)－诗歌－文学研究 Ⅳ. I561.072

中国版本图书馆 CIP 数据核字(2010)第 218600 号

书　　名:超越的可能:作为知识分子的乔叟
著作责任者:丁建宁　著
责 任 编 辑:黄瑞明
标 准 书 号:ISBN 978-7-301-18058-7/H·2688
出 版 发 行:北京大学出版社
地　　　址:北京市海淀区成府路 205 号　100871
网　　　址:http://www.pup.cn　电子信箱:zpup@pup.pku.edu.cn
电　　　话:邮购部 62752015　发行部 62750672　编辑部 62754382
　　　　　　出版部 62754962
印 刷 者:三河市北燕印装有限公司
经 销 者:新华书店
　　　　　　650 毫米×980 毫米　16 开本　11.5 印张　200 千字
　　　　　　2010 年 11 月第 1 版　2010 年 11 月第 1 次印刷
定　　　价:28.00 元

未经许可,不得以任何方式复制或抄袭本书之部分或全部内容。
版权所有,侵权必究
举报电话:(010)62752024　电子信箱:fd@pup.pku.edu.cn

序　言

丁建宁同志的博士论文经过修订，即将由北京大学出版社出版，嘱我写序。作为她的论文指导教师，我欣然从命。

记得当初丁建宁和我联系，报考博士研究生时，国内英语语言文学专业的博士点数量还不多，华东师大的生源也相对较好，指导教师选择的余地大。因此，这一年开始，我明确要求，如果希望我指导论文，就请研究中世纪英国文学，她接受了这个挑战。

我希望博士生去做中世纪英国文学研究，一方面是因为自己的博士论文是在这个领域，另一方面也是因为国内中世纪英国文学研究者偏少，需要加强力量。对于后者，我想多说几句。中国是人口大国，近年来高校的发展和变化，造成英国文学研究者队伍不断扩容。部分研究领域可能已经人满为患。与此同时，仍然有一些领域问津者寥寥。做学问是要关心学术人口学的，它是一种生产劳动，要讲究劳动效率和产出。一个特定领域研究的人多了，可能会带来学术的繁荣，可能会多出一些专著和文章，但同时也会有负面的作用，会付出人才和人力浪费的代价。现在有些研究领域，不是参与者人数越多越好，而是研究者个体的学术研究水平需要提高。况且，即使研究者学术水平都很高，也不一定保证人人都能开辟新的领域，或有新的发现。

对于这一点，德裔美国学者汉娜·阿兰特（Hannah Arendt，1906—1975）说过：

有一些研究领域，现在只能做到博学，却不停地、无意义地要求原创性学术,这或者导致地地道道的离题万里,即众所周知的那种对越来越无足轻重的研究对象日甚一日地刨根究底,或者导致伪学术的发展,从而事实上毁掉了学术研究本身。

(The ceaseless, senseless demand for original scholarship in a number of fields, where only erudition is now possible, has led either to sheer irrelevancy, the famous knowing of more and more about less and less, or to the development of a pseudo-scholarship which actually destroys its object.)

引用阿兰特的话,并非要给学术创新泼冷水,而是要说明学术创新不容易,有时甚至不太可能。中国的英国文学研究整体上说,还远没有到"只能做到博学"的地步,而一些领域研究者过多,大大压缩了个体学术创新的空间,却是应该引起注意的。因此,除非有特殊的理由,要少在学术研究领域使用人海战术,要关注不该冷落但实际被冷落的领域,如中世纪英国文学。从国家人才培养合理性的层面来说,研究中世纪英国文学,不是钻冷门,而是需要。这一点,入学时的丁建宁同志亦表示认同。

学术研究本身,是不分国界的。国内似乎是冷门,国际上很可能是热门。中世纪英国文学研究的情况就是如此。因此,这又不是热门冷门、人多人少的问题。作为一名学者,如果希望自己的研究真正具有某种意义,就应该让自己的视野超越国界,不投机取巧,不瞒天过海,不夜郎自大,尽力使得学术研究有一些价值。丁建宁同志勤于思索,为此用力甚勤。

进入新领域的丁建宁,入学之后遇到种种困难。她要迅速进入研究领域,大量阅读中世纪文本,积累研究的基础,尽早熟悉学术研究前沿。同时,作为读博的在职人员,她要承担原单位繁重的教学任务;作为妻子和母亲,她在家庭中依然要承担种种责任和事务。但她的一个最大优点,是关键时刻终不放弃。论文做得很苦,时间也长,但心态是积极的,目标是明确的,即尽可能使研究有一些价值。2004年,牛津大学麦尔科姆·戈登教授(Malcolm Godden)专程来上海为华东师大英语系中世纪方向的研究生开设系列讲座时,主持了她的论文开题报告,对她的探索精神和研究思路甚为赞赏。为了写好论文,她前往北京中国社科院外文所学习和研究半年,广泛求教国内一流学者,后又两次去英国牛津大学,一次为撰写博士论文在牛津大学英文系做了半年研究,另一次是提交论文后收到邀请,去参加中世纪文学研究国际学术会议。六年的时间,终于磨成一剑!

再说几句关于她的论著的话。受当代思想界知识分子研究的启发,丁建宁从知识分子的角度,重新阅读乔叟其人其作,揭示了作为知识分子的乔叟,所体现的一些超越时代的特征。这在西方乔叟研究领域,还没有谁如此明确地提出来和尝试过。她又将乔叟和中国封建社会的"士"进行比较,探讨英国中世纪身兼宫廷官员和文学家双重身份的乔叟所具有的知识分子特点,并且结合作品进行了新的阐述,从而又使乔叟研究获得了中国审视角度。如此转换研究的视角,言人所未言,且自成一说,就是我们所说的创新。它对西方中世纪英语文学研究长期以来的思维定式进行了冲击,为乔叟研究带来了活力。这也是为什么她的论文评审者之一,剑桥大学中世纪和文艺复兴研究教授(Chair of Medieval and Renaissance Studies)海伦·库柏(Helen Cooper)对丁建宁甚为赞赏的原因之一。

"作为知识分子的乔叟"是个很大的课题。我们不指望这部论著提供一个终结式的分析或解答,它只是这方面研究的开始。论文的一些方面,如乔叟和中国古代"士"的比较,限于论文主旨和篇幅,没有充分展开。有时,我们阅读作者的文字,饶有兴趣地聆听作者的分析时,她又很快从一个话题转向另一个话题,留给我们的,与其说是酣畅的分析,不如说是可能的思路。不过,当我们想到阿兰特关于学术创新之难的大实话,我们欣赏那些可能的思路中包含的思想火花,对论著中的不足不是宽容,而是理解。唯一希望的,是作者有机会能就这一研究选题作进一步挖掘和梳理。

我期待她此书出版之后,继续一步一个脚印,和同行们一道,将中世纪英国文学研究推向深入。是为序。

刘乃银

2010年11月

Acknowledgements

One of the pleasures of a first book is the opportunity given to its author to thank publicly those who have helped him in one way or another. The present book is based on my doctorial dissertation completed at East China Normal University. I have to first and foremost thank my supervisor, Prof. Liu Naiyin, who introduced, or in a sense forced me to enter such an academic terrain brand new to me, which turned out to be so fascinating: the medieval studies. He set a model for me with his academic penetration and preciseness, as well as his personal integrity. His vision in this field impressed me and directed me to the right route in the exploration of the present subject, while his sympathetic support when I was on the lowland in my academic exploration and personal life was always warm and encouraging. I could not imagine the present dissertation is possible without his guidance and help.

My six-month-stay in Oxford in 2005, helped with a grant from Jiangsu Overseas Academic Exchange Fund, is vital in widening my vision and upgrading the edging academic information. Prof. Malcolm Godden of the University of Oxford, who was also chair of the panel of my proposal judgment, made my visit to Oxford possible and pleasant. I would thank Prof. Vincent Gillespie of the University of Oxford for his being so supportive in providing advice on the subject. His remarks on Chaucer's literary strategies of presenting questions but leaving them open are especially inspiring to my discussion of Chaucer as an enlightener. Prof. Helen Cooper of the University of Cambridge is not only helpful because of her meticulously-written work on Chaucer. More than that is her constant academic and spiritual support. She never hesitates to help. I still remember clearly how nice she was to come a long way by bike to meet me in her office despite the heavy rain when I visited her in Cambridge! The reading list she recommended me, and the stimulating suggestions she gave me are significant in helping me frame my dissertation, especially the part on Chaucer's role of a counselor or a critic. These genius and generous people have helped better my understanding and interest in English medieval literature in general, and made my particular research on Chaucer go smoothly. Given all the help I received, any errors, for all my best attempt to avoid, I claim sole responsibility.

I would convey my cordial appreciation on my affiliated college: School of Foreign Languages and Cultures of Nanjing Normal University, which jointly funded my trip to the UK. I was supported to be away from work for one term in 2005 during my stay in Oxford as a visiting scholar, and for another term in 2007 for my academic visit to Chinese Social Science Academy. I was even privileged to have the accommodation financed by my school. I would like to thank my colleagues who understood me and helped share my teaching assignments. Thanks will be extended to all the teachers and fellow researchers for their ongoing encouragement and help.

I also wish to acknowledge my indebtedness to the many scholars who compiled, edited, and wrote about Chaucer. My main debt to the scholarly and critical work is listed in the selected bibliography.

My most profound debts are owed to my family. This dissertation would never have been possible without my husband Liu Hui's understanding and support. Though in a quite different field, he has spoiled my absence from time to time, one and a half year stay in Shanghai, half year in Oxford, another half year in Beijing! Thanks are to be extended to my mother Ma Youbi, who has taken such good care of the whole family since I started my PhD studying! Knowing nothing about English, she has been always ready to share my feelings, high or low. And I would also thank my son Liu Ruguan, who has kept my company along my academic journey from his primary school to his junior middle school. I guess he might be among the very few junior students in China who knows Chaucer! My gratitude to them is beyond words. I will always bear them in my heart!

前　言

　　知识分子研究在20世纪的西方人文科学界可谓如火如荼，话语纷呈。其关注的焦点是知识分子与权力阶层的关系，似乎知识分子就是对现状不满、对权力阶层说不的人群。将六百多年前的中世纪诗人乔叟与知识分子相提并论难免有牵强之嫌，成为犯"时代错位"的典型案例。然而，一味强调社会批判性是知识分子应共有的唯一品质似乎又明显带有"现代"偏见，至少是一种狭隘的理解。知识分子的概念和内涵远不止此，它本具有更加广阔的视阈。因此，本书试图从广义的知识分子概念切入，结合现代知识分子研究成果，重新审视英国文学之父乔叟，探讨乔叟的文学创作与社会参与之间的互动关系，并借此论证乔叟在文学创作和思想方面具有超越其时代的现代性。

　　本书的引言梳理了知识分子的定义和分类，指出广义层面的知识分子通常具备高度的智力水平、知识优势和理性倾向。但现代知识分子的研究和发展将这一广义概念逐渐狭义化，原本中性的词汇由于历史的原因带上"贬义"的色彩。但这种变化的意义在于，知识分子的概念从关注个人特质转向探讨社会属性，强调知识分子的独立人格和非功利性，特别是他们对权力、对现状所持的"对立"姿态。本书从广义层面的知识分子特性，即个人智慧入手，论证乔叟在文学和世俗世界中的博学和智慧，足以将他归入"智者"(an intellectual man)名列；继而结合现代知识分子研究中的社会关注要素，探讨他的社会属性，论证其成为现代意义知识分子（an intellectual）的可能性；并引出本文即将探讨的知识分子特质的三个核心要素：社会批评、启蒙和智慧及其相应的篇章安排。

第一章从现代知识分子概念中强调的社会批判角色与中世纪传统知识分子对王室的进谏、辅佐角色两方面，探讨作为宫廷文人的乔叟在愉悦王孙、谏言献策或是批评说教等多种职能之间的转换以及因此而面临的尴尬。笔者通过细读《坎特伯雷故事》中"梅勒比的故事"，论述乔叟运用"镜鉴文学"体裁写作的原因，是巧妙地隐批评于劝告中，是在模糊个人立场的表象下，传递自己的声音。继承"镜鉴文学"传统不是诗人文学创作所关注的全部，如何借诗传意，以及他本人的社会角色共同决定其文学选择。诗歌中的主题、风格、体裁选择以及对经典文本的取舍、改编都有一定的社会缘由。宫廷诗人乔叟不是纯粹的辅佐者或批评者，却在某种意义上兼扮两种角色。

第二章延续前章文学与社会语境互动的研究范式，在综述和分析当时社会结构的基础上，讨论乔叟所处的社会位置对他在进行社会评论时可能产生的影响。笔者认为，虽然乔叟作品中弥漫着观点并置、词语闪烁、回避或淡化社会事件的特点，因而对它们的解读不可避免呈现出多元性和开放性，但写作是"社会实践"的一种形式，文学文本的产生与社会势力之间的关系不可否认。与简单的文学社会决定论不同的是，两者之间不是镜子般的反映与被反映关系，而是存在一种不可分割的互动关系。因此，本章在讨论"女尼的教士的故事"时，比较了乔叟与同时代诗人或编年史者对1381年农民起义的指涉或描述，探讨乔叟对农民可能持有的同情和对社会阶层界限的模糊化倾向；之后，分别就乔叟在作品中对妇女和教会人员的刻画进行分析。本书选取《特洛伊斯和克里希德》中"不贞妇人"克里希德和《坎特伯雷故事》中的巴斯夫人为研究对象，指出乔叟对两者所作的圆形塑造，以及拒绝对他们的行为作简单的道德判断，这一行为本身实际上已超越了中世纪盛行的"唯道德服务"艺术观，同时也骚动了传统的父权观念。因此，他在某种意义上扮演了现代知识分子"搅局者"（disturber）的角色。本章在论述乔叟对当时教会问题的关注时，选取《坎特伯雷故事》中女修士、赎罪僧和牧师三个典型，指出乔叟对女修士世俗生活的温和嘲讽，以及对赎罪僧恶俗嘴脸的描绘，延续了他一贯的不动声色的风格。但是他对作为教会典范的牧师形象的理想化塑造,衬托了其他教会神职人员的腐败堕落,流露出诗人的不满。因此,本章通过分析乔叟在作品中对社会事件、妇女命运和教会问题的关注,论证乔叟承当社会批评者,或者至少是社会评论者的知识分子特质。

第三章重点探讨了体现在乔叟身上的启蒙精神及他所做出的启蒙努力。首先,本章重申乔叟宫廷文人的多重角色,指出乔叟不是一个纯粹取悦王孙的朝廷弄臣,也没有现代意义知识分子的公开对抗性;但他的诗歌寓教于乐,完美地将审美与教益相结合,诗歌中呈现的启蒙精神更从另一维度体现了他的知识分子特性,而这种启蒙精神主要体现在他与"权威"(the authority)和"权威文本"(the authorities)的协商中。然后,本章理清启蒙与权威的关系,并阐释中世纪权威概念独特的双重含义,继而论证乔叟在对待权威问题上的巧妙和悖反:一方面,他是运用各种权威文本的好手,通古博今;另一方面,他对权威文本的权威性并非盲目信仰、完全臣服,而是尽己所有,为己所用。在诗歌创作方面,乔叟通过对各种权威义本的翻译、改写和创新,确立了自己在文学领域的权威地位;在对待性别权威方面,他在质疑父权制的同时,触及哲学层面的知识与经验的对立。以女性为具象的经验和以男性为代表的权威二者之间的对立、紧张关系在巴斯夫人形象中得到集中体现。巴斯夫人对主要来自权威文本的男性权威话语的运用,和对男性权威本身的质疑恰恰折射出乔叟本人的影子。因此,通过与权威和权威文本的协商,乔叟实际上扮演了启蒙者这一知识分子的另一社会角色。

第四章将讨论的着眼点从知识分子的社会属性转回个人特质,探讨乔叟的才智在文学领域和世俗世界中的共同体现和相互作用。本章结合文本细读,选择性地讨论了乔叟诗歌中选用的梦境体裁,并置与开放、节制等艺术手法,论证乔叟不仅是在延承文学传统,或进行艺术创新,更是在扮演知识分子的角色,策略地实践社会批评。乔叟现世生活中智慧的讨论则被置于和中国古代传统知识分子"士"的比较中,着眼两者类似的亦官亦文的多重社会角色,探讨他们作为知识分子如何关注和影响社会发展,突出他们在文与道、形与心之间游走的智慧。

对乔叟的知识分子性研究试图从现代视角,重新阅读文学经典。本书以知识分子的智慧品质和社会功能为两条线索,结合文本细读和对当时英国社会、政治和文化历史原貌的追溯,探讨文学创作与历史语境的互动关系,解读诗人文本策略的社会意义。本书指出,乔叟不是任何单纯意义上的知识分子,但他身上却融合了知识分子的多种特质:社会批评、大众启蒙和为人、为文的智慧。讨论乔叟的知识分子性具有可行性和合理性,并可为阅读乔叟和理解知识分子的含义提供双重借鉴意义。

Foreword

The study of the intellectual was a heated academic area in the 20th century. Its focus was mainly laid on the intellectual's relation to the power, implicating that the intellectual was a special group courageous to say no to the authority. Therefore, to associate Chaucer, a medieval court poet, with "intellectual," a relatively recent notion, seems to be a forced or far-fetched attempt. The association could be the victim of anachronism. However, to privilege being a social critic the only feature commonly shared by the intellectuals is after all modern-prejudiced, or is at least a one-sided, narrow understanding of its meaning. "Intellectual," as a notion, basically has other implications than this particular one. This book therefore intends, from the perspective of the notion of "intellectual," its general sense and its modern sense, to revisit Chaucer the man and his works. It attempts to explore the interaction between his writing practice and his social engagement, and to argue that Chaucer transcends his age and can then be considered to be a modern writer not only for his literary creation but also his philosophical ideas.

After a retrospective study on the concept of "intellectual," and a review of those scholars who have touched on this issue, the introductory part primarily argues for the plausibility and significance of a systematic study on Chaucer as an intellectual. The definitions and classifications of the concept help to illuminate the bi-foci of the notion: one indicating the personal wisdom of an intellectual, the other concerning an intellectual's social function, a more contested point in modern intellectual study. Then Chaucer's intelligence and his social function as a court poet are discussed, and the three key aspects of the present study on Chaucer as an intellectual are introduced: his role of a social commentator, of an enlightener, and his wisdom exhibited in both his private writing and his public world.

From both a historical and a modern view, Chapter One explores the social roles traditional intellectuals in the court played as prince-pleasers and/or counselors, and the modern intellectuals' function as social critics. It elaborates the complex relationship of the roles Chaucer played as a court poet and a civil servant: his dilemma of pleasing the royal and aristocratic, or providing counseling advice and making criticism. Making a detailed analysis on the *Melibee's Tale* in the *Canterbury Tales*, especially its relationship with the genre of "Mirror for Prince," the chapter argues about the interrelationship between Chaucer's literary choices and the social roles he played. It argues that by adopting the genre of "Mirror for Prince" for the *Melibee's Tale*, Chaucer not only inherited the literary tradition but also achieved his social criticism strategically. The choice of subject, genre, and style may all have social reasons and significance. It is argued thus the inheritance of literary tradition is not the only factor that influences Chaucer's writing. Literary choices are determined by the interaction between literary tradition and the social roles the writer played.

The second chapter continues studying the relationship between Chaucer's work and his social roles under the frame of the interaction between literary texts and their social context. Based on a general survey of the medieval social structure, this chapter starts with a discussion about Chaucer's position in and on the society. In the second section, Chaucer's attitude toward the 1381 rebels is explored through a comparative study between Chaucer's treatment of the event in the *Nun's Priest's Tale* and the descriptions of it by other contemporary writers and chroniclers. The third and fourth sections of this chapter focus on Chaucer's depictions of women and clerics respectively. Sampling on two of the most contested women characters in Chaucer: Criseyde, "the false woman" in *Troilus and Criseyde*, and the Wife of Bath in the *Canterbury Tales*, the third section argues for Chaucer's denial of making any simple moral judgment. It argues that by so doing, Chaucer was in fact shaking the traditional idea of patriarchy. He was, therefore, in some sense playing the role of a "disturber" as a modern intellectual. The fourth section elaborates on Chaucer's attitude towards the clerics. Offering literary portraits of contemporary clerics, Chaucer betrayed his dissatisfaction with the corruptions of some of the clerics, though still in a cool and calm manner, without any radical attacks upon them. In all, Chaucer's concern with the social events, the fate of women, and the problems of the clerics in fact exhibits his role of an intellectual as a social commentator.

Chapter Three elaborates on Chaucer's role of an intellectual as an enlightener. After the mystery of "authority" in medieval time is cleared up, the chapter focuses on Chaucer's negotiating with the authority(ies), which is manifested in both his literary creation and his reflection on male superiority. It exposes Chaucer's ingenuity in taking advantages of the authorities and his paradoxical relationship with them, in the sense that he established his own *authority* in literature by exploiting these *authorities*, that is, the sources taken as canon. In terms of gender authority, the tension between the male and the female in his works is expanded to the conflict between the authority, which is usually embodied in men, and the experience, which is usually embodied in women. Being a constant issue in Chaucer's works, the opposition between authority and experience is illuminated in the *Wife of Bath's Prologue and Tale*. It is also argued that Chaucer's Wife of Bath mirrors Chaucer the poet himself: both apply the authorities against the authority.

Chapter Four turns to the discussion of Chaucer's personal wisdom. Nevertheless, the apparent shift of focus doesn't deny the interactive relationship between Chaucer's personal attributes and his public position. It is argued that Chaucer's artistic devices or textual strategies are not a pure matter of literary art, but a way of fulfilling his role of a social commentator. Compared with *Shi*, the group of traditional Chinese intellectuals, Chaucer's wisdom in both his private writing and his public life is manifested. Chaucer and *Shi* shared the same wisdom, knowing how to survive in an age of turmoil without giving up pursuing their spiritual ideal.

On the basis of a close reading of Chaucer's works, and with the reference to Chaucer's critical heritage and the related documents concerning the history and the culture of his time, the book tries to read the interaction between Chaucer's texts and the historical, social and cultural context of his time. Thanks to its double threads: the general sense and the modern sense, the notion of "intellectual" lends itself to an advantageous perspective of doing so. It allows a new angle to see the interaction between Chaucer's literary works and his social roles. Chaucer's intellectuality can be perceived, not only in his knowledge and intelligence, but also, more importantly, in his ambivalent and dual roles of both a counselor and a critic, in the skeptical challenge and enlightening effects in his poetry, and in his wisdom exhibited in both his literary and social life.

The attempt to examine Chaucer's poems both on their literary attributes and their social and cultural context is textually as well as contextually meaningful. The interaction between the text and the context helps us see not only the social and cultural significance of Chaucer's textual strategies, furthering a better understanding of the excellence of the writing itself, but also Chaucer's importance to and influence upon the advancement of society and culture as an intellectual.

CONTENTS

Introduction　The Problem and the Possibility ········· 1
　Chaucer as an Intellectual Man: A Review ········· 3
　Possibility of Chaucer as an Intellectual ········· 9
　The Layout of the Book ········· 20

Chapter One　Counselor or Critic? ········· 24
　Court Poet as Prince-pleaser, Counselor, or Critic? ········· 24
　Chaucer's Counseling: The Tale of Melibee ········· 32
　Between Counsel and Critique: Mirror for Prince ········· 43

Chapter Two　Chaucer as a Social Commentator ········· 48
　Chaucer's Position: in and on the Society ········· 52
　Writing as Social Practice: The *Nun's Priest's Tale* ········· 62
　Women in Chaucer's Society: Criseyde and Wife of Bath ········· 68
　Portraying of Clerics: Prioress, Pardoner, and Parson ········· 77

Chapter Three　Entertainer, Edifier and Enlightener ········· 87
　The Role of Enlightener: Authority Negotiated ········· 88
　Literary Authority and Chaucer's Poetic Innovation ········· 102
　Masculine Authority vs. Feminine Experience ········· 107

Chapter Four　Wisdom and/or Weakness ········· 111
　Wisdom in Art: Commenting with Strategies ········· 112
　Wisdom in Life: Chaucer and Chinese *Shi* ········· 136
　Weakness or Not? ········· 146

Conclusion　Possibility of Transcending ········· 150

Selected Bibliography ········· 154
　Primary Sources ········· 154
　Secondary Sources ········· 155

Introduction
The Problem and the Possibility

It may appear at first glance a forced attempt to associate Chaucer with the notion of "intellectual." On one hand, such an association may easily fall victim to anachronism. Chaucer was a late medieval court poet, while "intellectual," with its noun-form dating effectively not until the early nineteenth century, is essentially a modern word; it designates a social entity, if not a class, which emerges from a certain historical context. ① Additionally, relating Chaucer to the notion of "intellectual" might easily be refuted because of his lack of any systematic high education, which is commonly supposed to be essential for an intellectual. Although advanced education was available in Chaucer's time, we are left no official record of Chaucer as a student in a Grammar School, let alone a university. ② Chaucer's jobs as a royal servant and later a civil

---

① Many people in the English-speaking countries take "intellectual" as the synonym of "intelligentsia," which refers to a group of Russians emerging from about 1840s. They are social elites who have good manners, are well educated, but hold an oppositional posture to the status quo. Gradually, the word is used normally to emphasize the antagonist meaning.

② As for Chaucer's education, despite all the speculations by historians and biographers, Tout's opinion is more acceptable: "I am convinced that the excellent education which Geoffrey undoubtedly received was the education which the household of a king, or one of the greater magnates, could give to its junior members." (Pearsall, 1992: 34)

servant also seem to diverge from the career path of the then "educated ones," having little to do with ecclesiastics.

On the other hand, objections might also be raised to this connection because of the complexity of the notion itself. The multiple implications the notion has acquired over the years and the heated debates on the intellectual of last century in particular have brought to the fore the intricate relationship between the intellectual and the power. Some scholars even hold that only those who take an oppositional stance toward the power, who daringly criticize the government, are qualified intellectuals.[①] In this sense, Chaucer the courtier is apparently far from being an intellectual.

Yet, this association is by no means impossible or invalid if the notion is redefined, or, to be exact, confined within a certain scope and viewed from certain perspectives. In fact, in his famous *Intellectuals in the Middle Ages*, Le Goff argues strongly for the justifiability of this association.

> As in every pertinent comparatist perspective, if one does not separate the *sociological* approach, which sheds light on the coherence of types and structures, from the *historical* approach, which highlights conjunctures, changes, turning points, ruptures, differences, and the insertion of a historical phenomenon into the larger society of an epoch, then the use of the term "intellectual" is justified and useful (xiii).[②]

Venturing the application of this modern notion for medieval study, Le Goff confines the intellectual to only one select group: "the milieu of school masters" (1) emerging with the development of cities, especially with that of universities.

However, Le Goff's narrowing of the scope of his study on the intellectual does not mean his exclusion of others from the general group of the intellectual. Rather, for him, the group includes those "whose profession it was to think and to share their thoughts," "other groups of thinkers, other spiritual masters" (1). Thus, "the

---

[①] See Said, xiv.

[②] See Le Goff, Trans. Teresa Lavender Fagan, 1993, p. xiii. The words are italicized by the author because they denote the approaches adopted in the present book.

intellectual" is a general and inclusive concept. ① It is the certain qualities they share that determine their identity as intellectuals.

Therefore, to study Chaucer as an intellectual, we have to first of all explore the shared qualities of intellectuals, what intellectuals in general are supposed to be, and in what sense Chaucer can be regarded as an intellectual. The basic meaning of the notion shall serve as a good start. Meanwhile, the study will be invalid if it ignores the notion's developed meaning, its modern sense. Though modern intellectual studies lay emphasis on the social function of intellectuals, the concept of "intellectual" should not be nailed down to a simple political gesture or a social role one plays. The narrowing of the concept in fact manifests a kind of modern prejudice. But the implications of "intellectual" in modern sense do provide a new perspective to revisit Chaucer and his works. Thus, this book attempts to study Chaucer from the notion of "intellectual," and will discuss Chaucer's intellectuality regarding both the notion's basic meaning and its modern sense.

Chaucer as an Intellectual Man: A Review

Chaucer's intellectual character lies first of all in his intelligence, that is, Chaucer is an intellectual in the general sense. Regarding Chaucer as an intellectual man is dealing with the basic meaning of "intellectual." It concerns one's personal characteristics: being intelligent, having knowledge, knowing how to apply one's

---

① According to Le Goff, high-ranking and important theologians and scholastics, teachers and students with a high level of scientific and intellectual achievement and prestige, compilers and encyclopedists, writers instilled with university training and spirit, whose product is theology and scientific knowledge, all of them are categorized in one general group—the intellectual. He also regards as intellectuals professionals, such as men of the church, instructors of grammar and rhetoric, lawyers, judges and notaries, all closely related and playing important roles in the development of towns.

reason rather than emotion.① The core of it is intelligence. Thus, there is little risk in substituting "intelligent" for "intellectual" when it is used as an adjective. But when it is used as a noun, it indicates a group of people who have the capacity of using their intelligence. They are, generally and superficially, taken to be people with the knowledge or skills that they can employ in professional activities, and the intelligence that may potentially lead to the production of works of originality.②

---

① The word "intellectual" functions both as an adjective and a noun. When it is used as an adjective, "intellectual" has generally the following connotations: 1. of or relating to the intellect, especially to a high degree, or use of, especially creative use of, intellect; 2. rational rather than emotional, involving coping with difficult situations, using the power of reasoning, grasping abstract concepts. "It had been an ordinary adjective, from C14, for intelligence in its most general sense," and "retained a neutral general use," in Williams' words (169).

② Firstly and basically, the noun form "intellectual" indicates the faculties or processes of intelligence. See *The Oxford English Dictionary*, Clarendon Press, 1989: 1068. Later it means an intellectual person, that is, a person with high intelligence. It was not until the early nineteenth century that it began to indicate a particular kind of person, or a person doing a particular kind of work, though there were some isolated earlier uses of this sense as well. It is when the word is used in its plural form, which indicates a category of persons, that it begins to be referred to unfavorably. In the entry of "intellectual," Raymond Williams in his *Keywords*, rightly points out the main reasons for the negative senses round intellectual: "The reasons are complicated but almost certainly include opposition to social and political arguments based on theory or on rational principle. This often connects, curiously, with the distinguishing use of the more or the most intelligent as a governing class, and with opposition, as in Romanticism, to a 'separation' of 'head' and 'heart,' or 'reason' and 'emotion.' Nor can we overlook a crucial kind of opposition to groups engaged in intellectual work, who in the course of social development had acquired some independence from established institutions, in the church and in politics, and who were certainly seeking and asserting such independence through lC18, C19 and C20... From eC20 the new group term 'intelligentsia' was borrowed from Russian... Until mC20 unfavorable uses of intellectuals, intellectualism and intelligentsia were dominant in English, and it is clear that such uses persist. But 'intellectual,' at least, is now often used neutrally, and even at times favourably, to describe people who do certain kinds of intellectual work and especially the most general kinds. Within universities the distinction is sometimes made between specialists or professionals, with limited interests, and intellectuals, with wider interests. More generally, there is often an emphasis on 'direct producers in the sphere of ideology and culture', as distinct from those whose work 'requiring mental effort' is nevertheless primarily administration, distribution, organization or (as in certain forms of teaching) repetition (cf. Debray)." (169)

INTRODUCTION
THE PROBLEM AND THE POSSIBILITY

Chaucer has been well acknowledged as a man who has knowledge of diverse disciplines. His intelligence and creativity, as revealed in his literary works, have also been well recognized. It is in this sense that Le Goff regards Chaucer as an intellectual. He specifically expresses in his preface to the 1985 French edition of *Intellectuals in the Middle Ages* his regret at having excluded Chaucer from his study.

> But I regret not having included the great "writers," those instilled with a university training and spirit, a portion of whose works is a product of theology or scientific knowledge. I am thinking above all of Dante, a truly unclassifiable genius, and of Chaucer, in whom scientific curiosity and creative imagination were equally balanced, even if it is to the latter that he owes his renown (xviii).

What Le Goff wants to emphasize is Chaucer's scientific knowledge rather than his universally acknowledged genius in literary creation. He is, however, not the first, nor the only one who recognizes Chaucer's extraordinary command of scientific knowledge. In fact, it had already been well appreciated even in the age of Chaucer. Thomas Hoccleve in his *Regement of Princes* (1412), for example, refers to Chaucer as "flour of eloquence" and "universel fadir in science" as well (Sanders 5). Views of Chaucer as a great learned poet and "rhetor" are sustained across the sixteenth century; Sir Brian Tuke, in the preface to William Thynne's 1532 edition, again refers to Chaucer's "excellent learning in all kinds of doctrines and sciences" and his "fruitfulness in words" (Saunders 5—6). Recent criticisms also show interest in Chaucer's scientific knowledge. Scholars have covered different aspects of Chaucer's "scientific curiosity," with a unanimous emphasis on his achievement in applying his knowledge of science to his literary creation. For example, his use of medieval science in creating characters is systematically explored in Walter Clyde Curry's *Chaucer and the Mediaeval Sciences*. In his *Chaucer and the Country of the Stars*, Chaucey Wood focuses on Chaucer's use of astrology. Chaucer's knowledge of science actually goes well beyond astrology and astronomy. His poetic use of medieval medicine, physiognomy, dream psychology, and alchemy has also been a popular topic in twentieth-century Chaucer study. ①

Besides his knowledge of science, Chaucer's great interest and command of the other realm of knowledge, the humanities which include philosophy, religion and art, is also beyond doubt. Writers, being humanistic intellectuals according to the common view, show more interest in human beings than in nature or the universe they live in. They are concerned more about the situation of human beings, about what people believe and think, and whatever life they are actually living. The inclination toward the abstract thinking of aesthetics and philosophy is, in fact, one of the innate features of an intellectual. Thus philosophy, religion and art are either possible subjects discussed explicitly by writers, or something whose impact upon the writers can be at least implicitly discerned in their writing.

Previous studies on Chaucer in this respect have mainly examined the philosophical and religious climate in Chaucer's time, and where and how Chaucer responds to them in his poetry. Geoffrey Shepherd, for example, provides a brief but comprehensive survey of the religious and philosophical polemics of the late fourteenth century, including a summary of the attitudes of the major thinkers and Chaucer's response. ② Others have made attempts to figure out the relationship between Chaucer's exploration into these subjects in his works and his personal inclination. No matter how different their views are, they all acknowledge Chaucer's knowledge of religion and philosophy and its importance and influence upon his artistic endeavor.

If knowledge plays an important role in the making of a good writer, the knowledge of previous canons, especially that of literature, is naturally indispensable. It could in fact become the "anxiety of influence," to quote Bloom. Fortunately, Chaucer is well known for his familiarity with the classical and medieval Latin canons as well as the continental vernacular

---

① For other bibliography of Chaucer Studies on science, see Allen and Fisher, *The Essential Chaucer*, entries 215—224, 69—71.

② See Geoffrey Shepherd, "Religion and Philosophy in Chaucer", in Brewer, *Geoffrey Chaucer, Writers and Their Background*. London: G. Bell & Sons, 1974. Reprinted. Athens: Ohio University Press, 1976, pp. 262—289. For other bibliography on this subject, see Allen and Fisher, *The Essential Chaucer*, entries 205—214, 66—69.

works. The *Canterbury Tales* is envisaged by Cooper to be a medieval *summa* or *encyclopedia*, "*a bringing together of all knowledge*" (*Structure* 72), including not only that of nature, but of life, of the state of human existence. ① What Cooper sees in the work is a kind of literary compendium, which covers a full range of medieval genres: romance, fabliau, beast-fable, saint's life, moral treatise and sermon.

But Chaucer is far from being a mere follower of those ancient "greats," nor is his work just an exhibition or showcase of his familiarity with the canons. He professes his admiration for the greats, and makes use of the models and conventions, but he brings to them originality by experimenting in his own style. Meanwhile, he subverts some concepts such as chivalry or fin'amors. Despite the fact that much of Chaucer's writing is usually regarded as translation, and that he himself is regarded as an eminent translator, Chaucer is not a good one. His translation is distinguished by a lack of fidelity to the original sources. Yet it is just this infidelity that makes him a great poet rather than a mere translator. He adjusts the Latin sources through mistranslation or change of context to fit medieval conventions. By making use of French tradition and Italian works of his age, he nourishes his own skills in literary arts, and meanwhile succeeds in avoiding any possible censure for the demerits and errors in what he presents. As Pearsall says, "Chaucer was widely read, and used his reading intelligently" (*Life* 32). His creative rewriting of all the literary sources manifests not only his knowledge of them, but also, and maybe more importantly, his innovativeness, a quality that is essential to scientists and artists as well. Even in his own time, he was regarded as the inheritor of a great tradition as well as the inventor of a new one. In later years, his creativity gained even more attention. As Saunders points out, "In subsequent centuries, however, Chaucer came to be seen instead as the great innovator, the 'father of English literature'" (5). It is his innovative application of the knowledge he owns that elevates him

---

① See "An Encyclopedia of Kinds" in Cooper's *The Structure of the "Canterbury Tales"*, 1983. Reprinted in Corinne Saunders, *Chaucer*, 2001, 218—239.

超越的可能：作为知识分子的乔叟
Possibility of Transcending: Chaucer as an Intellectual

to such an elevated status in the history of English literature. ① The innovation in his literary writing presents Chaucer as a man of intelligence, which has been universally accepted.

His intelligence was given full play in his social life as well. To some, it is partly a factor leading to his favor in the court. "It may be thought he was unusually likeable, [. . .] because of his wide conversational interests and lively fund of unexpected knowledge," wrote Coghill (4). While there is no solid evidence to explain how Chaucer benefited from court life, his sensibility and adaptability to changing political situations allowed him to survive several reigns. This at least demonstrates him to be a man of intelligence, if not a man of shrewdness, which seemed particularly true in 1380s' London, where it was dominated by "conferracie, congregacion, & couryne" (Strohm, *Politics and Poetics* 83). ②

In addition, his intelligence in civil affairs was better brought forth in a time that demanded civil expertise, such as that of administrators, or financiers. In his age, a newly educated laity that held civil posts arose as a new class. They were advanced not because of their noble birth or devotion to the clergy, but for their capability in secular, practical affairs. It was fortunate for Chaucer to live in such an age when he himself was among this rising class. Although Chaucer's success through several reigns does not necessarily depend on his literary talents, or his efficiency in public affairs, one thing is certain: his intelligence both in receiving education through courtly training and in his later exercise of this knowledge contributes much to it.

Chaucer is, in brief, both learned and intelligent, which is the most essential feature of an intellectual in the general sense. In Wetherbee,

---

① For this part, I was inspired by Wang Zengjing's discussion of the "three 'I'" factors in defining "intellectual." According to Wang, intellectuals are those who are highly intelligent, have persistent and intense interest in nature or social issues, and meanwhile have produced something innovative. This definition, though to some extent repetition of the previous studies, such as intelligence, concern of one's social role, and the creativity, is significant because of the qualification of these features. The quality of being "highly," and of being "persistent and intense," distinguishes a minor group from the masses who are also intelligent and sometimes may also be interested in nature myth and social problems. Only those with the special "three 'I'" features, who have made great contribution to human life, are qualified for the title, and hence a study on them worthwhile.

② See Strohm, *Literary Practice and Social Change*, in Patterson, 1990, 83.

He was probably the most learned of medieval English poets, and though he offers nothing like Langland's intimacy with the habits and themes of contemporary scholasticism or the homiletic intricacies and discourses on political philosophy of Gower, he is also in many ways the most intellectual. (75)

Therefore Chaucer is an intellectual in the general sense, in regard to his knowledge of various disciplines and his intelligence in the application of them in his poetic art and public affairs.

Possibility of Chaucer as an Intellectual

Heated debates about "intellectual" in the last few decades of twentieth century have expanded the implications of the word beyond the general sense of having knowledge and intelligence. The modern sense of "intellectual" makes it possible to study Chaucer from a new perspective. Different from illustrating Chaucer's intellectuality in its general sense, to study Chaucer as an intellectual in its modern sense lays emphasis on Chaucer's social function instead of his personal characteristics.

The social function of an intellectual can be traced and related to the use of "intellectual" as a noun. "Intellectual," before it is used as a noun, remains a "neutral general use" (Williams 169). However, the notion becomes questionable, and begins to acquire negative senses, when it takes its noun form.[①] The connotation of the word

---

[①] As Raymond Williams rightly and also depressingly states, "Until mC20 unfavourable uses of intellectuals, intellectualism and intelligentsia were dominant in English, and it is clear that such uses persist"(170). The reasons for its negative senses are complicated, but among them one that is relevant to the present study is "the opposition to groups engaged in intellectual work, who in the course of social development had acquired some independence from established institutions, in the church and in politics, and who were certainly seeking and asserting such independence through lC18, C19 and C20" (Williams, 170). Wang Zengjing analyzes the origin of the word in Russian and in French. In Russian, the word has the implications of people who are 1. social elites; 2. morally concerned and advocates of social progress; 3. well-educated. In French, the word means 1. people who are well-educated; 2. who are the guardians of social justice. But in English, especially the modern use of it, it is rather a synonym of opponent, or dissenter, neglecting the original basic meaning of an intelligent person.

has since then been expanded beyond personal characteristics to include social attributes. ① Hence a shift of focus in intellectual study from one's personal traits to one's social functions. This shift is significant in studying Chaucer because it allows a new angle to revisit Chaucer the man and his work. But before exploring Chaucer's social function, a review of what the social role an intellectual is supposed to play in the field of modern intellectual study should not be redundant.

The social roles intellectuals are supposed to play are multiple. But modern intellectuals are a group of people who seem to share the same aura or trait of being oppositional and critical. This characteristic derives from a complex of negative implications of "intellectual."② The most significant and particularly relevant to the present subject is the use of it in France during the Dreyfus Affair. For the first time in history, the notion of "intellectual" was attributed a new sense—the critical feature. Those who signed on the protest of Zola's *Manifeste des intellectuals* during the Affair "produced themselves as a collective entity through their public identification with a critical, oppositional stance" (Copeland 25), an identification that crosses the bounds of established social and professional lines. ③ They were of many different professions, such as writers, scientists, lawyers, physicians, academics, industrialists. What counted more then and there was the common oppositional stance they courageously held rather than the differences between their professions and social status. They were intellectuals not only because they were people who had knowledge and intelligence, or to use Lipset's phrase, "who create(d), distribute(d), and apply

---

① This has been well echoed in Eyerman's categorization. He conveniently divides various attempts to define the noun-form intellectual into two broad categories: those attributing personal characteristics and those that look to social structure and function(1). Though apparently simple, this division is inspirational. It introduces two key factors in the discussion of "intellectual": one's personal characteristics and one's social role, with the latter being most contested in modern society.

② See Williams' *Keywords* for detailed history of the positive and negative implication of intellectuals as a group, 169—171.

③ See Copeland, 25. As for the case of Dreyfus Affair, see the same page and also Eyerman, 23.

INTRODUCTION
THE PROBLEM AND THE POSSIBILITY

(ied) culture" (311) , though many of them actually fulfilled this role, but also and more importantly, because of their critical and oppositional public attitude toward the status quo. Since then "intellectual" has become a sociological label. It refers to a group of people "who never seem satisfied with things as they are," as Coser points out (xiii). ①

Coser's identification of intellectuals with opponents is not a solo voice but one in the chorus. It responds to a recurring theme in the symphony of intellectual studies and has been frequently echoed. Even before Coser, Julien Benda has stated that intellectuals are extraordinarily intelligent and are highly moral philosopher-kings. They constitute the conscience of human beings. The real intellectuals are similar to ancient clerics in that both are devoted to non-material profit. As he says, real intellectuals are "those whose activity is essentially not the pursuit of practical aims, all those who seek their joy in the practice of an art or a science or metaphysical speculation, in short in the possession of non-material advantages" (43). Highlighted are the intellectuals' moral responsibilities rather than their individual talents, their responsibility for the society, for the human beings as a whole.

Though it is generally agreed that intellectuals should hold the responsibility of helping to advance the world towards perfection, academic focuses are somewhat different when it comes to ways of practicing that responsibility. How to give full play to this sense of responsibility, as well as to their intelligence, is suggested by Russell Jacoby. Similar to Benda in insisting on intellectuals' social responsibility, Jacoby lays emphasis on their specialty in participating in public affairs. His idea is best expressed by his celebrated self-coined phrase "public intellectual" (207). He advocates in *The Last Intellectuals* that intellectuals can and should play their roles in politics, society and cultural activities in addition to their respective professional fields. Otherwise, they do not have,

---

① To Coser, scholastic researchers and professionals are not necessarily intellectuals. Those who confine themselves within their professional fields are not qualified intellectuals. Only those who are attempting to explore the ultimate meaning and values, and those who are not satisfied with the status quo and conventions, deserve this title.

in Gramsci's phrase, "the function of intellectuals" (9). ①

The intellectual's social and public role is more explicitly put forward by Edward Said. His thesis is that "the public role of the intellectual" is as an "outsider, 'amateur,' and disturber of the status quo" (xiv). According to him, "the principal intellectual duty is the search for relative independence from such pressures" (xiv). And hence he characterizes intellectuals "as exile and marginal, as amateur, and as the author of a language that tries to speak the truth to power" (xiv). What grips him in the intellectual is "a spirit in opposition, rather than accommodation," though at the same time, he admits that "intellectuals are not required to be humorless complainers" (xv). In all, despite the variety and complexity of the definition, what has been receiving increasing attention is the notion that intellectuals, at least in the modern sense, share the quality of being critical and oppositional; much advocated are intellectuals' independence and disinterestedness.

This similarity can be elaborated further by looking into the classification of intellectuals. No less various than the definition, the classification provides another clue to examining the intellectuals' social roles. Gramsci's monumental classification of intellectuals into the "traditional" and the "organic" is based on their social function. ② Foucault's division into "specific intellectual" and "universal intellectual" (Rabinow 68) and Kellner's division into "functional intellectual" and "critical intellectual" (41—42), though different in

---

① See Gramsci, 5—23.

② In the first place there are the "traditional" professional intellectuals, literary, scientific and so on, whose position in the interstices of society has a certain inter-class aura about it but derives ultimately from past and present class relations and conceals an attachment to various historical class formations. Secondly, there are the "organic" intellectuals, the thinking and organizing element of a particular fundamental social class. These organic intellectuals are distinguished less by their profession, which may be any job characteristic of their class, than by their function in directing the ideas and aspirations of the class to which they organically belong. For Gramsci, organic intellectuals are a product of modern society. They are more closely attached to and more dependent upon a certain class, usually the dominant one. They are, to say the least, blasphemers if not betrayers, to borrow Benda's words, of the sacred ideal that intellectuals should regard their duty or calling as the pursuit of universal truth or goodness.

INTRODUCTION
THE PROBLEM AND THE POSSIBILITY

definition and dimension, both take into consideration the relationship between the intellectuals' specific knowledge or capability and their universal concern about human beings. ① Their classifications are similar to Gramsci's in that they all concern the intellectuals' social function.

Such classifications of modern intellectuals are also significant in respect of medieval intellectuals. Le Goff borrows Gramsci's schema and takes medieval intellectuals to be after all "organic", because they are under a double bureaucracy —secular and ecclesiastical, and thus faithful servants of the Church and the state. But he also finds that the gradual emergence of university academics, as the university acquired more "freedom," effectively cultivated a critical sense. Abelard, Thomas Aquinas, Siger of Brabant and Wycliff are in the list of such who are to some extent "critical intellectuals" (xvi). ②

All these studies on the intellectual share a few central interests. They all question what the same work intellectuals do, or should do, in common, despite their different professions; and what kind of relationship intellectuals have with the powers and the public. A study on Chaucer as an intellectual also seeks to answer these questions, with a review on Chaucer's personal characteristics and his social attributes.

As a medieval court poet, Chaucer's social role has something to do with another origin of the term "intellectual." In the medieval time, the referring of intellectuals was usually reserved for the clergy who knew Latin and worked in the Church. However, a group of men who were termed *laicus*, or layman, appeared. They were either unable to use Latin, regardless of their social status, or not connected to the Church, that is, they knew Latin, but they did not

---

① See Douglas Keller, "Intellectuals, the *New Public Spheres*, and Techno-Politics" in *New Political Science*, No 41—42 Winter 1997. Refer to http://www.brooklynsoc.org/toulouse/cyberpol/kellner.html.

② Critical intellectuals were traditionally those who utilized their skills of speaking and writing to denounce injustices and abuses of power, and to fight for truth, justice, progress, and other positive values.

work for the Church.① Thus intellectuals became involved in both ecclesiastical and secular affairs. Gradually, the dichotomy and distinction between the two realms were blurred because of these intellectuals. They played the role of the clergy, such as teachers and writers, although writing works of literature was not yet considered a profession in itself.

These laymen or intellectuals carried out the tasks which were once considered exclusively appropriate for the clergy. When they worked in or out of the court, they became more and more influential, especially when they wrote in the vernacular and their audience became the entire society at large. Those who wrote works of literature were later referred to as "men of letters." They sold their skill in writing for a living. Chaucer was doubtlessly an intellectual in the sense of a "man of letters." He shared much with those great poets in Italy, such as Boccaccio and Petrarch. They all took literature as the means to fulfill their own personal ambitions. So Chaucer had the convenience of playing his social roles as a poet.

Other than his literacy-enabled cultural identity, where Chaucer was socially located and how he played a double role in both the literary and social worlds are as, if not more, central to his possible identity as an intellectual in the modern sense.

The relationship between Chaucer the poet and Chaucer the courtier is a good starting point. Chaucer's identity as a poet and translator, connected with his position as a court functionary, may find precedence in his French contemporary Eustache Deschamps.② Deschamps' having such a connection and his similarity with Chaucer in both holding a governmental position and achieving well in poetry writing suggest the social dimensions of poetry writing. The connection between poetic composition and public position, that is, how poets may possibly express explicitly or implicitly their social views in their artistic endeavor, becomes a key issue. Although there

---

① Although some of these intellectuals might join the church, mainly for economic and social reasons, they maintained a strong interest in secular culture (e.g. Boccaccio).

② In the first line of the envoy of Deschamps' ballade, which appeared in a letter to Chaucer, he addressed Chaucer as "poete hault, loenge d'escuirie" [exalted poet, pride of squiredom] (G. Olson 567).

is no direct evidence that Chaucer enjoyed any special favoritism from patrons for his poetry, it will not be without foundation to predicate that his writing "served as evidence of capabilities that made him successful in court service and that in some cases could have constituted such service" (G. Olson 568).

Taken as a court poet, though, Chaucer wrote neither merely to please the royal audience, nor to seek patronage. He did sometimes seem to write for the sake of royal commission. The *Book of the Duchess* has been widely taken to be a piece written for John of Gaunt, who was grieving over the death of his wife Blanche in 1368.[①] But most of his other works have no direct linkage to any specific occasions of royal or magnate patronage. The final scene of the *House of Fame*, with the apparently unfulfilled promise by a "man of gret auctorite" (l. 2158), is no longer read as any particular social announcement. Instead, it is taken to be a reflection on literary authority and reputation. Scholars, who tend to search for evidence of occasional events in Chaucer's works, have been tempted to connect the *Parliament of Fowls* with Richard II's marriage negotiations. Yet, much ink on the formel's more arrogant attitude as to postponing her decision, and the diverse comments made by birds of the lower classes might be more offending than fawning to the monarch himself. The *Legend of Good Women* is taken as a response and apology to members in the court who were displeased by Chaucer's unfavorable treatment of women in *Troilus and Criseyde*. But this is also based more on speculation than on solid evidence. As G. Olson points out,

> Most of his work seems not to have been the direct product of commission, or at least of royal commission. Rather, within the combination of household and administrative cultures in which he functioned, he seems to have been more interested in finding a sympathetic audience for his work than in securing royal approval of it, preferring "lateral allegiance" to this group over the hierarchical relationship entailed in patronage. (570)

---

① See Strohm, *Literary Practice and Social Change*, in Patterson, 1990, 83.

In fact, no Chaucer manuscript survives as a presentation copy for a royal patron.

Despite the lack of direct connection between his literary writing and advancement in the world of affairs, Chaucer as a courtier, whose job was to serve and satisfy the kings and the royal connections, could hardly be expected to be an intellectual in the sense of being critical of and in opposition to the seat of power. At least, it is not sensible to expect him to be daring enough to offend the monarch publicly and directly by writing poems that would often be read aloud to the court audience. However, it is too hasty to decide that Chaucer is a court poet in the commonly accepted sense of a prince-pleaser. It might be true that his early writings, which were completed when he was a household servant, have the taint of catering to the royal tastes. But this is not the case with his later writings, especially with some tales in the *Canterbury Tales*, which were mainly written after he retreated from the public sphere. His separation from London and retreat to his library seems a result of his loss of office, a possible side-effect of Richard's loss of power. So by then, he seemed to have broken with the courtly tradition he followed closely in his early years, the tradition that dealt with love, toned to please the court audience. Now he commenced on writing social satire, such as some of the tales in the *Canterbury Tales*, and even turned his attention to some scientific writing, which might appear more objective and also safer from any censure. Therefore, to some extent, Chaucer's career experience at least helps to our understanding of his literary works even if it does not provide an explanation of them.

The foregoing analysis shows a complex relationship between Chaucer and the power. It is not sensible to draw a hasty conclusion that Chaucer is, or is not, an intellectual in the sense of being critical. Close to Richard II, he is naturally thought to have played the role of a counselor in the court. But his status and influence are not comparable to the monarch's tutors like Sir Simon Burley, for example. His close relationship with Richard II, which is partly proved by his being entrusted with several secret tasks abroad, will not, however, exclude any possible influence he exerts upon Richard II, culturally and politically. So as far as his relation to power is

INTRODUCTION
THE PROBLEM AND THE POSSIBILITY

concerned, a safer and more convincing conclusion might be drawn only after detailed examination of his role as a courtier, a poet and a counselor, which will be elaborated further in the chapters to follow.

Chaucer's relationship with the public is another important factor in determining the possibility of his being an intellectual. As Regis Debray points out in his study on the French intellectuals, it is the impact upon the masses rather than the education one receives that defines an intellectual. He describes this as moral action, mainly political, but not necessarily party political. It is an endeavor for the sake of the people, for their mind and thought (qtd. in Fruedi 33). Chaucer's impact upon the masses is best exercised in his vernacular imaginative writing rather than in any of his involvement with political and social affairs in reality.

Vernacular writings were international in the fourteenth century. Chaucer followed the example of the Italian "greats," such as Dante and Petrarch, and tried his hand writing in English, a language which was then still conceived as shameful and inferior both to Latin, the orthodox, and to French, the "noble" language in England. It is wrong to take Chaucer as the first who wrote in English at that time, though he was indeed the first who used it in literary writing in such a competent way as to bestow it the grace of French, and the solemnity of Latin. Significantly, it is his deliberate choice rather than an unconscious action following the emergence of the popularity of vernacular writing. On the one hand, his choice of writing in vernacular English apparently results from the literary influence upon him of other vernacular works that he probably acquired when traveling to those countries. On the other hand, it is arguable that Chaucer's complex social situation must have contributed to it too. The complexity of his social identity—merchant, court poet, and official—will inevitably contribute to his literary choices, including his choice of language, style, subject, and genre. The choice of both language and artistic devices would naturally be relevant to his awareness of the multiple audiences.

As a court poet, Chaucer was well aware of his audience, consisting of the royal members, the royal servants who were his equals or near equals, and also the possible existence of readers, instead of an audience, outside the court. Composing his poems,

Chaucer would inevitably consider the factors that would determine the acceptance of them. In fact, Strohm has argued forcefully for the interaction between Chaucer the author and the audience of his poetry in his *Social Chaucer*. Yet,

> Linked thus to a variety of communities—mercantile, courtly, administrative and humanistically bookish—and alert to the varied sensibilities of each, Chaucer maintained no complete identification with any single one. The resultant distinction between self and estate is reflected in a poetry that more than any other of its time gives prominence to individual subjectivity. (G. Olson 569)

This subjectivity, fully explored by Patterson in his *Chaucer and the Subject of History* as indicating reflection and self-questioning, is in fact one of the special features of an intellectual. Chaucer is a poet who has strong self-consciousness in not only his literary experiment and acceptance, but also in the wakening of self. In this sense, he was also an enlightener.

Chaucer's way of enlightening reminds us of Chomsky's agreement with Paulo Freire. Both Chomsky and Freire hold that writing "is an avenue to social and political empowerment of the disenfranchised," because it can lead to "critical consciousness" (Olson and Worsham 56). People who can participate in that have ways of enriching their own thought, of enlightening others, of entering into constructive discourse with others by which they shall all gain (Olson and Worsham 57). The "entering into constructive discourse with others which they all gain by" lays an adequate emphasis on both the role of a writer as an intellectual in using discourse to construct, and that of the audience, real or imagined, to whom he would transmit or share his ideas. The "enlightening of others" has special significance in understanding Chaucer as an intellectual.

Chaucer's writing in vernacular English, if not a deliberate choice, is at least a welcomed side effect, enlightening those who were lower in social status and had no access to Latin or French. In this sense, his vernacular writing played a similar role to Englishing the Bible at that time.

However, language is not the only factor that contributes to the enlightening role of his works. His artistic devices, such as questioning and leaving open the questions, also have significance on understanding Chaucer's role of an enlightener. In fact, Chaucer's works are, according to Belsey, mainly interrogative in the sense that they pose questions by enlisting the readers in contradiction (83—84). His aim of arraying questions without giving any answer is to arouse the audience's awareness of the problems and to urge them to think, judge and decide all by themselves. He is a prompter, an enlightener rather than a didactic instructor forcing people to accept certain doctrines. His way of teaching, as Chomsky puts it, "is not a matter of pouring water into a vessel but of helping a flower to grow in its own way" (Olson and Worsham 55). He "light(s) the world with sense and color," for he both lights the world with the rational sense of an extraordinary intelligence, and meanwhile actually challenges the authority of the privileged, of institutions, even of beliefs that have already been well received (Knapp 141). In this sense, he stood at the frontier of his age when hierarchical structure was still the mainstream, though some new classes or estates began to arise. Consequently his enlightening became a stability-shaking force in an age when the Church still exercised considerable power and authority and religion still permeated people's lives.

The stimulating effect of Chaucer's poetry was later echoed by Virginia Woolf in her comment in *The Common Reader*:

> Chaucer lets us go our ways doing the ordinary things with the ordinary people. His morality lies in the way men and women behave to each other. We see them eating, drinking, laughing, and making love, and come to feel without a word being said what their standards are and so are steeped through and through with their morality. There can be no more forcible preaching than this where all actions and passions are represented, and instead of being solemnly exhorted we are left to stray and stare and make out a meaning for ourselves. (18)

All in all, the notion of "intellectual" and its multiple layers offer some fresh perspectives to revisit Chaucer the man, and the man's works. The Chaucer-as-intellectual interrogation shall also enable us to partake in the discussion of "intellectual" as well. In a sense, this study may hopefully become a kaleidoscope of modern intellectual studies, and meanwhile the value and variety of Chaucer and his works will be more keenly recognized.

The Layout of the Book

Studies on Chaucer's intellectuality have been touched upon briefly. But no systematic discussion regarding Chaucer as an intellectual in both general and modern sense exists till now. Medievalists agree on Chaucer's intelligence in his social life and literary world, but they fail to see and argue plainly and systematically the interaction in between from this particular perspective. Even on Chaucer's role as a social commentator, there exist more disagreements than agreements due to the peculiar evasiveness in Chaucer's writing. No one has made detailed analysis on his ambiguous and evasive style by taking into serious account Chaucer's social position in his time. Nor has comparative study been made on the relationship between Chaucer and the traditional Chinese intellectual *Shi*. Their shared wisdom in living, writing and pursuing of spiritual freedom when they were bodily confined by the social circumstances has not yet been exposed. Therefore, the book attempts to study Chaucer's characteristics as an intellectual by examining the social roles he played as a medieval court poet, revealing his wisdom in both his worldly life and his literary career. In this way, the book hopes to paint a full portrayal of Chaucer as an intellectual, elaborating the interrelationship between his writing and his living, his text and his context.

After a retrospective study on the concept of "intellectual," and a review of those scholars who have touched on this issue, the introductory part primarily argues for the plausibility and significance of a systematic study on Chaucer as an intellectual. The definitions and classifications of the concept help to illuminate the bi-foci of the notion: one indicating the personal wisdom of the intellectual, the other concerning the intellectual's social function, a more contested point in modern intellectual study. Then Chaucer's intelligence and his social function as a court poet are examined in sequence and the three key aspects of the study on him as an intellectual is introduced: his role of a social commentator, of an enlightener, and his wisdom exhibited in both his private writing and his public world.

From both a historical and a modern view, Chapter One explores the social roles traditional intellectuals in the court played as prince-pleasers and/or counselors, and the modern intellectuals' function as social critics. It elaborates on the complex relationship of the roles Chaucer played as a court poet and a civil servant: his dilemma of pleasing the royal and aristocratic, or providing counseling advice and making criticism. Through a detailed analysis on the *Melibee's Tale* in the *Canterbury Tales*, especially its relationship with the genre of "Mirror for Prince," the chapter argues the interrelationship between Chaucer's literary choices and his social roles. It argues that by adopting the genre of "Mirror of Prince" for the *Melibee's Tale*, Chaucer not only inherited the literary tradition but also achieved his social criticism strategically. The choice of subject, genre, and style may all have social reasons and significance. It is argued thus the inheritance of literary tradition is not the only factor that influences Chaucer's writing. Literary choices are determined by the interaction between literary tradition and the social roles of the writer.

The second chapter continues studying the relationship between Chaucer's work and his social roles under the frame of the interaction between literary texts and their social context. Based on a general survey of the medieval social structure, this chapter starts with a discussion about Chaucer's position in and on the society. Agreeing with Barr on that writings are socioliterary practice, I explore Chaucer's attitude toward the 1381 rebels by comparing Chaucer's treatment of the event in the *Nun's Priest's Tale* with other contemporary writers' and chroniclers' description of it. The third and fourth sections of this chapter focus on Chaucer's depictions of women and clerics respectively. Sampling on Criseyde, "the false woman" in *Troilus and Criseyde*, and the Wife of Bath in the *Canterbury Tales*, the round and also most contested women characters in Chaucer, the third section argues for Chaucer's denial of making any simple moral judgment. The fourth focuses on Chaucer's attitude towards the clerics. Offering literary portraits of contemporary clerics, Chaucer betrayed his dissatisfaction with the corruptions of some of the clerics, though still calmly, without radical criticism upon them.

超越的可能：作为知识分子的乔叟
Possibility of Transcending: Chaucer as an Intellectual

Chaucer's concern with the social events, the fate of women, and the problems of the clerics exhibits his role of an intellectual as a social commentator.

Chapter Three elaborates on Chaucer's enlightening role as an intellectual. Clearing up the mystery of "authority" in medieval time, the focus is laid on Chaucer's negotiating with the authority (ies), which is manifested in both his literary creation and his reflection on male superiority. This chapter exposes Chaucer's ingenuity in taking advantages of the authorities—the sources taken as canon, and his paradoxical relationship with them, in the sense that he established his own authority in literature by exploiting the authorities. In terms of gender authority, the tension between the male and the female in Chaucer's work is expanded to a conflict between the authority embodied in men and the experience embodied in women. Being a constant issue in Chaucer's work, the opposition between authority and experience is manifestative in the *Wife of Bath's Prologue and Tale*. It is argued that Chaucer's Wife of Bath mirrors Chaucer the poet himself: both apply the authorities against the authority.

Chapter Four returns to the discussion of Chaucer's personal wisdom. Nevertheless, the apparent shift of focus doesn't deny the interactive relationship between Chaucer's personal attributes and his public position. It is argued that Chaucer's artistic devices or textual strategies are not a pure matter of literary art, but a way of fulfilling his role of a social commentator. Compared with *Shi*, the traditional Chinese intellectuals, Chaucer's wisdom in both his private writing and his public life is illuminated. Both Chaucer and *Shi* shared the same wisdom, knowing how to survive in an age of turmoil without giving up their spiritual pursuit.

On the basis of a close reading of Chaucer's works, and with the reference to Chaucer's critical heritage and the related documents concerning the history and the culture of his time, the dissertation tries to read the interaction between Chaucer's text and the historical, social and cultural context of his time. Thanks to its double threads: the general sense and the modern sense, the notion of "intellectual" lends itself to an advantageous perspective of doing so. It allows a new angle to see the interaction between Chaucer's literary works and his social roles. Chaucer's intellectuality can be perceived, not only in his knowledge and intelligence, but also, more importantly, in his ambivalent and dual roles of both a counselor and a critic, in the skeptical challenge and enlightening effects in his poetry, and in his wisdom exhibited in both his literary and social life.

The attempt to examine Chaucer's poems both on their literary attributes and their social and cultural context is both textually and contextually meaningful. The interaction between the text and the context helps us see not only the social and cultural significance of Chaucer's textual strategies, furthering a better understanding of the excellence of the writing itself, but also Chaucer's importance and influence as an intellectual upon the society and the culture.

Chapter One
Counselor or Critic?

An intellectual in its modern sense, as has been elaborated in the introductory part, is usually expected to be a social critic. Unsatisfied with the status quo, he should make efforts to improve the situation by combating social unfairness or discontent through his pen rather than his sword. Thus, Chaucer the poet, if regarded as an intellectual in modern sense, is supposed to write to expose the harsh reality, or to criticize the crimes and combat the corruption of his time.

However, Chaucer's identity of a courtier seems to have dismissed the probability of his being a courageous fighter against the evils of the society. His job determines that he should serve and please his court superiors; and poetry by him as a court poet is supposed to sing the royals praises, or to provide them with advice. So he might also act as a court counselor, not entitled to the name though. He is expected to feed his royal audience the morals or advice through his literary expression.

Then, was Chaucer a counselor who intended to help the authority to consolidate the existent power relationship, or was he a social critic who perceived the darkness of the reality and attempted to express his dissatisfaction? There is in fact a dialectical relationship in between.

Court Poet as Prince-pleaser, Counselor, or Critic?

Because of his multiple identities, Chaucer played several roles in the court. What role to play depended on what job he took. All his jobs however were related with each other and relevant to his

CHAPTER ONE
COUNSELOR OR CRITIC?

position in the court. As a poet, Chaucer had to take his audience into consideration when he composed poems. The reason is evident:

> The audience whether in social or in individual contexts brings to a literary situation certain expectations. [. . .] A poet's social functions are determined in some large measure by the occasion at which he performs and by the expectations of his audience (Bloomfield and Dunn 6).

Chaucer's audience, therefore, determined Chaucer's poetry writing in respect of his choice of subject matter, tone, and style etc. As a court poet, Chaucer would inevitably concern more about his royal audience.

So in the first place, he was apparently a prince-pleaser. He had to engage the interest of the royal audience, including kings and queens, aristocrats and other social superiors, and his colleagues. His image on the frontispiece of a manuscript of *Troilus and Criseyde* portrayed Chaucer's reading his poetry to what looked like a courtly audience. ① Chaucer's self-portrait as naïve, dim, bookish, though definitely fictional and tongue-in-cheek, couldn't be more appropriate for a court poet, who wrote and read poems to please or entertain his social superiors. In fact, the subjects of his early poems were mostly of royal events and to the courtly taste. He was expected to dedicate poems to the king, which though were not necessarily confined to praises. He could at least make use of any royal occasions. For example, the *Book of the Duchess* provided comforts for the "prince" who had lately lost his beloved. Thus, Chaucer the court poet was expected to play the role of a prince-pleaser. ②

---

① The frontispiece is now at Corpus Christi College, Cambridge.

② However, some counter-arguments have been raised in recent years to the effect that Chaucer's audience is confined to a small coterie of professional men like himself, unconnected with the aristocracy, the king, or even a wider reading public. These counterarguments are based on the absence of any records of payments to the poet for works commissioned and of public dedication of his works to royal or aristocratic patrons, and also the lack of manuscripts dating from his time. Compelling and persuasive though, they are not waterproof. Jones rightly points out that the poets of Richard's court are different from minstrels, who are professional performers. They are rather seen as members of the gentry, and direct payment for their literary endeavors was something the "gentlemen-poets" may therefore have wished to avoid. The lack of manuscripts from his time is not sound evidence of that Chaucer's audience did not include aristocracy. On the contrary, it might be the very proof of his close connection with them, because it is possible that his manuscripts were deliberately destroyed by the usurping regime of Henry IV (Jones, 4).

However, Chaucer's poems seemed never to have been devotedly and exclusively prince-pleasing. Chaucer was not a professional minstrel, who gave performance merely to entertain the court. He functioned as a poet in early society was generally expected to be. As Bloomfield and Dunn point out, "Early poets were teachers, diviners, prophets, and preservers of tradition. Part of their sacred office was to admonish and warn rulers and subjects alike, and to hand on the accumulated wisdom of the past" (4). Thus early poets served as teachers. Court poets functioned to provide moral or political models for his royal audience to follow. In a sense, therefore, Chaucer wrote and read to his royal audience to provide advice as a counselor.

Yet, his counseling role is debatably complicated. The complex nature is relevant to the controversy on Chaucer's politicalness and related to a rise of court poets over professional minstrels in late fourteenth century. The controversy on whether Chaucer is political or apolitical results from two aspects.

Firstly, the rare reference to any social events in his writings presents Chaucer to be a detached, low-profile courtier who accidentally had a hobby of composing poems. On one hand, Chaucer appeared to have no political interest, let alone ambition. Unlike Thomas Usk, he never sought to climb the slippery pole of political appointment by way of singing the royals praises. Most of his poems were not make-work projects for someone with connections, though he might include some court occasions. For instance, the *Book of the Duchess*, and the *Parliament of Fowls*. On the other hand, different from what his contemporary John Gower did in his *Vox Clamantis*, he never made any pointed and critical commentary on current conditions in his poems (though Gower did it in Latin from circumspection). Even in some poems that are apparently related to the court, it is always difficult to decide what the real political message is. For example, it is not correct to presume Chaucer's good standing with Henry IV if we judge from his short poem *The Complaint of Chaucer to His Purse*, in which he saluted him as a "true king" (verray kyng). The very fact that he had difficulty getting paid (though no difficulty getting approved by the King) after Henry IV's accession to the throne is on the contrary evidence of Chaucer's loss of favor.

Secondly, in his life, Chaucer seemed to have never played the power game, either. On the contrary, he made efforts to stay far away from any factional struggles. He distanced himself from Richard at some moments. His giving up the controllership of Customs, and relinquishing the lease on his house in Aldgate are ambiguously telling. It might be a by-product of the English crown's leaving Richard II's head, which means he was one of Richard's men and now stepped back. Or he might have sensed the threat after the execution of his associates in the king's affinity. It must have been a shock for Chaucer when he saw his colleague Thomas Usk's head displayed on a spike on London Bridge. So it is always difficult to detect or decide about any of his political involvements.

But Chaucer's turning away from any political issues in his work, especially in the *Canterbury Tales*, should not be understood as his lack of interest in, nor his being fully free from any political involvements. As Patterson correctly notes,

> (A)s one of the Richard's royal servants the poet did not, as is usually assumed, disclaim any interest or role in politics; on the contrary, he was very much the king's man in the crucial Parliament of 1386, suffered for his allegiance when the king's party failed, and was finally rewarded for his loyalty when the king regained power in 1389. ("No Man His Reson Herde" 122)

Chaucer's political attributes, as has been argued by Paul Strohm, are closely associated his connection with Richard II. While detailing Chaucer's social and political attitudes during the late 1380s, Strohm believes that Chaucer was not totally detached from the political turbulence, nor did he keep a foot in both camps as early scholars had believed. [①] Chaucer was after all Richard's man, at least for a certain period of time. His long and close association with John of Gaunt, ever a protector and supporter of King Richard, his various appointments, the annuities and fees he received from the Crown during Richard's reign, all contributed to Chaucer's standing

---

[①] Refer to Strohm, 1989, esp. Chapter 2: The King's Affinity.

with King Richard.

Jones's suspicion of the truth about Chaucer's death in his book *Who Murdered Chaucer*? also poses a question that has never been attempted. ① For Jones, the mystery of the total silence of any details expected concerning such an illustrious man has been odd and this fact is significant in contributing to what Chaucer really is. The quiet disappearance can be rather the result someone is trying to achieve than a mere historical coincidence. So his mysterious death could be an event with political color.

Based on the above elaboration of his politicalness, it is sensible to conclude that Chaucer had his own political views and would inevitably express them in one way or another through his poems. It is also possible for him to criticise the unreasonable and the unfair in the social and political life. But his way of expression to them was different and special due to his own position as a court poet. This is mostly illuminating examined against the background of the rise of poets over minstrels in fourteenth century court.

The fourteenth century witnessed the decline of professional minstrels and the rise of poets in the court culture. This change of fashion is significant. ② First, the relationship between minstrels or poets and their audience, especially the king had changed. Thus appeared poems which differed from the songs of the minstrels in subject, style, tone, and language. Second, the social role court poets played, for example, to instruct or give advice to the king had not been expected from the minstrels. Poets began to ascend to the centre stage of state affairs. They were not exclusively entertainers as the minstrels were. Hence there emerged special characteristics of court poetry. They were different in both subject and style from

---

① See Jones, 2004.

② The *Canterbury Tales* presents the reader with a good example of the contrast between a minstrel and a poet. When Chaucer the pilgrim recited the poem he had committed to memory a long time ago, that is, the *Tale of Sir Thopas*, he was cut off even at the third "fit" by Harry Bailey, the host. But immediately after that, Chaucer the pilgrim gave a highbrow example of the "advice to the princes" genre, that is, the *Tale of Melibee*. The switch from the role of a minstrel, who is simply entertaining, to an intellectual worthy of consultation by his monarch is striking. The different acceptance of the two tales by the pilgrims portrays the rise of poets as well.

CHAPTER ONE
COUNSELOR OR CRITIC?

minstrels' performance.

Minstrels, when they gave their performance, reciting old tales and songs, were granted certain authority. They would discourse authoritatively on subjects like battles, chivalry or courtly love, although they might never have been in a battle, or have experienced the grief of being separated from their beloved ladies. It was a tradition that they might address the court audience directly without fear of being blamed for their tone of authority, because that was what one might expect from a professional performer. However, for a court poet, it was unthinkable for him to address his courtly audience, including the king and his social superiors, in the manner of a minstrel. They must be more careful and cautious about both the subjects and the manner of his composing, especially in providing moral instructions or political counseling. This was determined by the status of a court poet.

Meanwhile, court poets remained lesser gentry, despite their access to the world of the aristocracy. They were naturally supposed to show due respect to their superiors. For example, Chaucer's writing was characteristic of self-effacement and deference to his audience. In *Troilus and Criseyde*, when dealing with the love-longing matter, which was supposed to be an exclusively aristocratic prerogative, he deferred to the judgment of his audience: "Thow, redere, maist thiself ful wel devyne / That swuch a wo my wit kan nat diffyne." (V. ll. 270-1)[①]

Therefore, when giving moral instruction or political advice, a court poet must be aware of his status in the court. His way of instructing or advising must be appropriate for his identity of a court poet. He should make efforts not to offend his audience, though he was well-intended. So to stay safe, he preferred to explore the wealth of the authoritative texts and to pass a message implicitly rather than revealing his views by direct and plain expression. The tradition of "Mirror for Prince" Chaucer followed is one example of such wealth.

The main purpose of this genre is to offer advice. Bloomfield and Dunn briefly analyze the point of writing in this tradition as

---

[①] The modern version of the two lines are: "You, reader, may easily guess yourself / That such a woe my wit cannot define."

follows.

> We find advice to the princes in various forms of literature, above all in praise poems, but we apply the generic term only to those works whose chief task is to advise the prince. [. . .] In these works the poet was carrying out in a more systematic way an ancient function: to instruct the ruler or any ruler in the ways of wisdom, that is, the rational processes in the universe and society so that he may fit himself into the proper cosmic and social roles he assumed or is about to assume when he becomes a chief, ruler, or king. [. . .] The recognized poets had a certain leeway in criticism and suggestion, but they had to be careful. Their advice was presented both in direct and indirect speeches and poems. (137)

It is generally taken that there won't be any provocation in the tradition of "Mirror for Prince" because they are usually political treatise thought of adopting the king's point of view. Thus it will be hard to find from poems of "Mirror for Prince" any provocative or aggressive elements. Besides,

> they are often seen as compilations of platitudes, clichés, and ancient stories so general, so distant in time and place, and so inert that they have no bearing on political concerns contemporary with their writers and translators [. . .] would have little to say to their specific contemporary contexts. (Ferster 2)

Therefore Chaucer employed this genre in his writing. The choice of the genre "Mirror for Prince" was consistent with his status and his role of a court poet.

The seeming impossibility of any opposition to the king in the tradition of the "Mirror for Prince" helps to lower our expectation of Chaucer's role as critic, even without consideration of Chaucer's own position. And the often general assembly of cliché and old stories demonstrates little in the way of contemporary events. However, the apparent distancing from contemporary events in a poem is itself significant. It was especially true in late medieval England.

The advice to the king supposedly embedded in this genre was

CHAPTER ONE
COUNSELOR OR CRITIC?

especially important when a king's incapacity to govern resulted from immaturity or illness. Under such circumstances, the council played an important role in government. Conflicts and struggles between the council, the monarch, the nobles and the king's friends became central; and the establishment and development of parliament complicated the situation further. The fact that this genre was so popular but had not any direct reference to contemporary events is thought-provoking. The writers were well aware of the dangers of criticizing the king and his advisers. ① Thus the choice of this genre is in fact a guise or strategy for voicing their own views. ②

On the other hand, "(a)dvice can become critique," as Ferster believes, "and the audience for the work may include not only the prince to whom it is nominally addressed, but his subjects as well" (4). The readers of this advice literature included not only royalty, but also those who were interested in the governance of the king, such as those who worked in or out of the court, holding an office. Thus the same poem may actually have two effects which could be different. It depends on the audience's hermeneutic reception. For the prince, it should at least sound like well-intentioned advice. For those who were almost Chaucer's equals in the court, and the readers outside the court, it could have the effect of criticizing. Chaucer couldn't be ignorant of this.

The deconstructive reading of the *Melibee's Tale* as belonging to

---

① To be an advisor of the king is a dangerous job. They may easily fall victim to factional struggles. As is easily understood, to attack the king himself would have been treason; to attack the king's advisers would avoid this charge while maintaining the pretence of loyalty to the crown. Chaucer was well placed to see the situation and tried to evade any possible blame of being a bad advisor. Even the king's old tutor, Sir Simon Burley, could not be effectively protected by the Crown despite of all the protest and appealing. His execution by the aptly named Merciless Parliament of 1388, though hard to understand and accept, taught a good lesson to other counselors, including Chaucer.

② The risk is that they may suffer from censorship or suffer from ineffectiveness, that is, the failure of the implied message to be decoded. So they have to balance the two extremes. In Ferster's words, "The predicament of the writer facing restrictions on speech, as Robert Lane describes it, is that 'strategies that would protect him also risked rendering unintelligible the sensitive material that required protection in the first place.'"(4)

31

the genre of advice, for example, is proof that Chaucer was a supporter, not an opponent, of the disempowered monarch. He used the deconstruction of advice to oppose the Appellants when they were in power.① He was in this case a critic of the Appellants because he stood by the monarch, his patronage.

To generalise, the role Chaucer played as a court poet is multiple. He was a prince-pleaser, a counselor, and sometimes a critic. It all depends on what position he took. It was his duty to compose poems to please his royal audience. Meanwhile, he had the opportunity to instruct and advise his superiors, though he had to do it in a wise way. In addition, his writing was a relatively safer place for his own political utterance, voicing his pros and cons in a muffled way.

To write by following the genre of the "Mirror for Prince" is a typical example of this. While political actors use it to oppose the king, as it has been part of political thought, writers make use of it to achieve political address with less danger. The *Tale of Melibee* makes a good case study, because it can illuminate Chaucer's role of a counselor through his poetry composing.

Chaucer's Counseling: The *Tale of Melibee*

The *Tale of Melibee*, as its genre indicates, provides general advice for its audience, though it is now frequently recognized as a political tract written specifically for Richard II.② The Chaucerian narrator temptingly associates the tale with Chaucer the author. Thus a detailed analysis of the tale will help further a better understanding of Chaucer's role of a counselor and his way of counseling.

Despite of its importance, the *Tale of Melibee* is not a tale often

---

① Detailed analysis, see Ferster, 176.

② In Cooper's words, "The most cogent evidence for such a purpose lies in its omission of the quotation from Solomon found in the original, that laments the state of the land where the king is a child: a text that would hardly have been tactful in late fourteenth-century England." (1989:311)

admired by modern readers, mainly because of its clogged prose style, with allegorical abstraction, moralizing didacticism and long catalogues of proverbs.① However, its reputation has recently risen. It has been considered as an essential structural unit in the *Canterbury Tales*.② More importantly, the interpretation of the tale as a satire on chivalry and as an attack on wars, including civil conflicts and the French War, helps to foster a better appreciation of it. The issues it discusses are still and even more significant nowadays: "They are problems of war and peace, of the maintenance of national honor and its relation to a policy of pacific disarmament, of how policy is made and of the proper roles of legislatures and advisers in formulating that policy" (Benson 17).

But the tale's peace-making subject is not irrelevant to nor does it contradict the subject of counseling. They are in fact two threads intertwined. The tale tells how Melibee, a landowner, takes counsel from "the grete congregacioun of folk" (l. 1004) on how to respond to the injustice done to his family in his absence: house invaded, wife beaten and daughter wounded. Prudence the wife argues with her husband Melibee on whether he should listen to any of the discordant counsels from the folk: to be cautious or to take revenge. She tells him to choose counselors carefully and to evaluate their advice based on their motives. She criticizes all the counsel he has received, and judges against open war or feud, both for practical reasons (Melibee is outnumbered) and moral ones, and provides remedy for it: to negotiate peace and leave all to God's grace and forgiveness. Thus, it is a tale about taking counsels and advocating peace.

Superficially, the tale is about a domestic issue entailing personal revenge. Judging by the order of it in the *Tales*, it has also

---

① See more in Cooper, 1989, 321.

② See *Riverside*, 17. For more, refer to *Riverside*, 924: "A number of recent critics regard it as having a central thematic function in the Tales. Howard (Idea of Ct, 309—316) considers it a 'major structural unit' in the Tales, part of the 'address to the ruling class' that is a recurrent theme of the Tales. Ruggiers(in Ch Probs, 83—94)considers the tale's emphasis on prudent action, the taking of wise counsel, and the right use of the intellect part of the main concerns of The Canterbury Tales." Mann asserts the centrality of this *Tale* and of Prudence in particular (1991,120—127, also Brewer, 1998, 364—369).

been considered as Geoffrey's revenge against the Host, who interrupts his telling of *Sir Thopas*. But the tale in fact addresses not only private but also public policy. It has acquired a wider vision concerning the war and peace, the counseling, and any other serious messages, moral or political. It becomes one of the rare samples of Chaucer's writing with topicality.

Peacemaking: *Melibee and Richard II*

The tale's subject of peacemaking, and the status and character of Melibee, associate the reading of it closely with Richard II, which endows the tale with a profound topical significance.

In the first place, Melibee's threat to exile his adversaries attributes to him kingly powers. This extends the tale beyond private matters to public concerns, and thus easily reminds its audience of the similarity of Melibee to Richard II. The similarity, according to Cooper, is also well indicated in the primacy of the virtue of mercy in a ruler in the more freely expanded closing part, plus Chaucer's rare but deliberate excision of the lament over a land governed by a young king. And the few additions, such as "the wilde hert" in "Ovyde seith that 'the litel wesele wol slee the grete bole and the wilde hert'," are also telling proofs (1324). "(T)he wilde hert" is a close association of the white hart, a personal badge Richard assumed in 1390 (*Guides* 312).

The tale's subject of peace-making is not, as it appears, to be confined within the realm of the neighborhood. The significance of the subject is as extensive as it is related to a society, which is constant of conflicts and wars. Hotson, for example, holds that "the Melibus is a political tract, designed to dissuade John of Gaunt from launching on the invasion of Castile in 1386" (qtd. in Stillwell 433).① Johnson takes it to be concerned with the war between England and France (137—155). George H. Cowling mentions the

---

① See Stillwell, note 6, 433; Hotson, Leslie, "The Tale of Melibeus and John of Gaunt", *Studies in Philology*, XVIII, 429—452.

Hundred Years' War as a reason for the timeliness of the *Melibee*: "Its [*Melibee*'s] appearance among the *Canterbury Tales* seems to indicate that the strain and loss in blood and treasure due to the Hundred Years' War with France had caused the prudence and pacifism of this allegory to appeal to others besides Chaucer." (qtd. in Stillwell 434)① In fact the tale may associate with other possible wars, such as the battle with John of Gaunt, and the riot in London.

Therefore, *Melibee* should be read from a wider perspective so as to see its social and topical significance. The advice it provides, especially on the superiority of reconciliation to war, could have had relevance to a series of events during Chaucer's career. The date of *Melibee* contributes much to the tale's topicality.

Melibee, together with others in the *Tales*, such as *Knight*, *Physician* and perhaps *Monk*, is commonly accepted to be among the earliest written in the *Canterbury Tales*, and thus in the mid of late 1380s.② The 1380s were a decade witnessing a series of domestic crises starting with the Peasant's Revolt in 1381. The tension of the Revolt was built up rather than resolved in the succeeding years and culminated in 1388, when the King's favorites were exiled or executed by the Merciless Parliament. Thus the military policy and the revolt of the Appellant lords against Richard II appeared to be events Chaucer was reminded of in his composing of the tale.

Peace-making was however not a policy Richard was unfamiliar with. On the contrary, he was himself a pacifist. And theoretically speaking, Richard's pacifism was not alien either. It reflected the trend of his time. Peace had in fact been seen by many influential thinkers of the day as an ideal of kingship and the desire for peace as the mark of a just ruler (Jones 11). Richard might follow other great monarchs in Europe in cultivating a new court culture. For example, both Robert of Anjou in Naples (1309—1343) and Frederick II in Sicily had been learned men, the latter having been the patron of Petrarch and Boccaccio. "They established a culture of literature, science and the liberal arts as the mark of the modern, sophisticated ruler," and thus most probably were examples for Richard to

---

① See Stillwell, note 1, 434; George H. Cowling. *Chaucer*. Methuen. London. 1927, 162.

② See Ferster, note 3, 90.

follow (Jones 18).

The peace policy might also have resulted from Richard's personal inclination and the influence upon him of his tutors, like Sir Simon Burley, or John of Gaunt.

> As Richard grew to maturity he showed increasing signs of refinement and sensitivity and his court "assumes a rather precious, even effete, character." It is the court of Venus rather than of Bellona, comments the hawkish chronicler Thomas Walsingham, with evident disgust. (Jones 13)

According to the Westminster Chronicler, when Gloucester nearly came to blows with his brother, the Duke of York, in the parliament over the king's old tutor, Sir Simon Burley, Richard was described as a king who "with characteristic mildness and good-will, [had] been quick to calm them down." "He was trying to change the English court from a war culture to a peace culture." (Jones 14)

But his pacifist inclination became his merit as well as demerit. To some, it was a sign of his lack of valor and prowess, his inability to deal with warfare, which was in striking contrast with his father, the Black Prince, who had a great reputation as a warrior. As his son, Richard II was expected to live up to that reputation. To their disappointment, he chose an alternative lifestyle and established a different ethos at court.

Contrast with his father, he was a peace advocator, especially with France. He married the seven-year-old Isabel for the clear purpose of consolidating the peace between the two countries.① It remained the objective of royal policy until the end of his reign. But his pacifist concern was not welcomed at home because the hostility between the two nations had developed over two generations. More forceful and effective opposition came from the magnates, the barons, and members of the nobility, among whom the Duke of Gloucester, the Earl of Arundel and the Earl of Warwick were the most constant thorns. They held the opposite opinion mostly for the sake of their own personal rather than the national interest. Their

---

① See Howard, 309—316.

difference in personal character and taste also set them and the king apart. They had a hearty distaste for the new court ethos. Thus there was a saying that Richard II's court was dominated by an effeminate ethos rather than the worship of valor.

Though peace-making was controversially received in the political life of Richard, a theme of such is to the taste of the current court inclination. So if it is an overstatement to say that Chaucer wrote the tale to cater for the king as a prince-pleaser, it wouldn't be entirely without foundation. It is, in some sense, true. But he had done more than that. In writing this tale, he seemed to have played the part of a counselor as well.

Counseling: Prudence, Sophie and Chaucer

The tale's discussion of counseling also possesses historical and social significance. Acknowledging the wide application of the tale's allegory though, Gardiner Stillwell also illustrates the possible references of counseling to contemporary figures and events. For instance, the comparison between Richard and Melibee in their hastiness, their being quick to anger, their lack of good counselors, and the comparison of Prudence with Queen Ann, Philippa, or Joan of Kent. [1] The tale's association with the domestic political situation highlights the importance of counselors' role. Cooper prefers the idea that it is a more general advice without referring to any specific one of the political crises (*Guides* 312). But as Ferster puts it, "When the tale appears to be referring to contemporary politics, it probably is. And when it appears not to be referring to contemporary politics, it may still be" (104). Chaucer's deliberate effort in making variations from the source texts in fact testifies the tale's contemporary significance.

Chaucer seemed aware of the possible political reverberations the tale may arouse. He tried to control them by making variations on the source materials. For instance, he omitted proverbs in his French source like "Woe to the land that has a child as a lord" to disarm any

---

[1] Refer to Stillwell, "The Political Meaning of Chaucer's Tale of Melibee", *Speculum*, 19, 1944,433—444.

possible political application of his tale. ① The proverb could easily be taken as a reference to Richard II because of his accession to the throne at young age. Thus the omission is a deliberate choice to avoid any possible association of the tale to the troubles of having a child king. The deletion limits the interpretation of the tale. ②

However, some variations on the source text direct to the political association of the tale. For instance, in line 1325, he quoted Ovid as saying that "the litel wesele wol slee the grete bole and the wilde hert." His substitution of weasel for the viper in his French source is significant, especially when it is taken together with the comparison of Alison in the *Miller's Tale* to a weasel. ③ The substitution contributes to the political possibility of the tale because the weasel was recognized to be Robert De Vere, and the hart, to be Richard, since it was the beast Richard had chosen to adorn the royal heraldic devices and badges of livery. Thus the mention of immature counselors may naturally be a reminder above all of Robert de Vere, one of those young counselors whom Richard was accused of paying too much heed to. ④

---

① See Ferster 92, note 13.
② See Ferster 93, note 15.
③ The weasel is an embodiment of both a playful little animal figure and an ill-omen associated with trickery and lust.
④ From 1377, the year of Richard II's coronation, there were criticisms against his advisors. But for the first four years of his reign, they were mainly from the Commons. The essence of the criticism was that Richard had patronized more of the new courtier nobility than the established aristocracy in royal access, which has determined the following more fierce hostility between the king and his counselors, and the royal aristocrats. The dissatisfaction was manifested in the continuous demands by the Parliament for investigation into the household expenditure. Facing such grumbles and challenges, Richard took hasty measures by letting the new council take control of the revenues, absenting himself from Westminster to be more closely connected with the young counselors represented by Robert De Vere. In the struggles, Richard played a role the effect of which is the inverse of his intention. He applied "violent, rather than constitutional" methods to fight against those aristocratic counterparts, and finally triggered the battle at Radcot Bridge between his supporters and the opposing royal aristocrats, the Appellants, who finally forced the ultimate destiny of the King's favorites: exile or execution. So from these events, Richard was shown to be the apparent protector of his counselors, but in fact helper of his opponents, because he had provided excuses for their action.

CHAPTER ONE
COUNSELOR OR CRITIC?

Although there is much speculation about who Chaucer's audience is—the court, the London intelligentsia, the new middle class or some combination of it—we can be sure that the members of Richard's court have access to it. ① The real purpose in his choosing to translate a pedestrian work like *Melibee* at this particular moment, and deciding to include it to the *Canterbury Tales*, is hard to know.

> Was he commissioned by the "court peace party" to translate it as part of the propaganda war against the hawks? Or did Chaucer choose to make the translation as his contribution towards a cause with which he agreed? Or, indeed, did Chaucer translate it in order to improve his own standing with the king and the court party? Whatever the truth, the fact that Chaucer chose this tale as his own contribution to The Canterbury Tales must have identified him indelibly as a member of the court peace party. (Jones 30)

The purpose of writing this tale is not to criticize, if it is only an analysis of the contemporary situation, but to offer valid and helpful advice. We cannot make an easy judgment on Chaucer's position. He might stand on the side of the King, as he himself benefited from him.

In fact, Chaucer was not within the advisory inner circle, yet he was never far away from the situation, no matter where he stayed at the moment, London or nearby Kent. He had the advantageous position of observing closely what was happening around him. The influence of the happening upon his writing would be inescapable, though silence has been well perceived as a characteristic feature of Chaucer's writing. He was to some extent a quasi-counselor, providing advice in his own way. Chaucer's addition to the original source serves to prove his role as a wise counselor: "Ovyde seith that 'the litel wesele wol slee the grete bole and the wilde hert.' And the book seith, 'A litel thorn may prikke a kyng ful soore, and a hound wol hold the wilde boor.'" (ll. 1324—1325) As Cooper indicates,

> The addition carries no special emphasis, and is a warning, not a

---

① For more, see Strohm, 1989, 26—27.

threat; but it would none the less serve to place Chaucer among the wise counselors of the treatise, not among the flatterers. His poem to the King on "Lack of Steadfastness" confirms his readiness to take up such a role. (*Guides* 312)

When he addressed Richard in the final stanza, "Shew forth thy swerd of castigacioun./ Dred God, do law, love trouthe and worthinesse" (26—27), we should not ignore the counseling role he was playing.

Interestingly, in their idea and way of counseling, there is an overlapping between Prudence and Chaucer. Prudence is a clear-headed political counselor, with great wisdom. She is an advocate of deliberation, which has been manifestive in Chaucer not only in his public life, but also in his relatively private writing where evasiveness is pervasive. Throughout the tale, Prudence doesn't spend much time in blaming the advisors' fault. On the contrary, she points out Melibee's lack of reason in choosing the advisors, his overwhelmed emotional situation before the real counseling, and finally his inability to make sound judgment after that. Chaucer might also hold that it was essential for a king to have a rational and objective mind, with the help of good counselors.

However, Prudence's "concern with the nature of power and thus with the ways in which political power can be manifested and sustained for the good of all" is debatable in Chaucer's case (Johnson 141—142). He actually showed deep concern over moral issues and common profit in his work. As Forster says, furthering Howard's view, "it unifies the double theme of 'commune profit' and personal salvation that had fascinated him since the 'Dream of Scipio' and which was emerging in the *Tales* as a whole" (408). [1]

Chaucer's naming of Melibee's daughter Sophie is also telling. Chaucer's assignment of Sophie, from the Greek for wisdom, to the

---

[1] The name of his daughter, Sophie, that is wisdom in Greek, is Chaucer's, which indicate Chaucer's view, politically or philosophically. (*Riverside*, 924: "Melibee's wounded daughter is not named in the Latin or French texts. Thundy (NM 77:596) suggests that the naming illustrates Chaucer's concern with the theme of wisdom in the tale; Sophie is Melibee's own wounded wisdom which needs to be healed.")

wounded daughter can be interpreted literally as well as figuratively. Literally, Sophie is wounded physically in the breaching of their house by the evil neighbors. But Chaucer seemed to attract the readers to the figurative meaning even more. At the very beginning of the tale, the naming of the daughter is introduced. And Prudence says to her husband after a long quotation from an old book praising the good of wisdom and women,

> And therefore, sire, if ye wol triste to my conseil, I shal restore yow youre doghter hool and sound.
> And eek I wol do to yow so muche that ye shul have honour in this cause. (ll. 1109—1110)

Thus his daughter's being wounded is the indication of Melibee's lost or damaged wisdom. It might be Chaucer's advice that at this political crisis, Richard should resolve the problems with reason. He, as Prudence, offered a remedy.

Chaucer's counseling is, however, strategic. His choice of being a translator protects him from any censure and danger. Choosing Prudence, the female spokesperson, is an even further cover of his own position. As Lynn Staley Johnson points out, "this suggests that Chaucer availed himself of a double blind" (154). The genre of "Mirror for Prince" has a truism that it is the prince who makes the final choices among the options given by the counselor. A counselor takes no responsibility for what the prince finally decides. Similarly, as a translator, or a compiler of the original source, Chaucer thus didn't need to take any responsibility for the ideas of the tale.

It is conceivable that Chaucer was well aware of the possible effect to read "his" tale wrongly. Or did he do it deliberately? In the *Prologue*, Chaucer the pilgrim exclaims to the Host and the audience that the tale is going to be instructive, and has been told many times, but he will do it in his way.

> It is a moral tale vertuous,

> Al be it told somtyme in sondry wyse
> Of sondry folk, as I shal yow devyse.
> (ll. 940—942)

Meanwhile he requires that he be excused if there are any variations, but assures them that the "sentence" of his version is unchanged:

> Blameth me nat; for, as in my sentence,
> Shul ye nowher fynden difference
> Fro the sentence of this tretys lyte
> After the which this murye tale I write.
> (ll. 961—964)

But as Cooper sensitively perceives, "when Chaucer excuses himself, something suspicious is always happening" (*Guides* 310). The "sentence" will remain constant despite the variation of words is suspect, especially when we consider how the rephrased tales differ from the original stories in the *Tales*.

On the other hand, what he cannot shun is at least the responsibility of the arrangement. There is in fact a paralleled line between the prince and the writer, or a translator or compiler such as Chaucer. He may excuse himself from any censure on the content. But it is he who made the translation at a particular moment. The choice to do this, in addition to his addition of, his deletion of, or his variation on the source material, all contributes his responsibility. It is the writer himself who performed the selection and adaptation of the sources, just as it is the prince who made the final decision on whether or not, or how, to take the counsels. This coincides with Foucault's notion of "author-function" well. [1] But to play the role of counselor as a court poet, Chaucer must have his own way. "He thereby positions himself, along with Prudence, on the periphery of events, farsighted, astute, and artfully disguised by the inherent limitations of the role he has chosen for himself" (Johnson 155).

Similar to Prudence, Chaucer is more like an educator who

---

[1] Michel Foucault, "What is an author?" in *Foucault Reader*, edited by Paul Rabinow. New York: Pantheon Books, 1984, 101—120.

appeals for rational and objective thought, who applies wisdom rather than force, who values brain rather than brawn. Because "(f)or all its stress on the processes of taking counsel, Melibee emphasizes that wisdom and understanding are a priori qualities, pre-existing good advice" (Cooper, *Guides* 318).

Chaucer, taken as "a shrewd and centrally placed political observer" of the immediate political situation, quite naturally engaged these issues in his literary activities, even if not directly involved personally in the political activities (Johnson 137). Together with other intellectuals at that time, including chroniclers of Richard's reign, and his contemporary poet, John Gower, Chaucer had a profound concern with the topical situation, the nature of governance, authority etc. Though all people at that particular moment in England would have been involved in or concerned with the topical situation, their reflection and participation were definitely different in perspectives and depth.

Between Counsel and Critique: Mirror for Prince

Apparently, Chaucer seemed neither to be a political counselor in the court nor a courageous critic against the dominating ideology as are expected from modern intellectuals. Nevertheless, he was both, in some sense.

Chaucer was not, in the strict sense, a counselor. He was out of the inner royal circle and had no formal opportunity to offer advice. Yet his poems, quite often read aloud before the court audience, including the prince as well as other court people, inevitably had an impact upon them. Writing poems became a channel to let his voice out, thus enabled him to play the similar role of counseling. The *Tale of Melibee* serves as a good example to show it. As Green puts it, "his [Chaucer's] position as court entertainer, successor to generations of professional minstrels, is belittled in the self-mockery of 'Sir Thopas,' but as the adviser to kings the author of 'Melibee' writes essentially without irony" (*Poets and Princepleasers* 143).

Chaucer was not a direct critic either. In fact, his writing was characterized as "indirect discourse." However, Chaucer was not the only one whose "indirect discourse" became a feature of his writing. Under the same environments of political pressures, it was natural for the Ricardian poets to adopt strategic indirection. No matter to what extent they were critical about the contemporary situation, none of them was radical in the sense of their anti-authority, though their poetry had been labeled as "public poetry" concerned with common profit. In Middleton's arguments, "poetry was to be a 'common voice' to serve the 'common good'" (95).① But these poets were not public intellectuals as might be expected from the modern view. On the contrary, they showed a kind of caution against any unfavorable interpretation of their works' ambiguity, as the alterations made by Gower, by Langland, as well as by Chaucer in *Melibee*, manifests. As Middleton points out, "their revisions seem largely dictated not by formal considerations, but by matters of social fact and currency"(98). Gower's alterations in the *Confessio* have incurred the suspicion of political trimming, and the C-vision of *Piers* might be an effort to mend the ambiguities which have been profited by those in the Rising of 1381, rather than the pursuit of fullness and clarity advanced by Donaldson (Middleton 98).

But on the other hand, Chaucer had written many poems that both counseled and criticized, especially in those of Complaint and Mirror for Prince. Many poems of complaints in medieval England shared themes similar to those of the Mirror for Prince, such as "the inadequacies of young counselors and the danger that flatterers will distort the king's perspective" (Ferster 10). For the similar reasons of shunning censorship, most of them were anonymous. For those who were known to the audience, such as Chaucer, they needed both protection from their patrons as well as their intelligence in applying devices through choosing

---

① "Common" here is set against the background of courtly or clerical values, thus more emphasis on common people in society. "Common love" can be shown from poets' concern with commons, as well serve the common as "public servants" in public service. See more in Anne Middleton's "The Idea of Public Poetry in the Reign of Richard II."

CHAPTER ONE
COUNSELOR OR CRITIC?

the proper genre and enabling intended ambiguity (Ferster 10). ①

The benefits of writing in the tradition of "Mirror for Prince" are many. One of them is that writers, in doing so, exhibit great admiration and respect for authority, because they simply provide options but leave the king to make the final choices. It is the king who is ultimately responsible for his decision. Thus, they will not have to take any responsibility for the consequences of the king's choice since they are only advisers, and therefore shun any blame. But this is not always true. In Richard II's time, the notorious "Appellants" accused some of Richard's advisers of treason in parliament. Advisers on the council and the king's personal friends and confidants became the focuses of conflict, since it was definitely safer to criticize the advisers of the king rather than the king himself. On the other hand, the repetitive morality of the literary works and their constraints and the veiled discussion of political issues become an effective way to protect the writers and translators from controversies and struggles.

But writings of "Mirror for Prince," in Ferster's view, "are not only more topical than they appear to be but also more critical of the powerful than we might expect. Their deployment of the comfortingly familiar stories and maxims of the advice tradition is often strategic" (3). The writings are camouflage for political commentary. Thus, the deliberate choice of the genre is in fact an indirect way for the writer to engage his contemporary political conflicts. The problem is that such strategies which protect the writers also risk being unintelligible to their readers and audience. The audience included not only the king or prince himself to whom it was nominally addressed, but also his subjects, including those in

---

① Ferster's analysis is convincing: "According to Coleman, the poems of complaint in the late fourteenth century 'can be classified thematically as mirrors for princes.' They share with works that are more clearly derived from the Secretum Secretorum themes such as the inadequacies of young counselors and the danger that flatterers will distort the king's perspective. But perhaps because of the risks of retribution for pointed political critique, many of these poems are anonymous. If the writer was known to his audience, especially if he was in a patron's employ or wished to be, he needed protection other than anonymity. As R. F. Green argues, the delicacy of the social positions of a number of the writers of advice whose names we know may account for the abstractions, generalities, and circumspection of their works." (Ferster, 10)

court who might be attendance at the reading, or those who read them or those who were read to outside the court. The advice to the king or prince may sound like critiques for his subjects. But there exists the risk that the criticism will not function if it is over disguised, "since if the critique is disguised well enough to 'fool' the government, there is no guarantee that it can be understood correctly by a wider audience" (Ferster 4).

So Chaucer is intelligent in choosing "Mirror for Prince" to be his genre. The difference between the tradition of "Mirror for Prince" and the outright topical criticism is that the former tends to be more general without contextual implications. Full of clichés, platitudes and ancient stories, they bear no political concerns contemporary to the writers and translators. And also to some extent, their sphere is more about morality than politics.① Of course, one cannot totally separate morality from politics, because blame cast on immorality could be fairly good evidence for attacking the opposition in politics. But the writings of "Mirror for Prince" appear to be more like advice rather than blame.

The writings of "Mirror for Prince," however, also have a mixed tone of challenge and deference. The mixture of criticizing and counseling is in fact one of the characteristics of modern intellectuals. They are not necessarily the opposers of the government. They sometimes contribute their thoughts, of criticism or of counseling, to good governance for the sake of the common people. This will in turn consolidate the governance. Counsel or critique, they are different in their ways of action, but similar in involving the use of the intellect and knowledge, the domain of speech or writing.

> (F)or all of them (Gower, Langland, and Chaucer), poetry is a mediating activity. This notion of the poetic enterprise reinforces the social ideals of a tonally felicitous middle style that was consciously chosen as appropriate to a particular expressive purpose. (Middleton 101)

---

① For more, see Ferster, 2.

CHAPTER ONE
COUNSELOR OR CRITIC?

Being the genre of "Mirror for Prince," and also the only one other than *Sir Thopas* that Chaucer attached to himself, the *Tale of Melibee* reveals Chaucer's double role of counselor and critic. His choice of the genre, the subject, and his variations on the source French text, direct the readers to his writings as well as his social strategies.

Chapter Two

Chaucer as a Social Commentator

The close relationship between Chaucer and the society in and for which he produced his works seems both beyond question, and is still called into question. On the one hand, it is self-evident that no one can conceive ideas and write them down in a vacuum void of any outside impacts. On the contrary, one is bound to be conditioned and shaped by the contextual environments within which he lives. This is especially true of scholars who approach Chaucer from the perspective of New Historicism or Marxism. David Aers, one of the outstanding representatives of this approach, makes the following remarks: "As our personal experience and identity is inextricably social, so the poet drew on language, ideas, practices and collective experiences which were given by the culture he inhabited" (*Chaucer* 1—2). Chaucer's association with his social circumstance is emphasized by other critics. Robert Swanson observes that "no more than any other author can Chaucer be divorced from his contemporary context" (397). Thus to achieve a proper and a relatively full understanding of Chaucer and his works requires an appreciation of the world of his time.

On the other hand, with the discouraging defiance of the sovereign author of recent theories, texts have taken the upper hand over contexts. "The fallacy of intention" rudely breaks the former relationship between the authors and the readers. The validity of studying the relationship between Chaucer and the society, by taking

CHAPTER TWO
CHAUCER AS A SOCIAL COMMENTATOR

his intention, his audience, the social and historical facts of his age into consideration, has seemingly been either ineffective or outmoded, and thus questioned. Apart from this, Chaucer's pervasive efforts to detach himself from any direct reference to his contemporary world puts such close association in doubts, if it does not totally deny it. The social structures seem not a necessity but a possible distraction for Chaucer reading.

Yet, Chaucer's choice of depicting or not the social events in his works should not be, or at least should not be the only dimension for evaluating how much he was involved in the world. The absence of the social events is as important as, if not more important than, their presence, because "the gaps matter" (Swanson 397). Though for a time some critics preferred to take Chaucer as an "aesthetic" experimenter rather than a "social" commentator, indicating a shift of focus in Chaucer studies, the tradition of serious, historically informed scholarship has always been sustained (Saunders 16). In fact, history is not, and will probably never be, far from medieval studies. On the contrary, it is getting closer to them no matter how capacious and contested the labels of theories are. [1]

In medieval studies particularly, it is highly recommended and appreciated that readers and critics situate themselves in that historical context, trying to figure out what the authors and the readers at that time might think. The failure to do this is both egoistic and futile. In Aers's words,

> our reading needs to be informed by a serious attempt to reconstruct the text's moment of production, its own contexts of discourse and social practices within and for which it achieved meaning. Without this we risk a monumentally egotistic and finally tedious projection of our own being onto every other human product, however alien. (*Chaucer* 6—7)

Therefore, an understanding of Chaucer and his works necessitates a study of the historical background, which to some extent affected his

---

[1] Fredric Jameson's exhortation "Always historicize!", for instance, has been hotly challenged in the field of literary criticism. (1981: 9)

perceptions and ideology.

> They (the texts) are, indeed, made by the actual people in living relationships, but made within determinate systems (social, political, linguistic, sexual, literary), and within circumstances they have not chosen. Any attempt to understand literature must include the attempt to re-place it in the web of discourses, social relations and practices where it was produced; the attempt to discover what problems, what questions it was addressing. (Aers, *Chaucer* 2)

P. Olsen also affirms the necessity of studying the context in the view of Austen's Speech Act theory and Wittgenstein's observation that to understand a language is to understand a way of life (17—18).①

Many Chaucerians have achieved remarkable agreement in reading Chaucer with strong awareness of the close relationship between the contextual climate the author lived in and the poetry he produced. As Rooney generalizes, "(t)he exploration of the historical background has ranged from the search for pertinent events which might elucidate references, to the study of intellectual contexts such as astronomy, science, memory patterns and rhetoric" (2). Knowledge of Chaucer's life, intellectual attitudes and disciplines, his familiarity with the literary texts and types and thus their influence upon him, all these do not hinder but enhance and enrich our understanding of the poet and his poetry. Knowing them

---

① Olsen is radically against critics who read Chaucer by projecting oneself, his age and his way of thinking. He remarks, "Surely understanding Chaucer's language and system of usages requires understanding his way of life: his Parliament, Chamber, wool quay, the ecclesiastical and civil courts that he knew, and the assumptions of the poets and rhetoricians who defined how tragedies and epics communicated in his age. When we have achieved this understanding, we have done the critic's first job. We may then, if we wish, look at him with modern eyes and even decide that we despise his vision and dislike his artifice. We ought not flinch. Better so to reject the poet than to make him the Narcissus image of our own historical or semiological fantasies"(17—18). But the problem is whether it is possible for a reader as well as a critic to be free from one's own historical or semiological fantasies. Unfortunately, all readings are a kind of subjective activity. On the other hand, it is the exact charm of a good piece of writing for readers of different age with different experiences to have different Chaucers.

CHAPTER TWO
CHAUCER AS A SOCIAL COMMENTATOR

in fact opens up new possibilities.

Exegetical or patristic criticism represented by D. W. Robertson reads Chaucer in relevance to the *Bible*, the most important and authoritative text in the medieval intellectual context. He is right to emphasize the importance of historical context to the reading of poems in such a statement as this:

> What does Chaucer's poem, then, mean to us? It means nothing at all in so far as "emotional profundity" or "serious thought" are concerned unless we can place ourselves by an act of the historical imagination in Chaucer's audience, allowing ourselves, as best we can, to think as they thought and to feel as they felt. (255—256)

As David Jeffrey observes, "Most critics of medieval poetry now agree that at least some understanding of medieval exegetical method is indispensable for a historical understanding of the language of medieval poetry."(xiv)[①]

Paul Strohm has fruitfully discussed the relationship between Chaucer's writing and the idea of medieval social organization from three aspects: socially and politically inflected topics, socially

---

[①] Robertson's argument of the moral function rather than emotional appeal of medieval poetry has been counterargued by many critics. They point out the limit of this approach of excluding other interpretations. It is neither valid if Chaucer is read as a mere moralist. According to them, if Chaucer himself intended all his works exclusively to direct the reader towards charity, he would hardly have felt it necessary to retract them. "The dangers of the Robertsonian mode are memorably captured in E. T. Donaldson's essay, 'Designing a Camel: Or, Generalizing the Middle Ages': 'the image of the Middle Ages now current looks like a camel achieved by a Committee on Medieval Studies trying to design a horse.' Donaldson demonstrates the need for a sophisticated critical engagement that allows for exceptions and originality, so that Chaucer may be seen as questioning and creating rather than simply preaching" (Sanders, 15). For all these counter-arguments, Robertsonian criticism can still be defended because it at least provides a possibility, a voice which speaks truth in some sense. In Saunders's words, "D. W. Robertson's allegorical readings, though frequently constrictive, provide a salutary reminder of medieval scholarship and the religious world in which medieval literature is necessarily grounded" (Saunders, 17). It has heightened awareness of historical context. For Bisson, "Critics who recognize the validity of exegetical principles without applying them single-mindedly often finds that 'doctrinal nuance constitutes not a fruit which is the essence of a tale, but a fruity flavour enriching a tale's bouquet'" (30).

grounded issues of literary taste and reception, and the generally held notions about the structure of society (*Social and Literary Scene* 1). Though it is hard to identify and elucidate Chaucer's personal tone from his works, it is by no means dispensable to be informed by the societal scene of his age, a time of both social change and resistance to social change. Burrow emphasizes the importance of present-day interpretation of old writers and works; meanwhile he admits the inseparableness between good criticism and knowledge of the writers and their age. As he puts it, "(g) ood critics... owe allegiance both to their author and to their own age" (*Critical Anthology* 118).

Therefore a glance at Chaucer's society and his position in and on the society is naturally a necessity to the understanding of Chaucer and his works. It is especially important for a study on Chaucer as an intellectual, which focuses on the poet's social role.

Chaucer's Position: in and on the Society

Chaucer witnessed one of the most dramatic periods in English history. It was an age of crisis and conflicts which covered every aspect of life: society, religion, politics, even economics. The Black Death, the Peasants' Revolt, the Hundred Years War, the deposition of Richard II, the Great Schism, and the emergence of the heretical doctrines of John Wyclif and the Lollards, all happened then. These conflicts, though difficult to be detected directly from Chaucer's works, constitute the specific historical contexts Chaucer's poetry was produced from and for.

Marked as an age of change, the most fundamental change of England in Chaucer's life time should be that of social ideology. This can vaguely or roughly be described as changing from tripartite to dichotomous, and consequently, from a supposedly stable, harmonious and organic state, to an unstable and conflicted one.

The orthodoxy of late medieval thought, deriving from a centuries-old "tripartite" conception, took the society as a divinely ordained hierarchical unity. ① As the Holy Trinity was composed of three persons, the society was seen to be made up of three estates: those who pray; those who fight; and those who labor. ② It is generally and positively held that social structures were essentially holistic, fundamentally based on ideas of community and interdependence. The concept of "body politic" embodies the conception of the organic relation between members. Each group contributes in its own way to the good of all. The failure of any part of the body will lead to the dysfunction of the whole.

The enduring influence of such a tripartite conception can be perceived within Chaucer's works as well. In the *General Prologue*, we meet three ideal characters who represent this conception: the Parson, who sacrifices himself for his parishioners (ll. 477—528); the Knight, who has devoted himself to crusading (ll. 43—78); and the Plowman, who works hard, lives in neighborly harmony, and always pays his tithes (ll. 529—541). However, it should not be taken for granted that there existed a harmonious and consistently mutually beneficial relation within the body politic. It was not realistically that simple, and there was always distance and difference between ideals and practices. In fact, the body politic was treated mostly hierarchically in the fourteenth century. The strong sense of degree in medieval social descriptions made the tripartite structure turn to a dichotomy between those high and low. Among those three estates, there existed a difference of status between the higher and the lower, as Bracton, the thirteenth-century legal commentator, tuned the traditional tripartite constitutors to those high in the ecclesiastical hierarchy, those high in the civil hierarchy and those remaining(Strohm, *Social and Literary Scene* 2).

---

① "It had been used back in the twelfth century by John Salisbury, in his Policraticus, to exemplify the notion of the commonwealth; it was also invoked in the statutes of Oxbridge colleges to indicate the relationship between the various ranks of their memberships." See Swanson, "Social Structure", in Brown, 2002, 399; The rise of the theory of the three estates between the eleventh and the thirteenth centuries in France is scribed by George Duby, *The Three Orders: Feudal Society Imagined*, trans. A. Goldhammer, Chicago/London, 1980, see Boitoni, 17. Also Mann, 1973.

② For the explanation of "estates", refer to Mann,1976, 1—16.

Bracton's division, as well as his commentary on the social structure, focuses more on the separation and opposition between the higher and the lower (those remaining). Meanwhile his version permits recognition of new classes of persons who are not accommodated in the tripartite system. "Those remaining," in Bracton's division, are a general category of "freepersons and bondpersons," which comprises the majority of the fourteenth century populace. Admittedly most of the remainder were agricultural workers bound to the land, though there were also a minority of city-dwellers, who constituted "those remaining." It was this "middle class," those gentils, such as the knights and squires, who enjoyed the status of aristocrats, yet without financial benefit, those non-gentils, such as the urban merchants who were usually entitled "citizen" or "burgess," who enjoyed wealth yet without high status, who served the city and the Parliament as knights and squires in the battlefield, who were becoming more important (Strohm, *Social and Literary Scene* 2—3). Factually, it was just their emergence that wobbled the presumably stable tripartite social structure. They were free to climb to a higher level of the hierarchy, though there were many who might possibly stay at the bottom.

On the other hand, those in the higher levels of the hierarchy might be shifted down to a lower stratum, for various reasons ranging from financial to political.① Thus a split within emerges, which represents one aspect of the conflicting state of that age. Therefore, it is naïve to hold the belief that the society in late fourteenth century was a divinely ordained hierarchy, which was free from social conflict. In fact, "(t)he period was characterized by social fluidity, rather than by the formal maintenance of traditional hierarchies" (Swanson 402). Hence, more conflicts and crises.

---

① One of the important factors that leads to the social shifting is the expansion of non-agricultural employment and the emergence and increasing importance of the traders and merchants. Rigby sees the structure of English society in Chaucer's time as pyramids but made up of two groups: the laity and the clergy. For the laity, besides their social status, the economic factor plays an important role in the hierarchy. Representatives in Chaucer's are the Franklin, the Merchant and even the Host etc. Details see Rigby in Ellis 2005, 27—28.

CHAPTER TWO
CHAUCER AS A SOCIAL COMMENTATOR

There existed distance and difference between the official ideology of the tripartite conception and the social reality of dichotomic division.

The mixed and masked relation between the higher and the lower on the social scale did not reflect the whole picture of the dichotomous state of the society. It constituted only part of the scene of the social conflict.

Its focus on the social and political position, however, excluded a special group: the women. Women belonged to no estate, being totally excluded from a male-dominated society. ① Though sometimes women did act independently in practice, for example the Wife of Bath in the *Tales*, no position and place was reserved for them in a male-oriented fourteenth-century society. No real attempt was made to accommodate female autonomy. As Rigby states plainly, "(i)f status (noble, gentle, or common; lay or clerical) and class were two key axes of inequality, a third major aspect of medieval social stratification was gender. [. . .] (G)ender was a key determinant of an individual's access to, or exclusion from, wealth, status, and power" (*Society and Politics* 29). Chaucer's characterization of women, his depiction of the man-woman relation, and his ambiguous attitude toward women, which is most controversial, makes Chaucer's role as social commentator more complicated.

Another aspect which demands great attention in considering Chaucer's social commentary is his view on religion. As Swanson says,

> No consideration of Chaucer's reflections of and on social structure can be confined to his portrayal of the lay world; it must also integrate his stance on the social role of the church. Even if we see Chaucer primarily as a secular writer, that secularity is explicitly medieval, and accordingly "worldly." His views on the church's place in society can also therefore be considered in terms of contemporary "worldliness," without bringing in modern notions of secularity as a rejection of religion and spirituality. (397)

---

① "Estate" is defined as "a class of person, especially a social or political class or group; also a member of a particular class or rank," and "a person's position in society ... social class" (Mann, *Estates Satire* 3).

超越的可能：作为知识分子的乔叟
Possibility of Transcending: Chaucer as an Intellectual

In a society in which Christian ideals are dominant and prevalent in routine life, the social structure is not complete without considering the religious and spiritual demands and function. The role of the church is as important as other social forces. Chaucer's reflection on the church's role rests mainly on his depiction of the ecclesiastics. The portrayal of them in the *General Prologue*, the stories told by them on the way to Canterbury, and also their responses to the stories, all these drew a picture of the religion at that time, which will be later illustrated in a more detailed way.

Generally speaking, whatever the aspect of society, there emerged a more conflicting relationship between two poles, between the socially high and the socially low, between man and woman (genderly high and low), and between the ecclesiastic and the secular, with those of high status being challenged. Instead of the idealized stability and harmony, there was in practice mobility and conflicts. The supposed stability of the society was threatened by the change in the social constitution, and even shattered by the concomitant Plague and Revolt. The shifting and changing of social structure from tripartite to dichotomous is manifestly revealed in Chaucer's short poem, *Lak of Stedfastnesse*, as the "so stedfast and stable" world where "mannes word was obligacioun" has been "turned up-so-doun" that "now it is so fals and deceivable / That word and deed" (ll. 1, 2, 5, 3, 4). "All that has been overthrown through greed and desire for power to such an extent that men are judged by their ability to oppress others" (Rudd 56). Thus, the conflicting rather than the co-operational relation in the society took place.

The conflict was even intensified because of the economic changes consequent upon the Black Death and later epidemics. Peasants and laborers were in an advantaged position to demand high wages and were no longer meek and obedient as they were supposed to be. The landlord and the like would not, however, submit to this new state, and thus tried to maintain their position by turning to legal and political power. The notorious royal Ordinance of Laborers of 1349 was an example of such efforts. ① But it was not easily put into practice. There were a series of efforts on both sides, so more supplements were provided. The House of Commons, made up mainly of gentry and rich town people, also made attempts to force the laborers to remain in their location and work on the land, which was their assumed place and role. ②

Under such social circumstances, then, what would and could Chaucer do as a court poet as well as a civil servant? How would he react to the changes taking place and address the consequent problems? These questions will direct us to Chaucer's position on the society.

To understand Chaucer's position on the social structure, the best and probably the only place to go is still his texts. Without the journals or reviews left behind, we have more difficulties in perceiving the personal opinion of Chaucer's than that of modern writers. His poetry becomes the only clue we can trace and infer, though the validity is highly suspected.

As the theory of the autonomy of texts goes, there exists no definite and certain meaning in any text. Consequently no final agreement is expected to be reached. As far as Chaucer's position on the society is concerned, there are even more disagreements than agreements. The polarity has been illustrated by Swanson.

> From one standpoint he appears as a staunch supporter of the accepted order, writing for the perfection of the society through the proper implementation of current social ideals, making criticisms in order to recall those attached to their proper social roles and functions (Olson 1986). From the opposing direction, he can be declared inherently subversive, explicitly challenging contemporary mores in order to overthrow false perceptions and align himself with a reformist trend which sought, among other things, to undermine contemporary denigration of women and the misuse of Christianity (Strohm 1989). (qtd. in Swanson 398)

---

① Details, see Rigby in Ellis, 2005, 33.
② See Rigby in Ellis, 2005, 33, also note 4, 48.

In Olson's view, Chaucer's poetry offers a positive view of his society, while others see their hidden subversiveness.①

For the critics who hold the former view, they see Chaucer as essentially an orthodox, conservative writer. In this camp are D. W. Robertson, B. F. Huppe, Sheila Delany, P. A. Olson, and Alcuin Blamires.② One example is chosen to demonstrate that Chaucer had ironic views on those who were not satisfied with their low status, seeking promotion and enrichment. In the *General Prologue*, Chaucer's description of the Guildmen is telling: they wear their daggers "chaped noght with bras / But al with silver" (ll. 366—367). This seemingly objective description easily reminds contemporary readers of the Sumptuary Act of 1363, which prohibits certain classes of men from having a superior style of life. Similar to the Act itself with its purpose of maintaining the privileges and distinctions of the elite, Chaucer's description subtly satirizes the Guildmen who go above their allotted place. And thus the description is actually morally loaded, allowing Chaucer's personal condemnation of them to leak out, though without telling it aloud, as what Gower did in *Vox clamantis*: "Nothing is more troublesome than a lowly person when he has risen to the top—at least when he was born a serf " (qtd. in Rigby, *Society and Politics* 36).

Such polarity mainly results from Chaucer's manner in addressing these issues in his poetry. This is quite different from Gower's direct and lengthy discussion about the topical revolt, relentlessly didactic in tone, where we are sure to arrive at Gower's attitude toward them. For him, it was nothing but moral decline in society. However, it is difficult for us to do the same with Chaucer. He never spoke directly about them. All that we can do to tease out his implicit view is to study the characters in his poetry, and the fictional persona of Chaucer the pilgrim, though they are still, admittedly, a no more secure way to establish the poet's own attitudes.

Still, Chaucer's personal view on the structure of society can be identified, highly speculative though, from the texts he left. Take

---

① See more in Olson, 1986.
② Details see Rigby, 1996.

the short poem, *Lak of Stedfastnesse*, for example. Some critics conclude that Chaucer endorses the monarchial system, by reading the last stanza of it as a highly topical utterance. One of the "Boethian ballads and envoys" that shares similar themes to those found in Boethius' *Consolation of Philosophy*, *Lak of Stedfastnesse* also shares with others in this group a certain common tone which is characterized by critics as "most straightforwardly reflective and socially critical" (Rudd 55). It starts with recalling the good old days when "things were secure and a man's word his bond" (Rudd 56). "Somtyme the world was so steadfast and stable / That mannes word was obligacion"(ll. 1—2). It is however immediately followed by a different and contrasted picture of the contemporary world, where

> Trouthe is put down, resoun is holden fable,
> Vertu hath now no dominacioun;
> Pitee exiled, no man is merciable.
> Through covetyse is blent discrecioun.
> (ll. 15—18)

Before an envoy addressed to Richard II, he comments that "The world hath mad a permutacioun / Fro right to wrong, fro trouthe to fikelnesse" (ll. 19—20). Though opinions about this poem are polarized, as elsewhere, between one argument for conventionality and another for topicality, because of the last stanza, those opinions are, however, not incompatible. Texts and actions, different but not necessarily totally divided, may be examined in the same environment within which both are produced and received. Paul Strohm reasonably associates this poem with the 1388 petition. For him, "(t)he emphasis on oppression and extortion within both petition and poem is explicable not because one document is a 'source' for the other, but because both petition [...] and poem [...] draw upon current language and concepts to address a current situation of abuse of power" (*Hochon's Arrow* 68).

So the last stanza might be read as Chaucer's imploring Richard II to reassert right rule by saying "Shew forth thy swerd of castigacioun" (l. 26). The apparent irony is that it is this oppression that has been criticized in the second stanza. Moreover, debates over royal prerogative and objections to its abuse characterized the later part of Richard's reign. But it was neither Chaucer's idea nor Richard's practice to solve by force the problem of the folk's "lacking steadfastness." Instead, Richard had already devised and enacted his own role as princely mediator, so that the rival factional struggles might be appeased. ① And coincidently, Chaucer urged him in the envoy to do the same:

> To submit to a series of voluntary self-curtailments ("Dred God, do law, love trouthe and worthinesse") and to efface his claims, in order to serve as mediator, go-between, and priest in the wedding between his subjects and their own lost virtue ("And wed thy fold agein to stedfastnesse"). (Strohm, *Hochon's Arrow* 69)

Strohm has also made a good analysis of the reasons for Chaucer's writing the poem for Richard from the perspective of his career. ② But his focus and objective is more than that. He holds the view that similar actions and texts emerge from a common environment, though in different forms. Thus whether or not the envoy was addressed to Richard should not be an essential question for understanding Chaucer's texts and his views. The social environment in and for which Chaucer produced his works accounts more for a better understanding of him, especially when it is examined simultaneously with the texts.

Currently many critics think that Chaucer's *Tales* is dialogical without arguing his own view, explicit or implicit. They "see Chaucer's works as disruptive of the claims of the dominant social ideologies of their day" and "in its insistence on the clash of different world-views embodied in the pilgrim's tales," the *Tales* "undermines the claims to authority of any single dominant discourse" (Rigby, *Chaucer in Context* 42). Chaucer's position on the society may be an

---

① See Strohm, 1992, 69.
② See Strohm, 1992, 69—70.

CHAPTER TWO
CHAUCER AS A SOCIAL COMMENTATOR

unresolvable enigma. ① However, despite the polarization of Chaucer studies on the issue of his social view, it was and still is a persistent magnet for Chaucer readers.

No attempt is made here to draw a unilateral and unconvincing conclusion about Chaucer's position on the society solely and absolutely from his own social position. That has been rejected and discarded as social determinism. It is nevertheless not, as those advocates of text-autonomy may hold, irrelevant. As has previously been argued, the poet cannot be totally free from the political and social web of the time in which he lived. But the problem is that it is difficult to fit Chaucer into the stratum or estate order of his society. As Swanson perceives, "The narrator—Chaucer has no estate identity other than as pilgrim. His liminal pilgrim state is perhaps one solution to the problem of fitting Chaucer himself into the estate system, given no indication of where he comes from, or where he will revert to" (400). He was a bureaucrat, taking his relation with John of Gaunt, but without any land. ② He was "non-productive, non-fighting (even making allowances for his capture and ransom in 1359—1360), and non-intercessory (except in a private capacity)" (Swanson 403) either. But his birth from a vintner, and his jobs, varied and changed, but mainly dealing with cash and commodities, made one distinguishing feature of his identity, that is, his identity with the newly arrived stratum of citizenship, the middle stratum, if not class. ③ His connection with financial issues will make a great, if not definitely decisive impact, upon his writing, because after all, writing is a social practice.

---

① According to Swanson, "The *Canterbury Tales* clearly say something about late fourteenth-century England. It is a reasonable assumption that Chaucer expected them to have immediate resonances, and they can accordingly be accepted as relevant comment on his world. Yet, despite an unending torrent of criticism and analysis, just how he reflects that world and its society, and the views which should be teased out of his works to reflect his own opinions, are questions still unresolved, and perhaps unresolvable" (Brown, 2002, 411).

② It is not only that between a patron and a servant, but also of family connection. He is traditionally counted as a brother-in-law of John of Gaunt because of the marriage between him and Katherine Swynford, usually identified on slim evidence as his wife's sister.

③ For the uncertainty about Chaucer's personal estate, see Patterson, 1991, 39.

Writing as Social Practice: The *Nun's Priest's Tale*

The tension of social conflicts was a pervading concern for people at that time, and writers were no exception. Gower predicted the impending revolt in *Mirour de l'Omme*, recalled nostalgically in his *Confessio Amantis* the past good time (though not specified) when

> The citees knewen no debat,
> The people stood in obeissance
> Under the reule of governance.
> (Prologue, ll. 106—108)

Langland even criticized those complaining laborers in *Piers Plowman*.① At the very outset of her remarkable book, *Socioliterary Practice in Late Medieval England*, Helen Barr puts forward explicitly that writings are examples of socioliterary practice. By using the term "socioliterary practice," she " 'locate'(s) the production of literary effects historically as part of the ensemble of social practices" (*Socialiterary Practice* 1).② To these critics, language is neither a mirror for reflecting passively anterior "reality," nor is totally independent of "reality." They actually interact and affect each other. Literary texts as part of these discourses are no doubt also affected by social forces. As Fowler notes, "it is a mistake to regard literary texts as autonomous

---

① According to Rigby, "By c. 1377 Gower's Mirour de l'Omme was predicting impending rural revolt: unless the lords awoke from their lethargy, the violent and impatient 'nettle' of the 'folly of the common people... will very suddenly sting us all' (26437—26508)". Rigby generalizes as follows, "Langland's Piers Plowman criticized those labourers who, unless they received high wages, complained against God and against 'Reason' and grumbled against the king's council for passing laws to restrict them. No longer would they follow wise Cato's advice: 'Bear patiently the burden of poverty.' Langland wistfully recalled an era when food was less abundant and labor less scare: 'When hunger was their master, none of them complained.'" (B. 6. 312—319) (2005: 34)

② For this part, refer to Barr, 2001: 1, note 1, 4.

patterns of linguistic form cut off from social forces" (qtd. in Barr, *Socioliterary Practice* 1).① Belief in the social determination of cultural production forces writing to be understood as above all social practice and therefore a detailed historical contextualization is necessary. In Barr's case, her proposition is that "the formal features of language used in literary texts are essentially freighted with social resonances and that to examine the literary language of texts in detail is simultaneously to examine the kinds of sociological work performed by literary texts" (*Socioliterary Practice* 8).

My focus here is however on the interactivity between the literary production and the social forces. I hold that the social forces embodied in the author and the audience plays an important part in the production of literary texts. It is almost inevitable that in writing an author will be influenced by his own social position. At least the position will decide his perspectives. Meanwhile the audience, whose reception and expectation function in writing as well. This attempt is of course not innovative but only a response to the widespread trend of "return to history" in the area of literary study.② Though no single label is available and valid for the diversity of interest and assumptions (the "New Criticism" for example), a common impulse does exist among critics who adopt "historical" approaches, new or old, an impulse "to traverse the terrain between literary texts and a material world that constitutes the not-literature of history" (Patterson, "No Man His Reson Herde" 1).

Chaucer's rare reference to contemporary events in his poetry might be naturally the primary source we could go to in order to tease out his personal position. The *Nun's Priest's Tale* has been held to be the only one of Chaucer's works that mentions the 1381 uprisings, though obscure hints in the *House of Fame* and *Troilus and Criseyde* have also been recognized by some scholars.③ The account of the chase at the end, the noise of the hunt being like the

---

① Qtd in Barr 2001, 1, note 5. The original source is from Roger Fowler's *Literature as social discourse*, London, 1981, 7.

② Lee Patterson emphasizes that it is a return with a difference, though. See Patterson, 1990, 2.

③ See Barr, 2001, 106—107, note 2; also see Bisson, 158.

uproar caused by the Peasants' Revolt, and the simile of the slaughter of the innocent Flemings, all contribute to the implication of the topicality of the poem. The furor that follows the attack of the fox on the hen run was described thus:

> Certes, he Jakke Straw and his meynee
> Ne made nevere shoutes half so shrille
> Whan that they wolden any Flemyng kille,
> As thilke day was maad upon the fox.
> (ll. 3394—3397)

It is clear that he knew of the events. As a controller of Customs himself, one closely allied with the crown, and also an associate of John of Gaunt—one of the principle targets of the uprising, whose Savory Palace being burnt down during the riots, Chaucer wouldn't have been ignorant of the events and the situation. Actually he himself might have been, or have felt himself to be a potential target of the rebels' wrath. But it is not clear what his personal attitude might be towards the societal tensions of which the Peasants' Revolt was a most dramatic manifestation.

It seems more natural to speculate that his position was against the rebels. As the Revolt resulted from the increasingly heavy taxation, brewed together with other tussles and tensions, Chaucer's own position in the government seems to have decided his position on this matter. As Delany confidently puts it after comparing Chaucer's the *Physician's Tale* with its Roman source in Livy, the glorification of popular rebellion, which the original version of the story espouses, "is utterly alien to Chaucer's world-view, our poet is a prosperous, socially conservative, prudent courtier and civil servant, directly dependent for his living upon the good will of kings and dukes" (Delany, *Shapes of Ideology* 137). Delany illustrates that Chaucer's silent reworking actually alters the significance of the story. By making Virginius a knight, not the common soldier in the original version, and by moving much of the action from public to private settings, the revolutionary possibilities of the *Tale* are markedly reduced. The theme becomes one of personal response, not public reaction (Rudd 174).

This view is also confirmed by other critics. David Aers explores

CHAPTER TWO
CHAUCER AS A SOCIAL COMMENTATOR

and appraises Walter's despotism in the *Clerk's Tale*. But for him, Chaucer's exposition of Griselde's ability to rule well doesn't imply his endorsement of a radical alternative to monarchical rule. As Tuttle Hanson puts it more directly, "If a peasant woman can so easily rule as well as a noble man—or even better—then Walter's birthright and the whole feudal system on which it depends are seriously threatened" (Hansen 191). Alcuin Blamires even regards him as identifying with the establishment he served throughout his professional career (qtd. in Bisson 158).

Yet, some scholars have also detected Chaucer's masked sympathy for the rebels in his work. Lee Patterson argues that Chaucer's distancing himself from "the forms and values of aristocratic culture" is "a conscious and deliberate decision" rather than "a function of the instinctive pull of a natural origin" (*Subject of History* 254). He further points out that "any turn toward alternative values will be marked with a powerful ambivalence," since Chaucer is least expected to have natural sympathy for the peasantry (*Subject of History* 254).

Helen Barr's analysis veers in this direction further and more explicitly. By comparing Chaucer's characterization of the 1381 rebels in the fox chase scene in the *Nun's Priest's Tale* with those in his contemporaries, such as John Gower and other chroniclers, Barr comes to a very different conclusion from other critics. To these critics, Chaucer held a view similar to that of his contemporary writers that the peasants were unruly, noisy and sometimes bestial, which is an argument Barr tries to counter. [1] To Gower and the chroniclers, the revolt consisted of peasants who were characterized as "roustic." In fact the revolt was taken part in by a social composition comprising artisans, tradesmen, and a minority of gentry and clerics in minor orders. [2] But they chose to recount the events as though peasants and bondmen were exclusively responsible for it. In doing so, they distinguished themselves from those "mobs"

---

[1] Barr, 2001, 107, note 3.
[2] Barr, 2001, 107, note 6: The social composition of the rebels is examined by Rodney Hilton, Bondmen made free: medieval peasants and the English rising of 1381, London, 1973, 176—185.

as far as possible. Their account and description of the peasants were flavored with the most unflattering tone. They were symbolized by animals: wolves and bears in Gower's *Vox*, "rabid dogs" running wild through the countryside, inhabitants of hell; their approach to London was monstrous and represented as the fall of civilization (Barr, *Socioliterary Practice* 108—109). Anyway, "(a)ccounts in the chronicles and poetic records, excluding Chaucer, are written from an utterly authoritative perspective, and seek to present the rebels in the worst possible light, and as far removed from any kind of civilized discourse as possible" (Barr, *Socioliterary Practice* 107).

Compared with his contemporary poets and chroniclers, Chaucer's treatment of this event however was different. Firstly, Chaucer chose English as his narrative language while others used Latin or French. I agree with Barr that the choice of language also has its political implication. While many narratives of the rebels are in Latin, and/or in French, Chaucer's choice of English, a vernacular language accessible not only to the highly ranked nobles, but also, and most importantly here, to the lowly ranked common people, including peasants, is significant. Thus, no matter whether conservative or revolutionary, the narrations in Latin or French are for an audience most of whom feared the rebels' actions. [①] As Barr takes it,

> While the educated prose of the chronicles may preserve the demands made by the insurgents, the narrative stance is relentlessly dismissive, refusing, either through narrative distance, or through choice of imagery, to give any political credence to the rebels' agenda. Dissident power is dispersed through discourses of filth, uncouthness, bestiality, madness, senseless destruction, grotesquerie, and noise. (*Socioliterary Practice* 113—114)

The very difference of Chaucer's choice of English over Latin in his writing not only shortens the distance other narratives obtain, but also indicates Chaucer's acute awareness of his audience, which

---

[①] See Barr, 2001, 113.

includes a shift of different constitutions, ranging from the king and his equals in the court, who may have the opportunity to hear his works, to those who might be lower, outside the court where his poetry would be read or heard. The choice of employing vernacular English rather than the high Latin or French is also an action that breaks the social boundary between the lower and the higher, if we temporarily put aside the emergence of vernacular writing already started in Europe and its literary influence upon Chaucer. So I believe, to some extent, writing in English is also a sort of violation of social decorum and hierarchy the revolt represents. From this perspective, Chaucer might possibly be taken as one of those who stood by the peasants.

Secondly, in contrast to other contemporary chronicles and poems, with accounts filled with disparagement and distance, Chaucer's narrative position is least authoritative. This is well elaborated by Barr in her detailed analysis of the description at the beginning of the widow and her meager life. Barr points out that Chaucer applies the strategy used in the *Parson's Tale* by letting the audience know what should be done. The widow lives in a small cottage by a little meadow, with little in capital or rent. She eats a slender meal with no sauce piquant, drinks no wine. In this case, what the widow has-not rather than what she has is put forth and emphasized, which reminds us of the portrayal of the Parson in the *General Prologue*. Here we see the combination of laborers and the nobility from their space, diet, and the rhetorical scheme of "descriptio" (Barr, *Socioliterary Practice* 114—116), thus social blurring is implied both in style and details. ①"Whan Adam dalf and Eve span / Wo was thane a gentilman?" because Adam and Eve represent both the laboring and the noble estates (qtd. in Barr, *Socioliterary Practice* 112).② As Barr generalizes, "While the textual strategies of Gower and the chroniclers strove to reassert hierarchical control over the third estate, the rhetoric of the *Nun's*

---

① As for the detailed analysis of the social blurring in the allegorical resonances of the tale, see Barr, 2001, 117.

② Qtd in Barr, 2001, 112. Original source is from Walsingham, *Historia Anglicana*, ii, 32.

Priest's Tale can be seen to reproduce the social equality demanded by John Ball" (*Socioliterary Practice* 118). Therefore, Chaucer's narration of the event, in spite of its evasiveness, is after all a social practice. It betrays his attitude and inclination.

Women in Chaucer's Society: Criseyde and Wife of Bath

As has been previously mentioned, the orthodoxy of the relationship between man and woman had undergone subtle changes in Chaucer's time. Because of the lack of labor resulting from the Plague, women in the late medieval period had the opportunity to take advantage of it. It "allowed and even encouraged some women to enhance their own estates and follow their own calling" (Knapp 117). High mortality and low male replacement rates secured jobs for women that were once preserved for men. It became more common for women to benefit from the death of men by inheriting property. But this doesn't mean that women had been advanced so far that by then men and women were on an equal footing. The fact is far from optimistic. In general, "any advances made by women in the late fourteenth-century were marginal and short-lived and women's fundamental position remained unchanged" (Rigby, *Society and Politics* 32).

But before an exploration of the problematic aspects of Chaucer's portrayal of women, some general attitudes towards women in medieval times should be reviewed. In the tradition of Christianity, women were either Virgin Marys—the embodiment of perfection—or seductive Eves—the source of evil and temptation. In fact a negative clerical attitude towards women, which was traditional and deep-seated, was intrinsic to medieval misogyny, though admittedly the gender relationship was never simple. In Bisson's analysis, "(c)elebrating Mary's perfections did little to ameliorate the perfection of women in general, largely because pursuing those ideals means denying central aspects of women's nature. The medieval cult of Mary had inherent contradictions and placed impossible demands on women" (201). She also mentions Bloch's analysis of the paradoxes

CHAPTER TWO
CHAUCER AS A SOCIAL COMMENTATOR

women confront because of the Christian stress on virginity.

> To urge a woman to chastity is to urge her in some profound sense to deny her femininity, since to transcend the body is to escape that which is gendered feminine... The logic of virginity thus leads syllogistically to an even deeper paradox... That is, if the feminine is elided to the side of the flesh such that the women is the body of the man, and if renunciation of the flesh is the only means to equality, then woman is put in the position such that the only way she can be equal is to renounce the feminine or to be a man. (qtd. in Bisson 201)

Thus women's proper role became a pervasive concern, and the gender tension a question. Against the background of a time full of conflicts and crises, dialogues took place in many social aspects, including a reconsideration of women's roles and images. However, the patriarchal social structures were still much in place by Chaucer's era. So how did Chaucer respond to the problem? Did he share his culture's misogynistic attitudes or was it possible for him to transcend them?

As Hansen states, Chaucer had an "apparently lifelong engagement with the women question" (Hansen 10). Chaucer was in fact "negotiating between the two literary traditions: the Ovidian one deriving from the *Heroides*, which explores the suffering of women wronged by unfaithful men, and the antifeminist one, which stereotypically focuses on women's faults" (qtd. in Bisson 192). Women are sometimes portrayed as his most virtuous and vulnerable characters, such as Griselde in the *Clerk's Tale*, who tolerates a series of tests from her husband and keeps her loyalty to him; Constance in the *Man of Law's Tale*, who maintains her faith and her virtue through a series of hardships that stretches over years and follows her across continents. Sometimes they are good counselors with reason and morality, Prudence in the *Tale of Melibee* for example, who succeeds in persuading her husband from the folly of revenge with patience and wisdom. And some women even play evangelical roles such as Cecile in the *Second Nun's Tale* who converts her husband, her brother-in-law, and numerous Roman officials. These women play a didactic role either by their own suffering or by their forceful employment of speech.① They are generally portrayed as positive and morally exalted. As Alistair Minnis observes, "In his poem women have in effect taken over the position of moral superiority supposedly enjoyed by men" (qtd. in Bisson, 208).

According to Bisson, "when a medieval woman sought her own features in her mind's mirror, she found reflected there a preexisting pattern that patriarchal culture had already shaped" (191). Was that true with Chaucer, when he depicted women in his works? As a fourteenth-century male poet who was well-read in the misogynistic discourse from clerical as well as classical canons, Chaucer, when depicting women, would inevitably be suspected of having the taint of the misogynistic tradition. Some women characters in his works can arguably be considered as counter-models to the ideal and moral women mentioned above. They do not possess the feminine virtues such as meekness, subservience and loyalty. Among the most notorious ones are Criseyde and the Wife of Bath, who are also the most complex images of women that have aroused constant and controversial interpretations.

Criseyde—"the false woman"

The story of faithless Criseyde has been one source of the charge against Chaucer by the God of Love, according to the text of the *Legend*. It is said in the text itself that it is a penance for Chaucer because of his spreading the disparagement of Love found in *Le Roman de la Rose* by translating it into English, and then further defaming the character of true lovers, and women in particular, by telling the story of Criseyde.② Thus, apparently, Criseyde was, at least for Chaucer's contemporaries, a symbol of being untrustworthy and unfaithful. Yet, Criseyde is far more complex than a mere image of a faithless woman. Chaucer portrayed her as a "round character."

---

① For women's employment of speech for positive moral purposes, see Bisson, 196—197.

② See Legend, F: 320—340 and "And of Criseyde thou hast seyde as the lyste, / That maketh men to wommen lasse triste, / that ben as trewe as ever was any steel." (F: 332—334)

CHAPTER TWO
CHAUCER AS A SOCIAL COMMENTATOR

His own attitude was also very ambivalent.

In portraying Criseyde, as David Aers has fruitfully discussed, Chaucer has transcended the simple, one-dimensional abstraction of morality which is one of the pervasive and mainstream currents in medieval literature. He wisely perceives that Criseyde's tragedy is inevitable not because of her own individual demerits in terms of morality, but as a result of the social structure. In Aers's words, "in creating the figure of Criseyde, Chaucer developed a social psychology which comprised a profound contribution to the understanding of interactions between individual and society" (*Creative Imagination* 118). Unlike critics such as R. O. Payne and D. W. Robertson, who together with others, believe that all late medieval poetry was governed by the same unambiguous "ultimate moral principles," Aers assumes that Chaucer's poetry, similar to Langland's, supersedes this "art for moral's sake" mode of medieval writing. They are both sensitively socially aware. That is, they are not blinded by moral doctrines, following the trend of creating their characters in the manner of moralists, though medieval poets were supposed to do so because their main task was presumably to convey already known "typical significances" through fixed symbols. For Aers, "individual action, consciousness and sexuality, the most intimate areas of being, are fundamentally related to the specific social and ideological structures within which an individual becomes an identifiable human being" (*Creative Imagination* 118). Before readers venture to remark on Criseyde's weakness, or "slydynge of corage" (V. l. 825), they have to face the situation that Chaucer emphatically presented, that is, Criseyde was situated in awesome and lonely circumstances under which her fear was justifiable and her reaction and action, though perhaps incomprehensible for some, are understandable.

The daughter of a traitor, Criseyde's sense of isolation in Troy is understandable, and it can even win sympathy. Her father's crime is so serious that all his kin "Ben worthi for to brennen" (I. l. 91). As a woman, a member of the conventionally subordinate group, she is vulnerable and needs protection as well. (Fortunately, she cleverly sees her only asset, that is, her beauty and sexuality, as a way out of the dangerous situation). It seems to me that Chaucer, by locating Criseyde in a socially inferior place and in a position of personal crisis, alerts readers not to make a simple moral judgment on her. In fact it is his implied sympathetic tone, the complexity of his women characters like Criseyde that could satisfy the feminists. Because in general,

> Chaucer seems no more able to portray a female who is both virtuous and three-dimensional than he is able to portray a cleric who is both good and human.... He means to be women's friend insofar as he can be, and it is this painfully honest effort, this unwillingness to be satisfied with the formulas of his age, which we as feminists can honor in him. (qtd. in Rudd 175—176)

Then why such detailed analysis of Chaucer's portrayal of women? What is the relationship between his role as social commentator and his portrayal of women? Although it is difficult to draw a clear-cut line between Chaucer the feminist and Chaucer the misogynist, one thing is certain: He is never a twentieth century feminist, nor is he a misogynist. What is more important is nevertheless not his personal attitude toward women. More significant and noteworthy is the role that Chaucer plays as an intellectual in the sense of being a *disturber*. In Minnis's description, "Within the framework of his patriarchal society, he creates a temporary space within which entrenched interpretive patterns are thrown into question; by so doing he disturbs, if not repudiates, the basis on which they rest" (qtd. in Bisson 208). In fact, Chaucer disturbs the patriarchal social structure by contrasting the position of women in the traditional court literature and their practical place in contemporary society. In the courtly tradition, women are idealized and women's marginalization is disguised. "Misogyny and courtly love are coconspiring abstractions of the feminine" (qtd. in Bisson 204). The romantic ladies are so idealized that they are actually dehumanized. There is in fact "a misogynistic thrust of romantic love behind its surface appearance of feminine empowerment" (Bisson 204).

In romance writing and literary work of courtly love, there is a conventional relation between men and women that is inverted and different from the actual practice. Women there are worshipped, served, and paid homage and devotion by the knights. Yet, in reality, women, no matter how high their social status might be, were in general inferior to their male social equals. They were subordinate beings and needed male protection. The opening scene of *Troilus and Criseyde* presents a clear picture of this.[①] And the conversation between Pandarus the uncle and Criseyde the niece gives a good manifestation of how Chaucer treated the conflict and contradiction "between aristocratic love conventions, in which woman was an exalted and powerful figure, and the reality in which she was a subordinate being to be manipulated and made to men" (Aers, *Creative Imagination* 123).

Chaucer's sympathetic attitude toward Criseyde can be further inferred by comparing his version with the source in Boccaccio. In Boccaccio's text, it is Criseida who actively organizes the consummation, and sends Pandarus to bring Troilus to her, and it is a private meeting with no other persons present on the night. While in Chaucer's version, Criseyde plays an inactive role in the whole process. She is not at all in the image of seductive Eve. In fact she has no wits and no way out under that circumstance. So finally she has no choice but to place herself in Pandarus' hands. She is actually being caught and cannot be a subject of herself. This passive or victimized image is further illustrated in Book III when Troilus is anxiously swooning at Criseyde's bedside. It shows clearly that the relationship between them is far from the conventional power relations in the courtly tradition. It is more like a picture of a predator and a prey. Only by then is the disguised reality revealed.

In a sense, Chaucer can be regarded as a prompter of questions who is aware of women's subordinate situation and tries to reveal the gender problem by contrasting the assumed with the real. In this way, he calls his audience to reconsider male-female relations and to some extent challenges the patriarchal social structure.

---

① See detailed analysis in Aers, 1980,120—121.

The Wife of Bath—"What maner womman artow?"

The Wife of Bath is another character that has been set as a negative role model in contrast to Constance or Griselda. Chaucer constructed her from the commonplaces of Latin clerical teaching and satire, and their vernacular derivatives on marriage and women, though, as was his custom, he did not mention the French works that he was more affiliated to.[①] The *Wife of Bath* shares many features with other sources. The depiction of female character derives from the rampant shrew and raging nymphomaniac of the satirical imagination. They are sexually aggressive, as the Wife of Bath's tormenting her old husband for instance: "As help me God, I laughe whan I thynke / How pitously a-nyght I made hem swynke!" (ll. 201—202) Her accounts recall those misogynist writings in "assuming a predisposition to masochism in women and must surely undermine any easy assertion that the Wife of Bath is a positive role model for women" (Rudd 121).

The Wife of Bath is also a representative of women who value experience rather than authority, which is exactly what the clerical as well as the traditional authorities warn against. Her fifth husband Jankyn owns and reads lots of such books full of bad wives. For men, women are aligned more with the body than the intellect; they are sexual rather than spiritual. The Wife of Bath has been an epitome of this, though more comically exaggerated and mocked. With five husbands in her life, she is implicitly referred to as gleeful, as she shares the name of Alison, the heroine of the *Miller's Tale*, and is also described in the *General Prologue* as having widely set gap-teeth and large hips concealed by a flowing mantle. All these contribute to the image of her as a sexually abused woman as opposed to an image of chastity and pure virginity. In this respect, she is closer to the women with carnal appetite that has been associated

---

[①] As Pearsall points out, "Chaucer does not mention the French works which he placed under even heavier contribution, namely the satirical Lamentations de Matheolus, which he uses extensively (see Thundy, 1979), particularly in the Wife's report of the abuse that she used to tell her three old husbands they would heap on her and her sex, or would have done if they had dared (235—378); and the Romand de la Rose." (Pearsall, 1985,72)

strongly with the exegetical tradition. ① In fact, the Wife embodies most of the faults for which medieval anti-feminist authors condemned women. This might easily make Chaucer's "all woman is frend" problematic. ②

There are also polarities in Chaucer's feminist reading. On the one hand, critics have found that in Chaucer's works, women sometimes become the centre, which is unusual for medieval writers. As Dinshaw has fruitfully demonstrated, the Wife of Bath actually "makes audible precisely what patriarchal discourse would keep silent" (115). However, Catherine Cox, in common with Susan Crane, "sees the Wife as an ambivalent figure, produced by, and reiterating, masculine, especially clerical, discourse, however much she might twist this for her own ends. The end product is 'anti-anti-feminist'" (qtd. in Ashton, *Feminisms* 371). On the other hand, though in the centre, a woman is usually represented as either Virgin Mary or Eve, the traditional opposition that Chaucer hasn't been able to escape. In E. T. Hansen's view, Chaucer replicates rather than transcends the concerns of his own culture. It is still men who occupy the centre. He is more concerned with men's place and men's anxiety. So for her, Chaucer does not supply anything new, but consistently, though maybe in a different manner, writes on the instability of gender. ③ From this angle, it is too simplistic to regard Chaucer as a proto-feminist. To some extent, he is more conservative.

In her *Prologue*, in the form of a long monologue, the Wife recounts her personal life and meanwhile condemns clerical and anti-feminist tracts seeking to define and contain women. But to her audience, those pilgrims who mostly comprise men or clerics, what

---

① See Bisson, 192—193.
② See Rigby, *Chaucer in Context*, 117. Also refer to note 2, 163.
③ Details, see Hansen, 1992. Ashton summarizes her view that "for Hansen, the Wife of Bath remains 'a dramatic and important instance of woman's silence and suppression in history and language' that endorses the anti-feminism the Wife rails against and that reaffirms traditional binaries. More generally, she hears in Chaucer's work not a genuinely female voice but 'something of a monotone making known both feminine absence and masculine anxiety'." (2005: 372)

she claims and performs consolidates her typical feminine features which they despise. Seemingly a feminist prototype, the Wife of Bath becomes the medieval anti-feminist stereotype. The authority of experience which she claims also becomes a target for mockery because of her own constant employment of authorities (authoritative texts). The more personal tone with so many personal pronouns, the repetition and inconsistency of her words, the loss of the thread of thought in speaking, all contribute to her feminine characteristics (at least in a man's eyes), and thus undermine/undercut her claimed authority. Of course, she asserts most forcefully her right to speak her mind. But for a performance that radically modifies clerical teachings about human sexuality, she earns the Pardoner's ironic praise for being "a noble preachour" (*WB Prologue* l. 165).

Comparison between Chaucer's *Wife of Bath* and his source texts will better our understanding the reason why Chaucer has made the character more complex, and thus resist a conclusion either way. Most of the source texts have the intention of mere didactics and satire upon the male-constructed evil women. For example, La Vieille in Jean de Meun's *Roman de la Rose*, the one which is very close to the Wife of Bath, is a loathesome, aging prostitute. She rejects any restraints on sexual appetite and teaches her young followers how to use their sexual power to seduce men, suck them dry and finally destroy them, gaining sovereignty over men and putting all their money into their own pockets. Similarly the Wife of Bath possesses this sexual aggressiveness which is best shown in her tormenting her three old husbands: "As help me God, I laughe whan I thynke / How pitousy a-nyght I made hem swynke!" (ll. 201—202)

However, La Vieille and the Wife of Bath are also different in many ways. The Wife is not a prostitute whose profession is to gain economic supremacy. She herself seems to be independent economically as someone in the cloth-making trade. The *General Prologue* shows more about her concern and interpretation of the marriage debt. "She has no implacable hatred of mankind, bears no vindictive ill-will towards her three old husbands, [...] There is a touch of affection. [...] Even her troublesome fourth husband she remembers with a certain of generosity (489—490) and she wishes him well (500—502)" (Pearsall, *Canterbury Tales* 74). Thus, "Chaucer, in fact, having taken over into his portrait of the Wife many of the traits of the traditional virago, has done much to subdue the element of the grotesque, or at least to complicate our response to the Wife so that we see in her something more than a monster of appetite and unreason" (Pearsall, *Canterbury Tales* 74).

Then what is the "something"? I think it is the Wife's self-conscious concern with the possible criticism of her own immoral or un-Christian behavior that is significant. She is thus not the stereotyped figure of female lust and domination. This is also another aspect of her difference from those in the source texts. As Pearsall points out after stating the inefficiency of the relation between the Wife's horoscope and her disposition, "the consciousness of a world of moral value in which mysterious entities like 'love' and 'synne' are sensed to have their being, and she herself perhaps not, are what lift the Wife of Bath out of the common run of trulls and termagants" (Pearsall, *Canterbury Tales* 75). Pearsall's comparing of La Vieille's discourse with the Wife's also demonstrates forcefully the complexity of the character of the Wife and its significance in contributing to the interpretation of the prologue and its teller, and perhaps, the poet himself. For convenience and conciseness, I quote them in the following: "The Wife of Bath's monologue is not so transparent: it demands to be looked into, puzzles and intrigues the observer, offers opportunities for contrary responses, creates, though itself a monologue, the effect of a dialogue, within the speaker and also within the readers" (*Canterbury Tales* 76).① Therefore, similar to the portrayal of Criseyde, the image of Wife of Bath Chaucer presented to us is not stereotyped. The two "round characters" will puzzle the readers, and then induce them to ponder and reflect. Thus, the characterization of the two most contested women characters reveals Chaucer's denial of making any simple moral judgment.

Portraying of Clerics: Prioress, Pardoner, and Parson

The Church in medieval time was not, as modern people suppose, monolithic and hegemonic. Though it was still an age when

---

① For the reading of the *Canterbury Tales* from Bakhtinian theory of dialogic interaction, see Liu, 1999.

faith dominated people and their everyday life, the problems of the Church had already been revealed. The problems became more evident and provoked more satiric attacks when the behavior of the clergy fell short of people's expectations. Their impotence in the face of the repeated epidemics of plague, their failure to perform their duties because of cowardice, or clerical abuses which resulted from placing their own interests above those of their people, in addition to their own internal strife, all these contribute to a ready understanding of any unfavorable comments upon the Church and its men.

Chaucer, like many of his contemporaries, was acutely aware of the clergy's weakness. His treatment of the clergy showed his concern with the subject current in his time. "He devotes more time to figures representing the Church than to any other group on the Canterbury pilgrimage, and *The Canterbury Tales* makes us acutely aware of their overt and covert tensions" (Bisson 50). If we judge from the number of the churchmen he depicts in the *Tales*, there are more anti-heroes than heroes. Roughly speaking, the Monk, the Summoner, the Friar, the Prioress and the Pardoner are all portrayed in one way or another negatively. Among them, the Pardoner stands out for his embodiment of extreme sinfulness, evil things committed, while the culprits are well aware of their evil intent.

As elsewhere, Chaucer's attitudes toward and ideas about religion are not immediately apparent. Again, his tales have to be interrogated so as to tease out the implicit message. On the other hand, the difficulty lies in the integration of his treatment of religion and other issues such as race, class and gender. For convenience as well as for the characteristic features they carry, only some of the clerics portrayed in his work will be discussed. They are the Pardoner, the Prioress and the Parson. [1]

The Prioress has attracted more critical commentary and controversy than almost any other character in the *General Prologue*. [2] Though much debate has been concentrated on the

---

[1] The prologues and tales by the Pardoner, the Friar, the Summoner, the Monk and the Prioress can be set against the ideal portrait of the Parson in the *Parson's Tale*.

[2] For the details, see Benson, *Riverside*, 802—803.

CHAPTER TWO
CHAUCER AS A SOCIAL COMMENTATOR

degree of the satire Chaucer offers, critics agree with Robinson that "if it can be called satire at all—(it) is of the gentlest and most sympathetic sort" (qtd. in Benson, *Riverside* 803).[①] Then what does Chaucer satirize in the portrait of the Prioress?

To generalize, the Prioress is in fact a violator against religious disciplines. In Cooper's words, she is the "Nonne" who is not in any simple sense nunly (Cooper, *Guides* 37). Her appearance is more secular than ecclesiastical: "Ther was also a Nonne, a PRIORESSE / That of hir smylyng was ful symple and coy" (ll. 118—119). As a nun who professes love celestial, many of her attributes show secular features. Her well-proportioned nose, grey eyes, pretty mouth, fair forehead, all direct to standard romance beauty. And her romance name "Eglentyne" ("And she was cleped madame Eglentyne", l. 121) has its associations with the white-and-red roses to which romance heroines are often compared. Her seemly manner of singing the divine office in a tonal voice, her exquisite table manner:

> She leet no morsel from hir lippes falle,
> Ne wette hir fyngres in hir sauce depe;
> Wel koude she carie a morsel and wel kepe
> That no drope ne file upon hire brest.
> (ll. 128—131)

and her sentimentality towards small animals: "She wolde wepe, if that she saugh a mous / Kaught in a trappe, if it were deed or bledde" (ll. 144—145) contribute to her figure as a romance heroine. The brooch she wears, with the inscription of "Amor vincit omnia" (Love conquers all), arouses more ambiguity because the word "amor" has been supposed to be dual in its meaning of divine and earthly love.[②] In the first place, nuns are forbidden to wear brooches.[③] Secondly, the motto, though interpreted by some critics as the Prioress's dedication to religion, has yet another possibility,

---

[①] This situation has been changed with more harsh criticism upon the Prioress because of the anti-Semitism of her tale. Details, see Benson, *Riverside*, 803.

[②] See Benson, *Riverside*, 805.

[③] See Benson, *Riverside*, 805, note 160.

of secular interpretation. From that point of view, the Prioress is condemned for wearing the worldly ornament and seeking secular love.① In addition, a Prioress, like the Monk, should not be travelling at all. Such leaving of office which she shares with the Monk has been more ironically condemned when the Monk is portrayed out of his cloister as "a fissh that is waterlees"(l. 180). She is also an imperfect prioress in having pet dogs, feeding them with fine food during an age lacking in material supplies and frequented by plagues and famines: "Of smale houndes hadde she that she fedde / With rosted flessh, or milk and wastel-breed." (ll. 146—147) The extravagance displayed also in her pleated wimple is itself what the rule of the Church is against. Therefore, she clearly violates many of the rules of her order, including going on pilgrimage, which is forbidden. In all, the Prioress's potentially secular nature epitomized by her brooch and her pets is frequently condemned as her demerits, if not evilness. ②

In spite of all the above, the Prioress lacks those failings traditional in satiric portraits of nuns, which are identical with those assigned to women in general. ③ But Chaucer's description of the Prioress does betray her fondness for nice clothes, which is akin to what characterizes secular women. What's more, "It is what remains unsaid—the image of what a nun ought to be—that gives the portrait much of its edge," no matter how Chaucer "keeps his air of innocent admiration" (Cooper, *Guides* 38). Chaucer reveals his hidden unfavorable attitude to the Prioress, though calmly and collectedly.

Contrasting to Chaucer's image as an innocent reporter of the Prioress, the Pardoner has been portrayed, with relatively overt

---

① The original lines are as follows: "Ful fetys was hir cloke, as I was war. / Of smal coral aboute hire arm she bar / A peire of bedes, gauded al with grene, / And theron heng a brooch of gold ful sheene, / On which ther was first write a crowned A, / And after Amor vincit omnia" (ll. 157—162). See also Benson, *Riverside*, 805, note 162.

② It has been generalized by Saunders: "Critics have frequently condemned the worldly Prioress, whose potentially secular nature is epitomized by the ambiguous words of her brooch, 'amor vincit omnia' (love conquers all), as well as by her lap dogs feds on white bread" (270).

③ See Mann, 1976, 129.

criticism. The Pardoner is in fact an epitome of a tension between "ideal" and "real" views of religion.

Firstly, a Pardoner's office is supposed to pardon people's sin by selling relics. Through the sale of indulgences, the church got financial income.[①] However, Chaucer's Pardoner has been working so hard not for the benefit of the Church, but for the benefit of his own. As Pardoners are supposed to be authorized by a religious house and licensed by the Pope, they should hand over most of the money they have collected. However, this Pardoner doesn't share the income at all.

Secondly, the relics he sells are supposed to be genuine. As he himself advertises, he has come from Rome. But whether he himself has been there is questioned. On the contrary, the forgery of supposed papal indulgences is suggested.

> "Ye, Goddes armes!" quod this riotour,
> "Is it swich peril with hym for to meete?
> I shall hym seke by wey and eek by strete,
> I make avow to Goddes digne bones!
> Herkneth, felawes, we thre been al ones;
> Lat ech of us holde up his hand til oother,
> And ech of us bicomen otheres borther,
> And we wol sleen this false traytour Deeth.
> He shal be slayn, he that so manye sleeth,
> By Goddes dignitee, er it be nyght!"
> (ll. 692—701)

Thirdly, the contrast becomes more evident if we examine what the Pardoner does and what he preaches in his *Tale*. Generally speaking, the *Tale* is apparently a sermon on the theme "Radix malorum est Cupiditas" ("acquisitiveness is the root of all evil", l. 334). It is in itself a moral tale against avarice and drunkenness.

[①] "The theory behind indulgences was that Christ and the saints had laid up an infinite treasury of merit under the guardianship of the pope, on which Christians could in effect draw cheques in return for a cash payment—a payment that supposedly demonstrated their penitence, and so fulfilled the punishment, poena, required as satisfaction or reparation for sin." See Cooper, 1983, 58.

However, the Pardoner's telling of it, especially while drinking in the tavern setting he fiercely condemns, turns it into a tale of immorality, a revelation of his own vice. His confession that he uses sermons to trick people out of their money becomes evidence of his selfishness and avarice.

The Pardoner's spiritual sterility is actually hinted at by his physical shortcoming even in the *General Prologue*, where it is suggested that he is a eunuch, or at least highly effeminate, with his thin, high voice, lack of beard, long hair, long neck, even his exhibitionism:

> A voys he hadde as smal as hath a goot.
> Ne berd hadde he, ne nevere sholde have.
> As smoothe it was as it were late shave.
> I trowe he were a geldyng or a mare.
> (II. 688—691)

It is true that the *Pardoner's Tale* reveals the problems current in Chaucer's age. But Chaucer's view, as usual, is still elusive. As Aers points out, "He is, self-consciously, no authority. His text leaves its readers to cope with its vision of the Church as seems appropriate to them" (*Chaucer* 49). Yet, the representation of the issue in his tales shows at least Chaucer's concerns. And in doing this, he actually presents the tensions and disturbance to the immediate audience of the pilgrims on the way to Canterbury as well as those not-immediate readers of it. Thus he holds the issue up for critical scrutiny. No matter how he tries to hinder any certain interpretation of his own attitude, allowing the Host to blame the Pardoner, an individual scapegoat instead of the holy institution he represents, and then mediating the tension between the Host and the Pardoner, symbolically through the Knight, by asking them to exchange a peacemaking kiss, Chaucer's critical power can still be sensed. It is especially true if it is considered together with the depiction of the group of clerics represented by the Monk, the Friar, the Summoner and the like. In fact, the *Canterbury Tales* "is a supreme and characteristic moment in Chaucer's poetry, revealing his critical power as he works over major problems of authority in the religious practice and discourses of his culture" (Aers, *Chaucer* 51). The Pardoner is perhaps only the culmination of the negative depiction of these churchmen and their practice.

Primarily the *Pardoner's Tale* is a sermon. But his prologue, one of the lengthiest in the *Tales*, functions as a confession, in which he brags of his techniques and success in exploiting members of his parish. It is the most sinful thing to commit the sin that one is well aware of. Thus the confession of the prologue emphasizes the Pardoner's negative image and contributes to more ironic criticism against him when he preaches in his tale on the same theme—"radix malorum est cupiditas"(l. 334) ("avarice is the root of all evil")—attacking the very sin of which he is guilty. Chaucer's treatment of the Pardoner as the chief hypocrite challenges the orthodox to address abuses without specifically attacking the doctrine on indulgences (Fletcher 117—120). Some critics go even further in pointing out that Chaucer expresses his distaste for the behavior of both the Church and the crown. The *Pardoner's Tale* becomes "a picture of a betrayed kingdom in which church and court have been consumed by corruption and avarice" (Brown and Butcher 114).

If the portraits of the prioress and the pardoner and the like serve as a foil, the image of Parson represents an ideal religious man. In fact, the Parson has often been taken as a contrast to characters like the Pardoner and even the Prioress. Again we need to glimpse back at the Parson in the *General Prologue* in the first place.

The Parson is a man of lowly religious office, but takes his duty extremely seriously. The first several lines in describing the Parson have given him the most positive and virtuous image: "A good man was ther of religioun, / And was a povre PERSOUN OF A Toun" (ll. 477—478). This ideal model image is restated in the near end of his part: "A bettre preest I trowe that nowher noon ys" (l. 524). Counterbalancing the ecclesiastical corruption evident in the Pardoner, the Parson is an example and representative of his impoverished parishioners. As a shepherd, he has set a good example for the sheep in his parish, not only by teaching but also by his own moral actions: "diligent," "in adversitee ful pacient," "wolde he yeven, out of doute, / Unto his povre parisshens aboute/ Of his offryng and eek of his substounce" while he himself "koude in litel thyng have suffisounce" (l. 483, l. 484, ll. 487—489, l. 490). Even within the portrait of the Parson, the ideal image is set against other unnamed churchman, who would preach not for saving the souls but to get paid, while the Parson "dwelte at hoom, and kepte wel his folde, / So that the wolf ne made it nat myscarie" (ll. 512—513). This testifies to his commitment to the apostolic life. He also regrets the abuse and corruption in the Church, adding after his teaching according to the Gospel: "That if gold ruste, what shal iren do?" (ll. 499—500) It is a shameful thing if the shepherd is foul while the sheep are clean.

Though spoken by the Parson, these words of criticism reveal Chaucer's attitude towards the misdeeds of the churchmen. Presenting much of what is admirable in the Parson's portrait in the negative rather than in the positive way suggests the failure and weakness of other practitioners. "The account of the Parson's virtues inevitably suggests the sins of the average priests, and his portrait thus becomes representative of the estate in both its good and its bad aspects" (Mann, *Estates Satire* 56). In addition, by telling his tale, in fact, not a fiction, not in rhyme but in prose, a treatise on penitence that reviews the seven deadly sins in detail, the Parson offers every pilgrim an opportunity for reflecting on their own sinfulness, and he himself plays the role of auditor as he regularly does in his parish each year.

The final mixture or mingling between Chaucer and the Parson is also implicitly telling. There is an inclination to read the *Parson's Tale* as Chaucer's own. The evidence is as follows.

Firstly the Parson's dismissal of rhyme is manifested in the parody of the rhymed forms of popular ballad in the *Tale of Sir Thopas*, a tale told by Chaucer the pilgrim but unluckily cut short. Secondly, the unfavorable remark on " 'rum, ram, ruf' by lettre" (*Parson's Prologue* l. 43) parallels Chaucer's own literary preferences. Thirdly, maybe the most current and acceptable reason for taking Chaucer and the Parson to be overlapping, if not totally identical, is the retraction. It is at this point where Chaucer's voice blends with that of the Parson's. "The opening reference to the 'litel tretys' and the tag 'All that is writen is writen for oure doctrine' easily apply to the *Parson's Tale*, and only possibly to the *Tales* as a whole" (Rudd 149). And the list of Chaucer's works in the

CHAPTER TWO
CHAUCER AS A SOCIAL COMMENTATOR

retraction further leads readers to confuse the poet with the Parson. The powerful tone of leave-taking is suitable for pilgrims who are approaching their destination, as well as being appropriate as Chaucer's final words for the tales at least, if not for his whole literary career. ① But again caution is needed. It is simple-minded to assume that Chaucer is a moralist as the Parson is. The fact is more complex than that.

In Chaucer's portrayal of the Church, one great absence is the contemporary papacy and the Schism. Chaucer's silence on this big event, which first erupted on his second major Italian journey in 1378, is surprising. He definitely knows of it and seems to have deliberately avoided treating this subject in his poetry. However cautious he is, his tone can still be inferred, though without certainty. The only mention of the contemporary papacy is made in connection with the morally bankrupt Pardoner, who comes directly from Rome with his pardons: "His walet, biforn hym in his lappe, / Bretful of pardoun comen from Rome al hoot" (ll. 686—687). This is telling of Chaucer's possible discontent, shared by John Wyclif and the Lollards, with the Church's wealth and abuses.

However, it is not intended here to include Chaucer among the Lollards. In fact, it is something Chaucer might be trying hard to avoid. Nevertheless, the influence of it is inescapable. Both Wyclif and Chaucer moved in John of Gaunt's milieu, and they shared some friends. Chaucer's thinking does parallel Wyclif's in a number of key areas: "his negative attitude toward the mendicants, his stress on the vernacular, his beliefs about authority, and his conviction about the importance of the reader's intention in interpreting a text" (Bisson 59). Yet, it is again a difficult task to define the extent of Chaucer's sympathy for and involvement with Wyclif and his supporters because of Chaucer's consistent elusiveness, possibly resulting from his cautiousness.

---

① Koff's chapter on "leave-taking" is an elegant example of the desire to read the *Retraction* and the *Parson's Tale* as Chaucer's final words (1988, 222—236). Howard (1976, 376—387) offers an elegiac reading of the *Tale*, also taking it as Chaucer's final words, a view tactfully countered by Pearsall (1992, 228, and 267—270). Cooper discusses the standing of the *Retraction* and its thematic links to the *Tales* as a whole (1996, 410—412). See Rudd, 150.

超越的可能：作为知识分子的乔叟
Possibility of Transcending: Chaucer as an Intellectual

Despite the difficulty of pinning down Chaucer's exact relationship with Lollards, his discontent with the corruptions of the churchmen can be easily perceived from his poems. He plays the role of an intellectual as a social commentator, if not a critic who expresses publicly his unfavorable opinions. His position in the society influences his views on social events, fate of women and the problems of the clerics.

Chapter Three
Entertainer, Edifier and Enlightener

Traditionally, a court poet takes the responsibility for pleasing the prince, the aristocrats and the like. From this perspective, court poets function like minstrels, who provide entertainment for the court audience. On the other hand, unlike minstrels, court poets are also supposed to provide mirrors for the princes. By retelling the audience old tales, they demonstrate what is good, moral and wise, and what is not. In this sense, they play the similar roles of princes' counselors, though they do not have the proper title and status that real counselors have. They feed the audience moral instructions or edification. Naturally, Chaucer as a court poet plays the double roles of both entertainer and edifier. What's more, Chaucer is not an edifier in the sense of giving moral teaching only. He is rather an enlightener, who does not air his ideas or pass the messages explicitly and directly. This enlightening job is, in Chomsky's words, "not a matter of pouring water into a vessel but of helping a flower to grow in its own way" (Olson & Worsham 55). Chaucer's writing helps his audience or readers discard their blind belief in authority, cultivate their self-consciousness, and enable them to make sensible judgment and decisions by themselves. He in fact plays the role of an intellectual in its multiple senses—an entertainer, an edifier and an enlightener.

The Role of Enlightener: Authority Negotiated

Entertainer and Edifier: a Dual Choice

The roles of a poet as an entertainer or an edifier, or both, and the function of poetry, have been constant topics in the history of literary criticism. The concerns can be traced back to Plato and Aristotle. Despite their opposing attitudes toward poets, they both attach great importance to art and its social and moral function. Plato emphasizes poetry's use "to states and to human life" (Zhang 29), and thus tends to be more utilitarian, while Aristotle stresses its educational role through the functioning of *katharsis* or purgation (Zhang 47). However, it is Horace who firstly observes and states directly that artists are craftsmen who both delight and instruct the readers or audience. He puts forward plainly in his *Art of Poetry* that "(t)he aim of the poet is either to benefit, or to amuse, or to make his words at once please and give lessons of life" (Zhang 96). In fact, as Bloomfield and Dunn summarize,

> Teaching has always been recognized as an important function of poetry. Early poets were teachers, diviners, prophets, and preservers of tradition. Part of their sacred office was to admonish and warn rulers and subjects alike and to hand on the accumulated wisdom of the past. (4)

Therefore, it is not surprising for a poet to play the role of an entertainer and an edifier at once. It seems an essential quality of a good poet to have a sense of social responsibility. However, specific individuals may certainly have specific traits, because "(a) poet's social functions are determined in some large measure by the occasion at which he performs and by the expectations of his audience" (Bloomfield & Dunn 6). This is also true of Chaucer.

As a court poet, Chaucer is presumably expected to play the role of pleasing as well as providing moral mirrors for an audience consisting largely of his social superiors: the prince and the aristocrats. Naturally, the courtly love celebrated in lyrics, romances, and dream visions by French poets becomes one of the

CHAPTER THREE
ENTERTAINER, EDIFIER AND ENLIGHTENER

main subjects of Chaucer's poetry. In this sense, it is not uncommon to understand Chaucer as an entertainer as well as an edifier. It seems a dual choice that he apparently can not avoid due to his position in the court.

In fact, he himself seems to be well aware of this role and acknowledges the dual function of poetry. He puts forward his criteria of assessing a good poet by way of the host of the inn in the *Canterbury Tales*. At the beginning of it,

> he foregrounds his concern about the relationship between moral edification and entertainment when Harry Bailly announces that the pilgrim who tells the tale of "*best sentence and moost solaas*" (GP 798) will win the contest, thereby implicitly suggesting that a balance between the two is mostdesirable. (Bisson 40)

Thus tales to be told are expected to be more or less entertaining, as it is a good way of killing time during the long pilgrimage journey, and meanwhile instructive, providing morals for the pilgrims, which might also be most appropriate to a pilgrimage toward Canterbury.

Even in some tales that are superficially more didactic, aesthetic elements can still be perceived. Take the *Parson's Tale* for instance. With the theme of penitence, this tale told in prose and styled like a sermon is undoubtedly rather instructive. But its aesthetic charm can not be ignored, "its attractiveness is at least partly aesthetic, bringing the collection of tales to a powerful and effective end" (Hirsh 84). As Hirsh further elucidates,

> it is also didactic, though in the end less admonitory than discursive, seeking more to awaken introspection than to impose morality. Given the Christian optimism in which it is grounded, it is in the end, as the Parson foretold, a "merry tale," one which will "show the way" to the celestial Jerusalem, and so engage that mixture of "sentence" and "solaas," of meaning and consolation, which the host placed before the pilgrims as the model for their tales while they were yet in his London inn. (84—85)

In Hirsh's view, the *Parson's Tale* can be an example of good tale for its good balance of delightfulness and instructiveness.

However, there exist different views on this point. For Burrow, the *Parson's Tale* is less aesthetic. As he analyzes it,

> The *Parson's Tale* is a treatise on the sacrament of penance. The literary approach to the Tale will emphasize its appropriateness to its teller, a priest who would have administered the sacrament, and also its dramatic fitness as the last tale before the pilgrims enter the holy city of Canterbury; but such attempts to reabsorb the Tale into the spectacle of the Canterbury pilgrimage do not, I think, entirely convince the disinterested reader. Followed as it is by the *Retraction*, the *Parson's Tale* seems to break out of the fictional world of the poem and confront the reader directly with the realities of penance. (*Medieval Writers and Their Work* 22—23)

Convinced or not, readers, as well as the pilgrims, will have no difficulty in getting the moral message from the *Tale* which they have read or heard. The difference lies in not the nature of but the extent to which each of the tales told is entertaining or instructive. In addition, as Alfred David summarizes,

> Both poet and audience, however, were responsive to an even more pervasive pressure, the requirement that all poetry to earn its right to exist must be moral, that the poet has the obligation to educate and uplift his audience, and the audience, for its part, must look for instruction and edification and not only for entertainment. (5)

Thus, there seems no question to recognize Chaucer as both an entertainer and an edifier. However, it is not such a double role bestowed on any poet, but his role of an enlightener that counts more, and thus is the crux to understanding Chaucer's social function as an intellectual.

Enlightener and Authority

It is essential at the start to elucidate the exact implication of "enlightener" and "enlightenment" applied specifically for this discussion. When Chaucer is attributed with the role of "enlightener," no intention is made to relate him directly to the movement of the Enlightenment and its relevant concepts, since the movement occurred many centuries after

CHAPTER THREE
ENTERTAINER, EDIFIER AND ENLIGHTENER

Chaucer. The relation even appears incredible taking John Dryden's summary in his translation of Chaucer into consideration. ① As Allen and Axiotis perceive, there is

> a latent but insistent contempt for the entire Middle Ages pervades the discipline of literary criticism as a condition of its very possibility. To Enlightenment thought, the Middle Ages was a precritical age, and therefore a pre-literary one also. For the Enlightenment's formal ideal of the rule of reason in culture carries with it a profound horror of culture differently (dis-) ordered according to custom and tradition. (2—3)

Thus Chaucer and Enlightenment seem to be irrelevant at all to each other.

On the other hand, however, it is impossible to separate them in a clear-cut way. The most impressive dimension of Chaucer's possible relation with Enlightenment is not the sense of order but the rationality it provokes. From this point of view, any form of authority, that of religion, society or state system becomes the focus for examination. ② It is the very essential meaning of "making people understand better" and "critical consciousness" or "critical reflectiveness" that contribute more to the present discussion of Chaucer's role of an enlightener (Dupre xiii).

However, it is dangerous as well as untrue to equate Chaucer with a radical critic. He never reaches that far. Neither is he a revolutionary who negates religious superstition and absolute monarchy directly and totally. He is rather a moderator, a negotiator in relation to authority(ies). Still his critical reflectiveness was so advanced in his age as to uplift himself to the status of an enlightener in the Middle Ages.

As Dupre states, "The particular merit of the Enlightenment did not consist, as some have claimed, in abolishing moral or religious absolutes" (Dupre ix). In his view, the merit lies in permanently inuring against people's "willingness to accept authority uncritically"

---

① For the original summary by Dryden, see *Chaucer, New Casebook* ed. Valerie Allen &. Ares Axiotis. Also see John Dryden, Preface to *Fables Ancient and Modern*, printed in Caroline Spurgeon ed. *Five Hundred Years of Chaucer Criticism and Allusion: 1357—1900*, New York, 1960, vol. I, 280.

② Quoted in Zhao Dunhua, 2001, 236.

(Dupre ix). His emphasis on the need to question as one that distinguishes Western culture from others is in a sense true.① Questioning, doubting and thus refusing to accept any authority uncritically have been the ways to be enlightened.

Dupre sees Kant's view of enlightenment as emancipation, or a "way out." In Dupre's discussion, "Kant's description of the Enlightenment as an emancipation of mankind through an unconditional acceptance of the authority of reason," "expresses his unambiguous opposition to any unexamined authority" (Dupre 7—8). Similarly, Foucault holds that

> Enlightenment is a process that releases us from the status of "immaturity." And by "immaturity," he means a certain state of our *will* that makes us accept someone else's *authority* to lead us in areas where *the use of reason* is called for. Kant gives three examples: we are in a state of "immaturity" when a book takes the place of our understanding, when a spiritual director takes the place of our conscience, when a doctor decides for us what our diet is to be. (Rabinow 34)②

Therefore enlightenment encourages one's own understanding, judging and decision, that is, as the motto of enlightenment indicates, "Have courage to use your own reason!" (qtd. in Dupre 8) But how can we use our own reason? Are we able to? Is there any reasoning that belongs to, and can be done absolutely and exclusively by oneself? Do we need someone or something that can help us become mature, being capable to make use of our understanding

---

① See Dupre, ix—x. His statement however reflects his somewhat Europe-centered, or European Chauvinistic inclination.

② I italicized the three words for the sake of emphasis. There is overlapping between Foucault's and Kant's idea of Enlightenment. For Foucault, "Kant in fact describes Enlightenment as the moment when humanity is going to put its own reason to use, without subjecting itself to any authority; now it is precisely at this moment that the critique is necessary, since its role is that of defining the conditions under which the use of reason is legitimate in order to determine what can be known, what must be done, and what may be hoped... The critique is, in a sense, the handbook of reason that has grown up in Enlightenment; and, conversely, the Enlightenment is the age of the critique." (Rabinow, 37—38)

CHAPTER THREE
ENTERTAINER, EDIFIER AND ENLIGHTENER

without any direction from others? This is not Kant's view, at least. On the contrary, "(f)urther in the text he [Kant] more specifically addresses the conditions needed for educating people toward thinking for themselves" (Dupre 8). It is, in fact, at this point that the role of an intellectual as a teacher, an enlightener needs to be highlighted. Diderot's description, as Dupre perceives, expressed a keen awareness of the social role of the intellectual:

> The magistrate deals out justice; the *philosophe* teaches the magistrate what is just and unjust. The soldier defends his country; the *philosophe* teaches the soldier what his fatherland is. The priest recommends to his people the love and respect of the gods; the *philosophe* teaches the priest what the gods are. (qtd. in Dupre 8)①

So people need to be educated to be enlightened.

Chaucer, in a sense, plays the role of an enlightener as well as an educator. He tries to educate his audience to make use of reason by themselves, instead of accepting any authority willingly and uncritically. In fact, as Foucault's brief but persuasive analysis states clearly, the three factors of Enlightenment, that is, will, authority, and the use of reason, are inherently related. So in spite of the fact that there are controversies over who has authority and what the decisive factors that decide the authority are, the key factor that an enlightener would presumably deal with is still *authority*.②

---

① This part is quoted from Dupre, 8. As for the original source, see note 12 in Dupre, 342.

② The following quotation is helpful to see the key factors of authority and the role of educator and education in the process of enlightenment: "Kant's educational project appears legitimate and, by today's standards, uncontroversial. Yet his definition of enlightenment as the 'release from a self-imposed tutelage' contains more than the need to think for oneself, which all educated people do and have always done. It has a polemic edge: many deprived themselves of that right by their willingness to accept uncritically the opinions of political and religious authorities. Kant condemns such a submissive attitude as immature (Unmundigkeit) and morally irresponsible. Still one wonders: Could anyone survive without accepting a number of unexamined ideas on the authority of others? Or, for that matter, what gives a decisive authority to the one whom the public considers a Gelehrter, a learned person?" (Dupre, 8) Also see note 13 in Dupre, 342.

Authority of/and Authorities: *"Who painted the lion?"*

Not a trick of word play, the authority of/and authorities is actually a constant concern of Chaucer and a focus that gets more and more heated in recent Chaucer study.① The focal point of its application is Chaucer's demonstrations of negotiation with authority, which may be traced to Michael Foucault's notorious claiming of the pervasiveness of power in the social net.② To expose this, the exact meaning of "authority" in its two forms—"authority" and "authorities"—should be explained first and foremost.

The word "authority" has its usual and superficial meaning of having power and being authoritative; while "authorities," has been taken more often than not in its medieval sense: the works by authoritative men which have been accepted as true and often cited.③ Thus, "authority," in its medieval sense, is not only power, but also, specifically, a text which could be cited to prove an argument. These "authorities" are references to an actual author or saying intended to augment the weight and affirm the standing of a work. "Thus an epic would refer back to the Classical writers, Homer and Virgil, while texts dealing with moral topics would cite the Bible or famous commentators such as St. Jerome" (Rudd 164). These "authorities" are the works not only by classical writers, but also by

---

① Notions of authority and its applications in Chaucer study is pervasive from the mid-1980s through to the early 1990s, ranging widely from gender implication of text (Dinshaw 1989), to social and ideological criticism (Strohm 1989; Wallace 1997), and the study of subjectivity (Patterson 1991), and the very discussion of the notions (Minnis 1984; Minnis and Scott 1991; Wogan-Browne et al. 1999). Refer to Brown, 2002, 23.

② In Andrew Galloway's "Authority," he traces the initial focus on Chaucer's negotiations with authority and pins the different directions to the work of Michel Foucault, "whose arguments for the pervasiveness of social power, defining both artistic and 'natural' aspects of identity and social life via the comprehensive notion of 'discourse', and especially 'authorship', were widely influential on scholars of Renaissance literature and helped put the topic of 'authority' in the air." See Brown, 23.

③ In Davis's *Chaucer Glossary*, authority has two forms in medieval English: auctoritee and auctour. Both terms share the same meaning of authority, that is, being authoritative and having power. But meanwhile each has different focus. Auctoritee implicates the emphasis of authoritative text, while auctour lays the focus on the originator, creator, or to put it roughly, the author of the authoritive text. However, the two terms are interrelated. Details, see Davis, 9.

CHAPTER THREE
ENTERTAINER, EDIFIER AND ENLIGHTENER

philosophers such as Plato, Aristotle, or by Christian philosophers like Augustine.

> The text itself was the repository of knowledge that could be regarded as true and be trusted, with the prime authority being, naturally, the *Bible*. An author, then, becomes one who writes such a text and is esteemed as a result. This is a more specific use of the word than our current "author" which simply means the writer of a text. [...] The word also had connotations of leadership and the ability to increase a thing. Thus God may be termed the chief auctor, as leader and enlarger of creation as well as the true author of the Bible, with the individual writers of it being in effect scribes under divine instruction. When it came to secular texts there was still a similar division. (Rudd 72)

Thus the authoritative texts as such and their authors are both considered to be the "authorities."

However, Chaucer never protests his being such an author, that is, an author who can exercise power upon the audience/readers through the impact of his texts. On the contrary, he repeatedly states his role as a "rehearsing"[①] compiler. The following extract in the *General Prologue* is an example of such a statement, although through the narrator of the *Canterbury Tales*.

> But first I pray yow, of youre courteisye,
> That ye n'arette it nat my vileynye,
> Thogh that I pleynly speke in this mateere,
> To telle yow his wordes and hir cheere,
> Ne thogh I speke hir wordes proprely.
> For this ye knowen al so wel as I,
> Whoso shal telle a tale after a man,
> He moost reherce as ny as evere he kan
> Everich a word, if it be in his charge,
> Al speke he never so rudeliche and large,
> Or ellis he moot telle his tale untrewe,

---

① "Rehearsing" means repeating or reciting. See Davis, 117—118.

> Or feyne thyng, or fynde wordes newe
> He may nat spare, althogh he were his brother;
> He moost as wel seye o word as anther.
> Also I prey yow to foryeve it me,
> Al have I nat set folk in hir degree
> Heere in this tale, as that they sholde stonde.
> My wit is short, ye may wel understonde.
> (ll. 725—746)

Chaucer seems to be content to remain a compiler. He may have perceived and taken its advantages. Playing a role of compiler, he can be excused from any responsibility for his compilation, good or evil, because "(a) reporter deserves neither thanks nor blame for what he repeats without fabrication or alteration: 'Blameth nat me...'" (Minnis, *Medieval Theory of Authorship* 200). So when he tells the *Miller's Tale*, he is absolved from the guilt of saying churlish words, for

> ...demeth nat that I seye
> Of yvel *entente*, but for I moot reherce
> His tales alle, be they bettre or werse,
> Or elles falsen som of my *mateere*.
> (ll. 3172—3175)

Thus, a compiler doesn't have to take responsibility for the materials in his compilation. This, in fact, indicates the compiler's freedom in choosing the materials. However, inclusion or exclusion, even if without alteration of any given materials, does amount to something. Each compiler selects and organizes the materials according to his own intention. He must be responsible for the intentio (entente), if not the materia (mateere), as the above quote admits.

However, most of the medieval writers "follow the compilers' theory and practice of *ordinatio partium*. The major medieval compilations were compendious, containing materiae to cater for a wide range of demands and tastes" (Minnis, *Medieval Theory of Authorship* 200). But, on the other hand, the compiler still cannot

CHAPTER THREE
ENTERTAINER, EDIFIER AND ENLIGHTENER

be authoritative in the sense of taking control of the materials, because such compilation of diverse materials also bestows freedom on the readers. "(T) he reader can isolate and believe whatever things he wishes to believe: no attempt has been made to force the auctores to speak with one voice, and it is up to the reader to make his own choice from the discordant auctoritates offered to him" (Minnis, *Medieval Theory of Authorship* 201). Minnis elaborates Chaucer's thorough understanding and good use of this feature.

> If a reader does not want a tale like the *Miller's Tale*, there are many other types of "mateere" on offer. [...] The common principle involved is that a compiler is not responsible for his reader's understanding of any part of the materia, for any effect which the materia may have on him and, indeed, for any error or sin into which the materia may lead a reader. "Blameth nat me if that ye chese amys," warns Chaucer; "Avyseth yow, and put me out of blame." (I, lines 3181, 3185) (*Medieval Theory of Authorship* 201—202)

Thus, despite the inferior status compilers often claim to authors, one responsibility that they cannot shun lies in what materials they choose to include and how they organize them.

Chaucer's compilation features not only in diversity of subject matters, genres, styles, but also, maybe more significantly, in multiplicity of voices. It is difficult to perceive any authorial opinions from his work. Thus it seems that the author presents no intention. But "no intention" might be just his intention, since this way of organizing is not only consistent with the literary theory and practice of compilation in medieval times, but also in harmony with his social position and perhaps his personal views. As has been elaborated previously, the diversity of material and the multiplicity of voice help him utter something that is not utterable. It is a wise way of escaping any censure that may result from his writing, because as Alcestis defends the dreamer in the *Legend*, he is just a translator or reteller of old tales:

> He may translate a thyng in no malyce,
> But for he useth bokes for to make,

And taketh non hed of what matere he take
(ll. 341—343)

Certainly, it is not irrelevant to the fact that in medieval times knowledge of tradition is superior to originality for a poet. Poets make good use of the reservoir of those authorities not to exhibit and show off their knowledge, but to augment the weight of what they compose, that is, those authorities may lead to the authority of their own work. Chaucer is among such writers. His works are filled with authorities of diverse origins. By applying so many various authorities of different levels in his work, Chaucer actually establishes his own authority as an author, a poet, a maker, instead of a mere compiler.

In fact, Chaucer himself is well aware of the matter of authorship and authority. He constantly mentions his identity as the author of his texts. The *House of Fame* is acknowledged twice by Chaucer as his own work. It is listed in his early work in the *Prologue* to the *Legend of Good Women*, and again among the "translacions and editynges of world vanitees" (*Parson's Tale* l. 1085) at the end of the *Canterbury Tales*. In the *Prologue* to the *Legend of Good Women*, he portrays himself as a poet who so devotes himself to books that only daisies in May may draw him away. The introducer of the dream is no longer the Latin Canons but his own poem. Though it is speculation based on his own statement: it is presented to Queen Anne (ll. 496—497), Chaucer makes it clear that he is the author of his works by listing them (ll. 414—425). Again, in the introduction to the *Man of Law's Tale*, Chaucer, through the Man of Law, mentions his own name and his occupation as a story-teller/author (ll. 47—56). The *Retraction* mentions not only the tales in *Tales*, but also many of his other works (ll. 1085—1087). Meanwhile, from time to time he includes himself in the text itself: as "Geffrey" in the *House* (l. 729) or as one of the Canterbury pilgrims. His concern with the reliability of scribes and the accurate transmission of his text is manifested in *Chaucers Wordes unto Adam, His Owne Scriveyn* as it is expressed in *Troilus* (ll. 793—798).

CHAPTER THREE
ENTERTAINER, EDIFIER AND ENLIGHTENER

Chaucer's naming of himself and listing of his works in his own texts contrasts sharply with the general anonymity of medieval writers. The anonymity results from the importance of texts rather than authors in the Middle Ages. In the Middle Ages, writers/authors/poets were generally divided into two levels: those who wrote sacred texts and those who wrote secular ones. Although the former were relatively superior to the latter for the assumption of their divine inspiration, the position of a human author was not important, even in scripture writing. Gregory the Great, in discussing the author of the *Book of Job*, articulates this position by comparing the human author to a pen:

> If we were reading the epistle of some great man with his Epistle in our hand, yet were to enquire by what pen they were written, doubtless it would be an absurdity, to know the Author of the Epistle and to understand his meaning, and notwithstanding to be curious to know with what sort of pen the words were marked upon the page. When then we understand the matter, and are persuaded that the Holy Spirit was its author, in stirring a question about the author what else do we then in reading a letter enquire about the pen? (qtd. in Bisson 34)

The author thus acts as a scribe, simply taking down what God dictates. It is the truth he conveys that is all-important. His purposes and personality are excluded from serious consideration. [1]

But the High Middle Ages witnessed a shift towards elevating "auctours": from scribe to maker, from "an essentially passive conduit of divinely inspired truths" to "a more active creator whose own mind functions as a shaping instrument" (Bisson 34). [2] The auctour's task was to pass on ancient stories that were derived from

---

[1] See Bisson, 34.

[2] According to Minnis, "The term 'auctour' may profitably be regarded as an accolade bestowed upon a popular writer by those later scholars and writers who used extracts from his works as sententious statements or 'auctoritates,' gave lectures on his works in the form of textual commentaries, or employed them as literary models. Two criteria for the award of this accolade was tacitly applied: 'intrinsic worth' and 'authenticity'"(1988: 10).

other established authors and preserved old truths.① Chaucer was more aware of his role as a maker. Though he declared that what he was doing was the mere retelling of old tales, he seemed not satisfied to be only a reteller/scribe, a passer-on of old wisdom. On the contrary, by associating his work with the authorities, those Canons, he established his own authority as a poet. The authorities give power to and augment the level of his own works. As Rudd generalizes,

> This self-identification asserts Chaucer's place in the literary canon as is described in The Man of Law's Prologue (*Tales*, II: 46—56) and at the end of *Troilus*. In this way he claims authority through a process by which the identity of the creator of a text (author as we think of it today, as distinct from scribe) and the standing awarded to it (authority) enhance each other and are themselves enhanced by the respect accorded to any quotations cited in the text (authorities, in medieval term). (153)②

It is worth noting that Chaucer is not the only one who, as an author, acts as a character in his own poem. John Gower, to whom, together with the philosopher Ralph Strode, Chaucer dedicated his *Troilus*, identified the Lover with his own name near the end of his *Confessio Amantis*, and referred to himself as being old and sick, as

---

① See more in Blamires, 51: "an assumption that stories relay auctoritee: i. e. that inherited stories communicate the 'authority' of past wisdom, and that the poet ideally preserves or reinforces the wisdom inherent in a story as he transmits it. A story's 'authority' derived in fact from considerations such as (a) its antiquity, (b) its association with some celebrated past writer, and (c) its continuing capacity to exemplify general truths (e. g. 'Fortune is fickle')."

② Rudd later summarizes what modern scholarship's reflection on this issue: "Modern scholarship reflects the way Chaucer presents himself as both author and authority in two major ways. First, the appreciation of his works and the respect accorded to him in 'Lives' and critical biographies have created and maintained a reverence for him as a great literary figure. [...] Second, critical analysis and scholarly endeavour have taken up Chaucer's own interest in the origin of stories (evident in *House* and *The Clerk's Tale*), the concepts of authority and authorship (reflected throughout Troilus and in the vexed questions of transmission of manuscripts ['Adam Scriveyn' reveals Chaucer's own anxieties on the topic of scribal error])" (153).

CHAPTER THREE
ENTERTAINER, EDIFIER AND ENLIGHTENER

Gower might well have been at the time of writing. The dreamer in *Piers Plowman* was named "Will," which was the same as that of the author William Langland.

Contrary to the general anonymity of medieval writers, there was usually some degree of correspondence between the narrator and the author. This "may be simply one more manifestation of the medieval desire for authority, the reluctance to cut the audience off completely from the known world. Or it may be a natural result of oral delivery" (Hussey 192). There was in fact a new rising awareness of authorship and authority among medieval writers in late fourteenth century in England. However, how authoritative were they? Did such texts and their authors really have authority or power? How could they acquire such authority?

Chaucer is, as Delany persuasively elaborates, skeptical of the authority of authorities, despite so much of his searching for them, as is manifested in the *House of Fame*.① No one will be surprised by the (non-)ending of the poem. It is ended or unfinished at the very moment when the dreamer sees a man of "great authority" whom he can not name. The promise of meeting the "man of grete auctorite" is broken. The breaking off of the poem at this point, at least implies, if not explicitly expresses, Chaucer's own uncertainty of the existence of authority. In the *Prologue to the Wife of Bath's Tale*, the rebellious Wife queries the authority of those authorities by men authors:

> Who peyntede the leon, tel me who?
> By God, if wommen hade writen stories,
> As clerkes han withinne hire oratories,
> They wolde han writen of men moore wikked-
> Nesse
> (ll. 692—695)

It is a hasty and naïve inference to equate the poet's own view with

---

① Rudd generalizes that "Delany regards the poem (HF) as enacting the conflicts between the different kinds of truth found in literature, philosophy and religion." See Rudd, 76.

the Wife's. But it is undeniable that Chaucer had been continuously dealing with the vexed question of text and interpretation. In fact, he had been negotiating with authorities from various aspects. Due to the limitation of space and my ability, the following discussion will be confined to literary authority and gender authority only.

Literary Authority and Chaucer's Poetic Innovation

> Go litel bok, go litel myn tragedye,
> Ther God thi makere yet, er that he dye,
> So sende myght to make in som comedye!
> But, litel book, no makyng thow n'envie,
> But subgit be to alle poesye;
> And kis the steppes, where as thow seest pace
> Virgile, Ovide, Omer, Lucan, and Stace.
> (*Troilus and Criseyde*, V: 1786—1792)

The lines above on one hand show Chaucer's respect for "the greats" and his admission of inferiority occasionally made in his works. On the other hand, however, by so doing, he places his works, with all due modesty, in the classical tradition, and thus asserts his status as an authorized poet.

Tim Machan directly expresses the paradoxical sense of the passage above in the following quotation.

> It is in the *Troilus*, where Chaucer utilizes the fiction of Lollius and his text, that the various relations between the modern vernacular work and the ancient authorial book are most fully explored. In the poem's famous conclusion, for instance, Chaucer affirms the culturally subordinate status of vernacular poetry by admonishing his "Litel bok" to "subgit be to alle poesye; /And kis the steppes where as thow seest pace/Virgile, Ovide, Omer, Lucan, and Stace. (5. 1790—1792) [...] At the same time, however, he validates his own composition by situating it in this literary tradition only one step below these culturally recognized "auctores." And the implication is that Gower, inasmuch

CHAPTER THREE
ENTERTAINER, EDIFIER AND ENLIGHTENER

as Chaucer sends the book out to him, is not even on the staircase. (177—178)

While Machan's understanding of the passage is in a wide context under which the relationship of vernacular writing characterized by Chaucer and Latin authorities is discussed, E. T. Donaldson probes this matter from another angle, to a somewhat deeper level. According to Donaldson, "(t)his is the modesty convention again, but transmuted, I believe, into something close to arrogance" (95). Donaldson is right at this point. Even if Chaucer was not arrogant in boasting his literary achievement, he at least knew that he was successful as a poet, despite the repetitive assertions of his own inferiority that appeared in his works.

His success lies, at least at the beginning, in his knowledge of old wisdom. As one of "the most learned," Chaucer exhibits in his work his wide range of knowledge, from science to art, especially of the classical canons. As T. S. Eliot remarks, one test of a great poet is what he does with his borrowings.[①] Chaucer's works are full of influences from and references to other authors and their works, ancient and modern, secular and religious. The range of the extraneous knowledge and authorities are wide, and his methods of applying them are equally various.

Admittedly, source study has been a major trend in Chaucer studies. Critical research in this area has yielded many fruits. Though their perspectives and focuses are diverse, they agree at least on this point: Chaucer's poetry has much to do with the major sources of the classics, literary, philosophical, and theological. This view is also affirmatively presented by Salter: "No other English medieval poet had such a complex pattern of indebtedness and independence in his relationship with major sources" (142).

The reasons why Chaucer so frequently referred to other sources may be various. Some critics consider it a good way to cater for his immediate audience, on the assumption that Chaucer's audience had a ready familiarity with those source texts. This idea is, however, challenged by other critics, who raise more questions on issues like

---

① Quoted in Hussey, 2. See also note 3, in Hussey, 218.

what other texts were present in Chaucer's texts, and how familiar the audience was with them. If this problem is unresolved, it is not convincing to draw conclusions about Chaucer's intentions in referring to sources. The way Chaucer used source texts complicates this problem further, but paradoxically, serves as a key to the problem.

Truly, Chaucer shows great admiration in his poetry for "the greats" by somehow imitating their styles or borrowing directly from them. His admiration for and reverential attitude toward "olde bookes" is expressed by presenting himself as a hermit who devotes most of his time to reading books until his eyes are dazed (*House of Fame*, ll. 647—660), and by his frequent cryptic allusions to "the greats", such as Ovid. ① However, his references to source texts are not simply decorative frills in his own work. In addition, his fidelity to his sources is both superficial and incomplete. He is actually making use of them to achieve his own goals. In fact, in one way or another, he works change on them. By doing so, he apparently salutes the classical, but meanwhile sets up his own authorship of his own texts. In other words, his "originality often depends upon his precise manipulation of other texts" (Blamire 7). And the "very fidelity actually highlights any deviations. They communicate his distinctive aims and qualities" (Blamire 11). At the extreme, some critics even perceive that "even the smallest change is full of significance" (Salter 145). It is actually not difficult to perceive his indebtedness to other writings since they are pervasive throughout the tales.

In medieval times, when being erudite seemed more important than being original, the sense of tradition was strong. "Plagiarism was no sin, and many of Chaucer's stories, like Shakespeare's, are borrowed from other writers... That is why Chaucer sees himself in the quotation above as a humble follower of the great classical writers" (Hussey 2). The prizing of tradition over invention in medieval times makes it natural for Chaucer to borrow from those authorities more often than not. As C. S. Lewis puts it in *The*

---

① Details, see Blaimire, 7—8.

CHAPTER THREE
ENTERTAINER, EDIFIER AND ENLIGHTENER

Discarded Image, "If you had asked Layamon or Chaucer 'Why do you not make up a brand-new story of your own?' I think they might have replied (in effect) 'Surely we are not yet reduced to that?'" (211) The importance of tradition and its relation to a medieval poet has recently been discussed and confirmed in the landmark volume on medieval authorship, *The Idea of the Vernacular*: "Authorship in the Middle Ages was more likely understood as participation in an intellectually and morally authoritative tradition, within which [...] a writer might fill one of several roles, copying, modifying, or translating, as well as composing" (Wogan-Browne et al. 4—5). Therefore, it is not strange to read many authorities in Chaucer's works.

However, Chaucer never lacks creative gifts. In Chaucer, much is transformed in the process of such "participation." As Alfred in *The Strumpet Muse* suggests, Chaucer's creative gifts "carried him, in spite of himself, beyond anything taught to him by the old clerks he read and sometimes translated of whom he always speaks with affectionate if not precisely reverent regard" (6).

Take the *Parliament of Fowls* for instance. It is well and early recognized that it follows the form of French love-visions. It is, however, never a mere imitation. Chaucer actually furthers this genre by combining love-vision and the *demande d'amour* forms, or parodies the form of dream-poetry by combining realism and convention. Thomas Reed focuses on the form of literary debate, suggesting that a form demanding choice and resolution turns out, in the *Parliament of Fowls*, to be one in which no choice needs to be made and multiplicity can be accepted. ① It is a similar story in the *House of Fame*: Chaucer introduces it as a love-vision, borrowing the form of love-vision. But what it is actually preoccupied with is not love but literary creativity and the nature of Fame. ② It is no wonder that many critics recognize it to be unbalanced, ill-formed or

---

① Refer to Rooney, 85.

② According to Bisson, "This poem reveals him self-consciously exploring his role as poet and his doubts about language's capacity to capture truth (Jordan, *Chaucer's Poetics* 24)." (39)

incoherent.① The reasons for its arrangement, as elsewhere, are more often than not speculative. But one thing is certain: Chaucer is never satisfied with retelling or repeating old tales only. He is in fact telling his own stories. He is a maker rather than a compiler.

Such certainty, however, will be vulnerable to modern literary criticism, because the capacity of an author to exercise authority over the meaning of his writings is doubted, especially with the famously proclaimed death of the author by Roland Barthes in the 1970s.② Chaucer seems to have been aware of this and does something in what he writes to avert possible doubts. He is "uneasy about literary authority and so self-conscious about his own authorship that he keeps on minimalising his responsibility for his narratives" (Blamires 1).

Chaucer's uneasiness on literary authorities is manifested in his frequent reference to them but in a way that subtly changes them, if not challenges them. As Rudd sees it, "Chaucer's references to his 'auctor' indicates the composer of the text or story he is following, half suggesting that he is a mere scribe, recording what he is told" (Rudd 72). But what sources to choose and how to follow/adapt them, which are among the questions posed in the *House*, indicates Chaucer's self-reflexiveness in writing. Chaucer never follows "the greats" unconsciously. The authority of the authorities is his constant concern of his works. However, Chaucer's attitude toward authority is complicated not only because of his somewhat contradictory juxtaposition of the pros and the cons, but also results from his authorizing of himself, which is particularly special in an age when most authors are anonymous. David Aers shares with Larry Sklute in that the *Parliament of Fowls* "rejects authority and asserts the value of individual opinion" (Rooney 86). For them, the

---

① Some critics, however, have persuasively argued that the superficial disorder is suitable and matches well with the real state of the House of Rumour, and the confusing and conflicting elements of love.

② "Barthes's obituary was of course deliberately polemical, in order to draw attention to (and endorse) the emergence of a new set of cultural assumptions governing literary interpretation: a shift away from the author towards the reader." See Evan, in Ellis 2005, 10. See also note 2 of this chapter.

poem "challenges the timeless and objective nature of authority, which tends to turn exploratory concepts into dogma. The dreamer rejects such exclusive interpretation of his own dream which has multiple viewpoints and no moral boundaries, making dogmatic assertion impossible" (Rooney 87). Thus, in Rooney's summary, "Having undermined authority, Chaucer moves away from using it, both in PF and in other works, towards presenting multiple views and voices, most obviously in CT" (Rooney 87).

Therefore, in the field of literature at least, the relationship between Chaucer and the authority(ies) is paradoxical.

> [It was] Chaucer's unwillingness to claim to his own authority that, according to Machan, paradoxically enabled poetic "origininality." Such a fluid concept of authority, along with Chaucer's own claims that his rewritings depend heavily on his sources, suggests that Chaucerian texts resist any global attempts to determine how and why they were rewritten. (Prendergast 2)

In this sense, Chaucer himself sets an example of a great poet who knows well how to establish his own authoritative status in writing by employing the authorities of various sources, which itself manifests a way of negotiating rather than completely and blindly following the authority(ies).

Masculine Authority vs. Feminine Experience

> Experience, though noon auctoritee
> Were in this world, is right ynogh for me
> To speke of wo that is in mariage.
> (*Wife of Bath's Prologue*. ll. 1—3)

In this way begins the Wife of Bath when it is her turn to tell a tale. At the very start of the *Prologue*, the Wife lays bare the oppositional relationship between experience and authority with a gesture of feminist defiance. Claiming that her experience is the foundation of her authority apparently makes her a modern feminist, who refuses to be defined as inferior according to the logic of "patriarchal binary thought." In fact, there are two intermingled threads in a discussion with the above title: one is the antagonism between male and female, the other is that between authority and experience. The two threads intersect at the point that authority is usually embodied by the male while experience is often symbolized by the female.

First of all, how Chaucer deals with the gender issue in his poems opens the way to such exploration. With the development of feminist scholarship, gender study has come to the fore in literary criticism, and consequently the impact of it has also expanded to medieval study. As is always the case with Chaucer, there is more controversy than agreement on many questions related to Chaucer and "his women." Chaucer was on the one hand a "womanis frend," as Gavin Douglas put it in 1513, while on the other hand one of those misogynists popular in the medieval period.① While Mann puts the view that Chaucer's *Nun's Priest's Tale* is a satire on male supremacism characteristic of medieval intellectual orthodoxy, Delany and Hansen perceive Chaucer's misogynist tone in it.② Similarly, the variety of women, even in the *Canterbury Tales* alone, ranging from Emily, the romantic ideal to be worshipped (*Knight's Tale*), Cecilia as Virgin Mary (*Second Nun's Tale*), to the lustful, deceitful wife, such as Alison (*Miller's Tale*) and May (*Merchant's Tale*), to name a few, provide more obstacles to our understanding of Chaucer's view.

However, a focal examination of the Wife of Bath will reveal something not only on the issue of gender, but also on the relationship between authority and experience. This is actually a central problem of Chaucer's art. In the *Prologue* to the *Legend of Good Women*, he has already "attempted a rather abstract and intellectual reconciliation between the books in the poet's chest and his experience in the meadow" (David 136). The clash between authority and experience is evident even in *Troilus*. But it is in the *Wife of Bath's Prologue and Tale* that such matters become so

---

① See Rigby, *Chaucer in Context*, 117. Also refer to note 2 in Rigby, 163.
② See Rigby, 117—118. Also refer to note 4 in Rigby, 163.

sharp and complex.

Superficially or apparently, the Wife is the epitome of experience. She boasts of her rich experiences in marriage at the very outset of her tale-telling round. Married five times, she is qualified, as she claims herself, to be authoritative at least in the field of marriage. Paradoxically, in the process of presenting her own history, she frequently and abundantly employs those authorities, citing Jesus, Solomon, St. Paul, St. Mark, Ptolemy etc, in addition to a great body of anonymous wisdom. In fact, she becomes "one of the great users of authority in Chaucer's poetry" (David 136). However, she "turns Jerome's arguments inside out" to serve her own purpose, and meanwhile "employs anti-feminist commonplaces to create the speeches of her five husbands" (Saunders 284). ① But this, conversely, does not always function well to meet her purposes. On the contrary, the authorities that she employs to authorize herself may often work against her or at least undermine her authority. However, this does not fully negate her attempts, because "her very citation of those authorities reveals a knowledge of life that challenges the theoretical moralist in a much more profound way" (David 141). In fact, the Wife of Bath "enters the competition for authority by using male language and thus is better described as 'quasi-feminist' than feminist" (Rudd 178).

> In creating the Wife of Bath, Chaucer drew upon a centuries-old tradition of anti-feminist writings that was particularly nurtured by the medieval church. In their conviction that the rational, intellectual, spiritual, and, therefore, higher side of human nature predominated in men, whereas the irrational, material, earthly, and therefore, lower side of human nature predominated in women. [. . .] Jerome's diatribe and other antifeminist and anti-matrimonial literature provided Chaucer with a rich body of bookish male "auctoritee" (authority) against which the Wife of Bath asserts her female "experience" and defends her rights and justifies her life as a five-time married woman. (Abrams and Greenblatt 253)

---

① For the details, see David, 136—140.

超越的可能：作为知识分子的乔叟
Possibility of Transcending: Chaucer as an Intellectual

Yet, I would rather agree with Alfred David that the Wife of Bath is Chaucer himself. ① He, in the form of her actions, challenges the authority of the authorities by quoting the authorities.

> It is by using these stereotypes, rather than attempting to convey "how women feel," that Chaucer addresses "the problem of speaking in the voice of a woman." This is a complex manoeuvre that works by setting the speaker, the Wife, against her speech, which voices the conventional arguments of clerical thinkers. The Prologue works subversively, as the Wife of Bath sets up her own "experience" against the "authority" of the clerks-to become herself another kind of authority. (David 284)

The authorities are themselves not dead. So by glossing them, their meaning may change and, more often than not, become self-serving for the glosser. Therefore, the application and the choice of the authorities are, in my opinion, Chaucer's strategy. Chaucer's handling of the relation between received authority and observed experience in fact points to the exploration of the nature of knowledge and power.

In view of Chaucer's paradoxical relation to the authorities in his literary creation, and his potential subversiveness to gender authority, I hold that Chaucer is not a blind follower of any form of authority, nor is he in any sense a public challenger to the authority. Authority to Chaucer is something he can negotiate with, something he can make use of for his own benefit. It is his "critical reflectiveness," his courage to use his own reason that decides his identity of an enlightener. Through his negotiating with the authority and/or authorities, Chaucer plays the role of an intellectual as an enlightener.

---

① Refer to David, 135—158.

Chapter Four
Wisdom and/or Weakness

Intelligence, as has been elaborated in the introduction, is one of the key factors in determining whether one is an intellectual or not. Chaucer's intelligence or wisdom had been well recognized even during his own age. "'Thomas Usk... praised him as 'the noble, learned poet in English...' who 'in wisdom and in soundness of judgment... passes all other poets'" (Jones 3). Chaucer's prominence as a poet resulted from his learning from "olde bookes" and sharp perception of his contemporary situation. He actually established his authoritative position as an outstanding poet by making wise choices in making use of source texts, allowing multiple view points and inheriting traditional genres with innovation, to name a few.

His wisdom also manifested in some other ways than literary innovation. It has been universally agreed that Chaucer played well among his multiple-facet roles: as a courtier, a royal civil servant and a poet. Despite his living in a time of turmoil, Chaucer successfully protected himself from any possible harm resulting from the crises of his day, whether religious or political. By keeping a low profile and staying away from the court circle promptly, he shrewdly survived a series of factional struggles and political upheavals. In the following discussion, I will focus on the relation between his literary choices and his social comment, arguing that his literary strategies manifest not only his literary innovation but also his wise social engagement. Then a brief comparison between Chaucer and the traditional Chinese intellectuals, *Shi* is made to further elucidate the wisdom they shared: they knew how to survive in an age of turmoil without giving up pursuing spiritual freedom.

Wisdom in Art: Commenting with Strategies

Some remarks need to be made before the discussion proper of the literary strategies Chaucer employed in his poems. The strategies listed below are neither exclusive to Chaucer nor exhaustive. Chaucer made good use of many other literary genres and styles in his poems, among which some, such as irony, have been well elaborated, by Earle Birney for example.① Due to limitation of space and my interest and ability, it is impossible to include all that are relevant to this subject. But I hope the examples I have chosen are illuminating enough to show that his artistic wisdom is not merely confined to his choice of poetic form, but has hidden impetus as well. It will be argued that Chaucer employs the following artistic devices to play his role of an intellectual as a social commentator.

Dream Vision— Not a Pure Matter of Convention

Chaucer's surviving "dream visions" include the *Parliament of Foules*, the *Book of the Duchess*, and the *House of Fame*. He might have written more since this genre was popular in medieval times. What I will discuss here is not on the genre itself, but the relationship between this artistic device and the writer's social position, between his formal principles and his political or social attitudes.

Chaucer's social position at least influences, if not determines directly and exclusively his literary choice. Though not the only factor leading to his manner of poetic composition, his position is without doubt one among many others. The adoption of the dream frame in his poetry, for instance, results from its popularity, or

---

① See Birney, 1985.

CHAPTER FOUR
WISDOM AND/OR WEAKNESS

literary trend in medieval times.① It was probably the most popular literary genre, with the exception of the romance, with medieval writers. The advantages of writing a dream poem, as Philips generalizes, "is easy [. . .] to move between narrative and lyric, or between narrative and debate or didactic speeches, and dreams readily accommodate both allegorically and realistically conceived characters and landscapes" (*Dream Poems* 3). No wonder many medieval writers adopted dream vision for their works. It left freedom and space for their plotting the narrative and articulating ideas, to list only two of the advantages.

Dreams in general are recurrent subjects for Chaucer's writing. The appeal of dream vision to Chaucer was evident, especially in his early writing. His first three poems were all in the form of dream vision. After a break from it, Chaucer returned to this form in his later poem the *Legend of Good Women*. It is a tradition with a twofold origin: the philosophical or religious mode of instruction, and the courtly dream vision form made popular in French writing. Yet, I hold the same view with Knight that for all its literary conventions, dream vision potentially has the function of social criticism:

> The dream itself was a basic mode for medieval analysis of society. Dreams were taken seriously as ways of revealing a truth that the waking individual could not attain. [. . .] When he adopted the dream mode Chaucer was not only using a form appropriate to a leisured aristocracy: he was enabling himself to adventure into the highest ranges of medieval art and social analysis. (*Chaucer* 7)

The very genre may be especially significant if it is considered from the point of view of the social climate and the precise circumstances in which Chaucer composed. Chaucer's double role, as a courtier and a royal civil servant, and as a poet, influences his

---

① Chaucer's dream vision poems have lots of other issues to deal with: truth and interpretation; the difficulty of writing, the reputation or fame etc., which are also of interest. But due to the space, it is impossible to discuss them all here.

literary choice. Though it is difficult to decide whether his dream poems were aristocratic commissions, or how far they contained topical references, the very choice of the dream frame for his poems, I believe, manifests Chaucer's wisdom in a way.

It is not hard to imagine what kinds of poems Chaucer was supposed to present before his court audience, comprising the king and queen, and other aristocrats. A court poet, as a prince pleaser according to tradition, was expected to compose and present what catered for the taste of his court audience. Issues concerning court life and court culture, such as courtly love or chivalric romance, were appropriate subjects for his poems. Yet, in my view, Chaucer's poems overstep the boundaries by disturbing the audience with penetrating anxieties and tensions, though still within the dream vision form.

Unlike the French dream poems he chiefly used as models, Chaucer's dream poems were characterized by their denial of a comforting solution to the problems mentioned, and even denial of conclusive closure. This becomes intelligible if his role in the court is taken into consideration. To be a court poet, inferior to his audience, he was not expected to provide answers or solutions for his superiors. He should take a low position, presenting the problems but seeking solutions from his supposed wise audience. On the other hand, this method is good for the performance because it may open discussion. For whatever reason, it has been recognized as a characteristic feature of Chaucer's writing, not only of his dream poems, but even throughout his career. It seems that Chaucer persistently "produce(d) texts full of contradictory impulses and often radical discordances whose presence is half-veiled from us by a humorous and elegant surface and undogmatic manner" (Phillips, *Dream Poems* 4). The dream frame thus has become a kind of concealing surface, through which something may nevertheless leak out—something unspeakable.

A traditional literary genre though, dream frame is not purely a matter of inheritance for Chaucer. In fact the tradition of dream vision itself is not a mere literary issue. Many ancient dream narratives presented messages from God or the gods. Many classical, Jewish and early Christian dream narratives revealed heavenly truths

CHAPTER FOUR
WISDOM AND/OR WEAKNESS

not normally accessible to human knowledge.① Thus, the serious nature of sending holy and moral messages is innate in this literary tradition. One aspect of the tradition of dream narratives, describing journeys to the next world, continued into medieval literature and was further developed. In the dreams, the living receives warning messages from the dead, and thus dreaming becomes a process of purgation.

However, dream narratives, though fictional, are not irrelevant to reality. True, poets adopted the fictional device of the dream for his literary structure. But on the other hand, dream poetry is such an appropriate genre for court poets like Chaucer because it transmits teaching and messages through the dream while shunning any possible responsibility for them. As Phillips analyzes, "The serious and moral, indeed divinely sent, teaching that characterized early dream narratives made the genre an obvious one for political comment, giving powerful authority to what was presented, while distancing the speaker from personal responsibility for the message" (*Dream Poems* 375). She further points out that dream poetry in medieval time did include social and political issues, though there was not really a separate concept of the political in the period. *Piers Plowman* for instance combines spiritual and political reform as the twin subjects of its visions. Thus, "(t)opical observations may be obscured in dream poetry by allegorical and generalized treatment and merged with timeless motifs of moralization or regret, such as Reason, Fortune or worldly mutability" (*Dream Poems* 375—376).

The dream frame actually sets its dreamer at some little distance from his listening audience, which is analogous to Chaucer's distancing himself from telling his own opinion in the writing and reading of his own poetry. In dreams, fictions and reality can be fused, which casts doubt on the relationship between the first-person narrator and the author. Therefore, by adopting the genre of dream vision, Chaucer can make his social comments, positive or negative, with no anxiety of being censured.

In addition to this, a shared pattern in Chaucer's dream poems is also tellingly significant. In his dream poems, the main subject is

---

① Examples of such dream narratives are listed and briefly analyzed by Helen Philips and Nick Haveley in their *Chaucer's Dream Poetry*, 4—5.

超越的可能：作为知识分子的乔叟
Possibility of Transcending: Chaucer as an Intellectual

not reached until a long journey is made. There are always many other materials to be negotiated before the reader comes to the core of poems. In the *Book of the Duchess*, Chaucer's first dream poem, the main subject of a mysterious man in black bewailing the death of his wife takes a long roundabout course, from the dreamer / poet's complaint about sleeplessness, to his reference to the book he is reading (the story of Ceyx and Alcyone), to the dream that he dreams of the woman in white and man in black. And it is even later before we discover that the woman is the Duchess commemorated in the title.① The same pattern occurs in his other dream poems as well. Take the *Parliament of Fowls* for example. Again it starts with a poet who has difficulty sleeping. Then he starts to tell about a book he was reading in bed, this time "The Dream of Scipio." And then he falls into sleep, a dream begins and soon melts into another dream in which the poet is shown the temple of Venus and the goddess Nature upon a hill of flowers. After all these, we finally get to the "parliament of fowls" itself. This roundabout way is suitable for the dream form: some apparently irrelevant things are mingled, scenes are shifted and perspectives changed. However, the superficial jumbling and confused things have inner logic.

If we consider it by relating the narrator to the narrative,

---

① The function of the device of the book in the dream has been elaborated by Phillips: "The relationship of book to dream in Chaucer's dream poems is elusive and suggestive, never directive. The message voiced in Chaucer's retelling of Ovid's Metamorphoses tale of Ceyx and Alcyone, before the dream in the Book of the Duchess, about accepting transience, perhaps suggests a stoical consolation which the reader can apply to the Man in Black's sorrows later, within the dream. It is, however, instructive that critics have differed in what message they believe this Ovidian section provides. The juxtaposition of Dido's story and the dream in the House of Fame similarly challenges the reader to create interpretation, rather than providing a guide to the poet's meaning. The device of the book read before the dream is one of the 'layering' structures beloved of dream poets (the concept is Jacqueline Cerquiglini's) and such layering and the juxtaposition of often puzzling elements can make the characteristic structures of this genre inherently dialectic as well as didactic. Authors may cite a famous book and set up a creative conflict between that written existing text and the data in their own new vision. Chaucer questions the place of sexual desire in an ordered cosmos in the Parliament of Fowls after introducing the world-denying, transcendental vision of Cicero's somnium Scipionis. ... seem(s) to be challenging the other-worldly ideologies of the classical texts they cite." See Philips, in Brown 2002,381—382.

CHAPTER FOUR
WISDOM AND/OR WEAKNESS

something more will be revealed. The way Chaucer presents himself in his dream poems is crucial. In the poems, he is always presented as a shy and unassuming figure, with the color of naivety and clumsiness. He shows himself unable to make decisions facing a variety of perspectives and attitudes. In this poem, when he cannot decide which gate to enter, it is the guide of Afrianus who pushes him inside. It is not he himself who makes the choice. In the final scene of the parliament, when we, like the fowls, do not know what it all means, the poet simply wakes up, denying the possibility of any explanation. The function and effect of this device is to offer the framework with multiple attitudes and perspectives. By leaving them all there, Chaucer stimulates the readers' response without giving any explicit judgment himself. In fact, at this moment, he is enlightening his audience or readers, functioning partly as an intellectual. So Chaucer's adopting dream vision in never purely a matter of following literary convention.

It is easy to understand Chaucer's choice of the genre of dream vision for his poems if we examine the context in which they are composed. The *Parliament of Fowls*, like the *Book of the Duchess*, is sometimes seen as an "occasional" poem. The context has conditioned the self-image Chaucer could project. When he dealt with the sensitive matter of a wife's death, especially when it was associated with a poem commemorating the death of Blanche of Castile, the first wife of John of Gaunt, to be discreet and considerate was the only appropriate thing for him to do. Even in the freer atmosphere of a St Valentine's Day celebration in the *Parliament of Fowls*, the relaxed and chatty tone was balanced with respect and decorum. Facing members of an audience composed mainly of his social superiors, it is appropriate for Chaucer, as a courtier, to adopt such an attitude and employ such a literary device.

Although the *Parliament of Fowls* is a poem about love, as dream vision poems, especially those of French origin usually are, it also includes other aspects of life. The quarrelsome classes in parliament raise questions about the chivalric social myth of gentilesse and the hierarchical social order, as well as the cosmic order symbolized by Nature. The same is true of other dream poems. "The G prologue of his *Legend of Good Women* offers sharper warnings about tyranny (perhaps relevant to Richard II in the 1390s) than might be suspected initially from its elegant dream of the God of Love" (Phillips, *Dream Poems* 377). A dream vision poem, as the origin of the genre shows, is a perfect place or field to mingle and mix different messages, of courtly love, as well as of politics, morality and religion.

Of course, Chaucer was not the only poet who excelled at dream vision. This form had great popularity among his contemporaries. John Gower, for instance, also wrote his *Vox Clamantis* in the genre of dream vision too.① Both Gower and Chaucer saw the advantages of using dream frames and first-person narratives. They did not follow the convention rigidly. On the contrary, they made use of it for their own purposes. Both of them employed the dream frame to explore subject more than mere love. They included in their poems social issues. They dealt with these subjects however in an implicit way. But the way they chose and arranged the dreams was significant. The setting of the dreams chosen might show a poet's intention. For instance, the June setting in *Vox Clamantis* matches the month when the 1381 Rising took place. Similarly, in the *House of Fame*, the dream begins in December, a month which is used to foreground and foreshadow a darker or more complex theme: "contemplating the reputation of poets after death, the tragedy of Dido and a period of creative barrenness suffered by the poet" (Phillips, *Dream Poems* 378).

---

① Phillips has made a wonderful analysis of John Gower's *Vox Clamantis*: "John Gower began Book 1 of *Vox Clamantis* by describing wandering out on a sunny June day, then lying in bed visited by strange terrors. He finally falls asleep and dreams towards dawn—a time marked in classical dream theory as likely to bring significant dreams. His Prologue alludes to the apocalyptic visions of the Bible, referring to St John, author of the book of Revelation, and Daniel, whose dream of Nebuchadnezzar's statue being toppled was often taken by fourteenth-century writers as a warning of the fall of governments and decline of society. Their dreams, he says, were significant dreams, not idle ones. Often a troubled, melancholy dream narrator of this kind is suffering lovesickness but here, as in some other dream poems, his anxiety is moral and social. Gower's first subject is the 1381 Rising. He presents the rebels as animals, maddened with rage, irrationally destroying civil order. Gower's perspective is strongly pro-government, like that of many chroniclers, with fervent praise for those who crushed the rebellion." (*Dream Poems* 376)

CHAPTER FOUR
WISDOM AND/OR WEAKNESS

The importance of the role of a dream narrator in the poem also contributes to our understanding of the author's choice of dream vision. As Burrow points out, "the presence of a narrator inside the poem's fictional world is a very common feature of Ricardian work" (*Ricardian Poetry* 38). But unlike "Dante," who reported his journey through the regions of the dead in the *Divine Comedy*, Ricardian poets like Chaucer limited the perceptions of their narrators more strictly. The narrator's representation of the author is rather limited. Even though in some cases the narrator bears the author's name, as Will in *Piers Plowman*, and "Geoffrey" (1. 729) in the *House of Fame* for example, it is the poet's last resort to commit himself directly to the poem (Burrow, *Ricardian Poetry* 39). This on the one hand, "leaves the poet free to exploit possibilities in the contemporary vernacular which he might otherwise have found it difficult, as an educated man acquainted with politer languages, to come to terms with," on the other hand, "provides [...] the chief means by which Ricardian poets articulate their own kind of irony" (Burrow, *Ricardian Poetry* 39). The proper distance between the author and the narrator frees the poet from taking any responsibility when an unfavorable response to the poem occurs, because "'Disblameth me, if any word be lame, / For as myn auctour seyde, so sey I.' (Troilus, ii. 15—21) But that is Will (or Geoffrey) speaking, not me" (Burrow, *Ricardian Poetry* 40).[1]

In fact recent critics stress the "polyphonic" nature of the narrative voice in Chaucer. For them, there are "a variety of roles in relation to the narrative: author, hero, listener/recipient of the text, lover filled with desire, courtly retainer serving a prince or patron, translator or redactor, scribe or complier" (Phillips, *Dream Poetry*

---

[1] Burrow emphasizes the distinctive significance of the trick of self-depreciation which is common in medieval and Renaissance writing to Ricardian poet as Chaucer in the following remarks: "But the self-depreciation of Ricardian poets ... is more significant stylistically..., because it is closely associated with a persistent verbal irony whereby simple, 'lame' and conventional expressions—expressions of the kind we have been prepared to accept from the narrator—prove to be charged with subtle and often damaging implications for which the author seems hardly to be responsible: 'Disblameth me...' Very often in such cases the narrator's voice, acting as the ostensible voice in a two-voiced ironic utterance, will employ some familiar turns of expression which carry clear points of social or moral criticism." See Burrow, 1971,39—40.

13). The physically passive, mentally uncertain dreamer-narrator, like the dream narrative itself, offers opportunities for variety of subject and sophistication of structure. Meanwhile the multiplicity of the dreamer-narrator role allows more freedom and space for the poet to gloss both the fictional narrative and reality as well.

Chaucer's writing of dream poems thus cannot be taken as a singular case of following the tradition of dream vision as a literary decision. He was among a tide of dream poem writing which was important in late medieval times. Virtually all the major poets of that time composed dream poems, and this generated more successors in fifteenth century. Nevertheless it is not fair to say that Chaucer's dream poems were only a genre choice following the then literary fashion. The political and social implications always bear upon the literary choice.① Thus Chaucer's writing dream poems, in my view, is not a pure matter of following literary convention. Rather, it is Chaucer's social practice: he was playing the role of an intellectual as a social commentator.

Juxtaposition and Denial of Closure—Judgment Yours!

Similar to dream vision genre, juxtaposition is another device Chaucer often chooses for his poems, I believe, for the reason of his artistic concern and his social role of an intellectual. As texts in dream poems are usually presented as raw material in need of interpretation, juxtaposition functions in the same way: they invite the readers to complete the process of understanding and making judgment. By putting many things, especially those that are contrastive or seemingly irrelevant together, Chaucer articulated no explicit views, and thus would shoulder no responsibility for whatever they were. Such attempts to shun responsibility have already been revealed in the *General Prologue*. What he did here was more like a reporter, recording what had been observed, rather than

---

① Such dream poems loaded with topical or political significance have later witnessed further development. Piers Plowman, for example, is such an influential dream poem that a number of poems, though not specifically presented as dreams, take on the subject of contemporary political crises and abuses, and have developed into the "Piers Plowman Tradition."

CHAPTER FOUR
WISDOM AND/OR WEAKNESS

telling something to convey any intended messages. Some seemingly unfit connections between the portraits of the pilgrims and the tales they later tell in the pilgrimage are in fact internally logical. It is, according to Pearsall, only an illusion that Chaucer keeps consistently in touch with, and an illusion that Chaucer makes efforts to maintain, while "(t)o develop portraits so as to make them accord with subsequent revelations would disturb this illusion" (Pearsall, *Canterbury Tales* 52).

On the other hand, I believe, by juxtaposition, Chaucer provides multiple points of view for his audience, and thus to some extent subverts monolithic moral judgments. This has also been manifested in his portrayals of the pilgrims in the *General Prologue*. As Pearsall states, people are not only grouped according to their estates, there are other kinds of grouping, such as the Parson and the Plowman by blood and spirit; the Knight, Squire and Yeoman by kinship and service; the Prioress, Monk and Friar by religious profession; the Man of Law and Franklin by common interests, to list only some (Pearsall, *Canterbury Tales* 58). Thus, the traditional hierarchical ordering of the estates is at least disturbed, if not totally subverted.

However, Chaucer never articulated any significant message explicitly. Even the disturbance of orthodox ordering took place in the context of sweet and overarching harmony from the beginning of the pilgrimage, and also from the outset of the *General Prologue*. The first eighteen lines demonstrate the poet's mastery of his poetic craft. The lines run smoothly and musically, with no imperative or forcing impact upon the audience. In Pearsall's words, "the technical skill... is the harmonising of an unobstrusively 'natural' syntax and metre into a long flowing verse paraphrase which has something of the character of inspired conversation" (*Canterbury Tales* 54). Nature and the supernatural are celebrated for their harmony in Chaucer's description of springtime, "under the canopy of a wise and amiable governance" (Pearsall, *Canterbury Tales* 55). Even the circumstance of the inn, where the pilgrims get together, is filled with a harmonious aura: with the physical comfort of the inn itself and the comfortable relations between the pilgrims, since all seem desirous of "felaweshipe" (l. 32).

But this superficial harmony is disturbed in the course of the poem, which is manifested in the example of the ordering of the portraits. The introduction of the pilgrims follows broadly the order of descending social class, "passing from the landed gentry through the professional classes and the lower mercantile and trading groups to the Plowman," to a group that has been termed "a rogues' gallery of miscellaneous predators" (Pearsall, *Canterbury Tales* 58). Yet, the general impression of hierarchy and the traditional ordering of estates are not without faults. The last group is a mixture of both secular and clerical portraits. What's more, the Summoner and the Pardoner, representing the second estate, follow the Miller, the Manciple and the Reeve.

The juxtaposition also manifests in Chaucer's way of detailing the portraits: unsystematic, random and vague, seemingly from the observer's memory. In this way, Chaucer creates the readers' desire to figure out the implicit significance, "the missing link that will rationalise the discontinuity" (Pearsall, *Canterbury Tales* 59). ① Irrelevant observations in the *Wife of Bath* (*GP*: ll. 459—460), and different proportions of portrait details are two other examples of Chaucer's juxtaposition. ②

Juxtaposition seems to be a more sensible device if it is examined by considering the fiction of his poems in the mean time. Pearsall has recognized the fiction of the *General Prologue*: It is only what the poet has seen or heard of them. He agrees with Cunningham that the fiction is similar to dream-poetry, both allowing a poet to talk with some degree of seriousness about what he has seen and "experienced," a kind of subject-matter that would conventionally be regarded as of utmost triviality (Pearsall, *Canterbury Tales* 60). As Pearsall rightly perceives: "The fiction is of the greatest importance to Chaucer, since it relieves him of the obligation to systematise his presentation of the pilgrims according to some single unifying moral

---

① Detailed analysis, see Pearsall,1985,58—59.

② For the irrelevant observations in the *Wife of Bath's Tale*, see the following lines: "She was a worthy womman al hir lyve: / Housboundes at chirche dore she hadde fyve." No detailed portrait is provided for the Parson and the Plowman, while some are in full-scale and fully developed portraits: Prioress, Monk, Friar, Wife of Bath.

principle" (*Canterbury Tales* 60). In fact, its importance to Chaucer is even more than relieving him of this obligation. It also relieves him of the obligation to make any explicit moral judgment. All the choice and judgment are left to the audience. That might be one of the purposes which Chaucer consistently bears in his mind in his poetry writing. Juxtaposition is one means through which he achieves this goal.

The denial of closure, though significantly common among many late-medieval poems, also functions similarly to juxtaposition in inviting the audience's own judgment. Take the *Canterbury Tales* for example. Only twenty-four tales survive, which is drastically short of the 120 tales promised in the *General Prologue*. Among them some are unfinished, because of the interruption of the pilgrims Chaucer introduces, as in the cases of the *Monk's Tale*, *Tale of Sir Thopas*, and the *Squire's Tale*. One tale, that is the *Cook's Tale*, has been truncated, by Chaucer the author himself. Seven out of the thirty pilgrims introduced in the *General Prologue* have not even been given the chance to tell any tales at all—the Plowman, the Knight's Yeoman, and the Five Guildmen. However, the Canon's Yeoman is inserted in the tale-telling, unexpectedly, without having been introduced together with the company of pilgrims in the *General Prologue*. The deletion and addition can't be interpreted as merely the poet's carelessness and poetic failure. On the contrary, they acquire much political significance. They are in fact the author's intentional arrangement. As Bowers rightly indicates,

> The insertion of the *Canon's Yeoman's Tale* renders the absences of these other sections, promised but not delivered, matters of willful neglect, making them subject to interpretation as issues of authorial intention. The disruption caused by the unexpected entry of a new tale-teller casts Chaucer's decision to omit others into sharp relief. It renders them silent, allows them to slip into partial invisibility, and thereby makes them available for later appropriation or continued neglect. (13)

Thus, it won't be hasty to conclude that Chaucer arranged the tales in such a way for two reasons: for one thing, it was safe to put something inappropriate aside; for another, he himself disturbed the construction with a view of attracting later readers' attention, and allowing them to make their own judgments. As Prendergast interprets Bower,

> The fragmentary nature of the *Cook's Tale* or Chaucer's failure to assign tales to seven of the pilgrims seems to result not so much from carelessness as from self-censorship in a politically controversial age. Yet far from lying unnoticed or untended—as Chaucer might have intended—these incompletions tended to invite later writers to shape additions that answered their own political concerns. Hence, [. . .] unfinished tales are given closure while complete tales are put into the mouths of formerly mute pilgrims such as the Plowman. These more "complete" versions of the *Tales* satisfied the aesthetic desire for closure and also both authorized and were shaped by politico-literary concerns, such as the desire to claim Chaucer as a champion of Wycliffism. (3)

So politics has been one of the factors that shaped and mutated early versions of the *Canterbury Tales*.

The accepted conclusion of the *Canterbury Tales* is also questioned by some scholars.① They point out that the uncertainty and fluidity of the text itself suggests the resistance of any global attempts to determine how and why they were rewritten. Chaucer is well aware of this. As Steven Justice puts it, Chaucer's texts demonstrate the poet's "consciousness that the author cannot control the social reach of his text, and that there are potential though unimagined audiences who might make words spoken in innocence something guilty" (224). But it might be Chaucer's willing choice rather than poetic impotence. If Tim Machan is right in holding that the conflation of medieval and modern notions of authority is precisely what "obliterates" the author-function of vernacular literature, then it might be acceptable to conclude that Chaucer is in

---

① See Miceal Vaughan, "The Invention of the Parson's Tale", in *Rewriting Chaucer* edited by Prendergast and Kline, 45—90. Vaughan argues that it is the scribes who invent the Tale to provide a fitting conclusion to a work that may have ended with the Parson's Prologue.

fact unwilling to lay claim to his own authority. ①

Chaucer himself also claimed repeatedly that his rewritings depended heavily on his sources. His unwillingness to claim his own authority for the texts he wrote or rewrote is suggestive, not only in politically shunning any responsibility, but also in poetically, in a paradoxical way, forming his own "originality." As Colish states, "With an unfinished work, we can never know how, or if, Chaucer would have drawn conclusions and achieved closure. But the *Canterbury Tales*, as we have them, present a specifically Chaucerian outlook, a serene, playful, non-judgmental enjoyment of variety for its own sake" (222). At this point, again, Chaucer achieves a good balance, or to be more exact, a combination between his worldly wisdom and his literary innovation.

Thus similar to dream vision genre, juxtaposition and denial of closure are not merely literary devices in Chaucer's poems. They are again Chaucer's strategies of either making social comments, or enlightening the audience to make their own judgments. His poem writing serves to be his social commitment as an intellectual.

Restraint—*A Play between Virtue and Subversion*

If it is inaccurate or exaggerated to say that the *Canterbury Tales* are composed with a tone of restraint, it won't be too surprising for readers of Chaucer to notice the importance of restraint in one of the *Tales*: the *Clerk's Tale*.

Restraint was regarded as a virtue in medieval times. In the *Clerk's Tale*, the heroine Griselda embodies this virtue to excess. As the wife of a marquis who rules the land, Griselda's total obedience, passivity and restraint seem to have been taken for granted and welcomed in a society of male supremacy and hierarchy. However, it is more than a secular virtue. The moral of the tale is at the same time religious. As has been claimed in the Lenvoy de Chaucer at the end of the tale:

> This storie is seyd nat for that wyves sholde
> Folwen Grisilde as in humylitee,
> For it were inportable, though they wolde,

---

① Refer to Machan, 177—199.

> But for that every wight, in his degree,
> Sholde be constant in adversitee
> (ll. 1142—1146)

Griselda is an example that is supposed to be followed not in secular life, but in one's spiritual life.

> For sith a womman was so pacient
> Unto a mortal man, wel moore us oghte
> Receyven al in gree that God us sent
> (ll. 1149—1151)
> ......
> And suffreth us, as for oure exercise,
> With sharp scourges of adversitee
> Ful ofte to be bete in sondry wise;
> Nat for to knowe oure wyl, for certes he,
> Er we were born, knew al oure freletee;
> And for oure beste is al his governaunce.
> Lat us thanne lyve in vertuous suffraunce.
> (ll. 1156—1162)

Thus, Griselda's restraint can be considered a virtue, and the *Clerk's Tale* provides morals to be taken by its audience.

However, the statement can be argued against and become problematic, if Griselda's restraint is studied from another perspective. M. L. Warren's discussion of Griselda is a signpost for the recognition of this significance. Warren examines Griselda's unquestioning obedience in the light of Michel Foucault's "technology of the self." According to Foucault's definition, technologies of the self are those "which permit individuals to effect by their own means or with the help of others a certain number of operations on their own bodies and souls, thoughts, conduct, and way of being, so as to transform themselves in order to attain a certain state of happiness, purity, wisdom, perfection or immorality" (18).

Thus Griselda's "unnatural restraint" can be argued as a technology of forging or constituting herself as subject. Her constancy or *stedfastnesse* in the face of the three or arguably four tests is not simply

CHAPTER FOUR
WISDOM AND/OR WEAKNESS

passive submission of wife to husband, or the ruled to the ruler. Instead, it is an active self-improving process of one's own volition. To illustrate this, Warren further puts forward the example of the desert monk in eastern tradition and states that exagoreusis is "founded on the capacity of the master to lead the disciple to a happy and autonomous life through good advice" (Foucault 45). The monk deliberately entrusts himself totally to his master so as to be directed to God. The similarity of Griselda to the monk lies in her total obedience to Walter as disciple to his master, or in another name, his spiritual director. When she chooses to accept Walter's proposal of marriage, she makes this promise:

> And here I swere that revere willingly,
> In werk ne thought,I nyl yow disobeye,
> For to be deed,though me were looth to deye
> (ll. 362—364)

This promise is not an ordinary one but of great significance. As Jill Mann says: "Griselda's unquestioned obedience to her husband is not the simple result of her marriage vow, but something that she takes upon with the unique promise that is the special condition of her marriage" (*Chaucer* 146). The promise has extended the wifely duty to a total obedience, which is akin to that of a monk's ascetic entering into a relationship of exagoreusis with a spiritual father.

An example of radical obedience in Cassian's "Institutes" can serve to make Griselda's attitude towards her loss of the two children relatively understandable. The example is of a father's entering a monastery with his small son. He is in such total obedience that he not only consents to see his son beaten daily without any reason but even proceeds to throw him into the river as ordered, which is stopped by some of the brothers "who had been purposely sent to watch the banks of the river carefully" (qtd. in Warren). [1] This is evidently reminiscent of the loss and return of

---

[1] The original source information, according to Warren, is as follows: Cassian John. Institutes. Trans. E. C. S. Gibson. *A Select Library of Nicene and Post-Nicene Fathers of the Christian Church*. Eds. Philip Schoff and Henry Wace. 2nd series. Oxford and London: 1984. Vol II. 24.

Griselda's children. The ascetic spirituality of Christian monasticism was in fact very influential through the spiritual movement of the Middle Ages. Christianity, as a religion of salvation, is to guide "the individual from one reality to another, from death to life" (qtd. in Warren). It involves one's transformation in the ascetic-like process. Griselda's transformation is overtly indicated in the tale: from her initial poverty, dirty and uncombed hair (ll. 375—380), to jeweled glory; the stripping to her smock and her final reclothing, which is an easy reminder of rebirth. And the religious reference can be easily perceived in the details: "oxes stalle," "as a lamb" for example (l. 207, l. 538) etc. All the tolerance of adversity is the path to the goal of being morally perfect, or religiously, of the closeness to God.

Fortunately, all these extreme sufferings are not a vain effort in Griselda. In the practice of asceticism, Griselda's virtues, which was initially recognized by Walter, (a spiritual father is supposed to have the ability) get highlighted. By promising to totally submit to Walter, she gains the opportunity to win the popularity of the people. Her renown travels so far and wide that people travel a long way simply to see her. When Walter is away, she is provided the opportunity of proving herself able to settle discord and dispute with her "wise and rype wordes" (l. 438). Her radical obedience finally forces Walter to recognize her innate nobility and restore her to the palace "... ther she was honored as hire oghte" (l. 1120). She is gradually reaching the state of perfection under the direction of Walter. The two do not appear as enemies at all but mate in the same direction to God. Yet this is too hasty a conclusion.

As Elain Tuttle Hansen suggests in her discussion of Griselda, "woman's insubordination is ... a derivative of her subordination" (189). Then does the subordination imply the possible insubordination? Or to put it more directly, is there any insubordination hidden behind the subordination? Can we understand Griselda's subordination as a kind of strategy, or to borrow Foucault's term, "technology" of insubordination?

Foucault points out that the technology of revealing one's self in total obedience may not necessarily lead to self-eradication. It might be a self-forging or self-constituting process, because "(b)y telling

CHAPTER FOUR
WISDOM AND/OR WEAKNESS

himself not only his thoughts but also the smallest movement of consciousness, his intention, the monk stands in hermeneutic relation not only to the master but to himself" (Foucault 47).

So we won't run a grave risk if we infer that by full submission one may be more aware of his subordinated position, which might finally lead to insubordination. Two pieces of evidence from the *Tale* can be employed to support this hypothesis. When she is recalled to the palace to prepare for Walter's second wedding and to say how she likes the new wife, Griselda, obedient as ever, wishes Walter well with his young bride. Meanwhile she warns him without any malice not to treat the new wife of noble origin as unkindly as he did others, meaning in fact herself:

> O thing biseke I yow and warne also,
> That ye ne prikke with no tormentinge
> This tender mayden, as ye han don mo:
> For she is fostred in hir norishinge
> More tenderly, and, to my supposinge,
> She coulde nat adversitee endure
> As coude a povre fostred creature.
> (ll. 1037—1043)

This is the first time in the *Tale* that the insubordination spirit creeps in silently and secretly. The final outburst of her feeling when she regains her two children is in striking contrast to her former meek and "coy" character. It is a good demonstration of how strong a release may be after one has been repressed too much and for too long. The *Tale*, according to Hansen,

> suggests on one hand that Griselda is not really empowered by her acceptable behavior, because the feminine virtue she embodies in welcoming her subordination is by definition both punitive and self-destructive. On the other hand, the Tale reveals that the perfectly good woman is powerful, or at least potentially so, insofar as her suffering and submission are fundamentally insubordinate and deeply threatening to men and to the concepts of power and gender identity upon which patriarchal culture is promised (190).

The power of the totally submissive Griselda is evident at the end of the tale, with the final restoration of her fame, her children and her deserved position. To some extent, Walter is right, or at least understandable, to test Griselda's loyalty in respect of hierarchy. As Hansen writes, "... Walter's decision to torture and humiliate her comes, according to the narrative, after she has been acclaimed as a saintly ruler" (191). Griselda gradually becomes a threat to her ruler and director. This, on the other hand, proves that Griselda's "unnatural restraint" is not a total passivity but a sort of preparation for or a roundabout means of insubordination.

Interestingly, there is an easily perceivable similarity between Griselda and the Clerk, who tells the *Tale*. The resemblance of the Clerk to Griselda is made clear by the Host in the prologue, though it is in fact a commonplace comparison of an ideal clerk with a maiden.

> "Sire Clerk of Oxenford," oure Hososte sayde,
> Ye ryde as coy and stille as dooth a mayde
> Were newe spoused...
> (ll. 1—3)

And so too is the Clerk's response to the Host's request that he takes part in the storytelling:

> I am under youre yerde;
> Ye han of us as now the governance,
> And therefore wol I do yow obeisance,
> As fer as resoun axeth, hardily.
> (ll. 22—25)

That "obeisance" is a natural reminder of Griselda's "obeisance" to Walter. The description of the appearance of the two echoes with each other too. Both are "povre creature" (l. 232), with the Clerk in his old, threadbare garments and Griselda in her old threadbare garments (Dinshaw 135—136). The significance of all these echoes, in my view, lies in the reminding of the possible overlapping of both characters. Restraint though thought "unnatural" and excessive, is definitely the key aspect in Griselda's personality. But what about

CHAPTER FOUR
WISDOM AND/OR WEAKNESS

the Clerk? Does the Clerk, who has a similar appearance to Griselda, also possess the same character of restraint? The answer may emerge from a careful examination of the relationship between the Clerk and the Wife of Bath.

According to John A. Alford, the Clerk mirrors the Wife of Bath and the vice versa. The opposition of the two begins even in the *General Prologue*, where they are given opposite sets of attributes, with one dressed in rich "coverchiefs" (l. 453), being obviously well-off, having five husbands, outgoing, fond of "compaignye" (l. 461) and appealing to experience, while the other a "ful thredbare" (l. 290), "povre" bachelor, a recluse who speaks no more than necessary and "sownynge in moral vertu was his speche" (l. 307), and who values philosophy and logic more (l. 109, l. 125). Besides, the literal fighting of the Wife with her fifth husband, who is also a clerk of Oxenford, makes the two stand somewhere in opposition too. The Wife's claim in her long *Prologue* that

> ... it is an impossible
> That any clerk wol speke good of wyves,
> But if it be of hooly seintes lyves
> (ll. 688—690)

has in fact thrown down a challenge for the Clerk to pick up. The Clerk, however, does not interrupt the Wife's speech as the Summoner and the Friar do. He keeps to his usual quiet manner and is patient enough to wait for his opportunity to respond to the Wife. He does not hurry to tell his tale till the last moment when the Host urges him to take part in the "play" of story-telling. Yet he is in fact well prepared in counter-arguing with the Wife, but still not in a direct, extreme way. He achieves his goal of insulting the Wife through the following devices: He tells a story of so good a woman as Griselda, though not a saint; he praises women in general for their virtue of humility while conceding that "clerkes preise women but a lite" (l. 935); and finally he delivers a mighty insult to the Wife herself by the mock-encomium of the Envoy. From the above, we may see that the apparent submissive, "coy" and quiet Clerk is not so "pacient" as he appears to be. Behind the dumb Clerk stands a very smart, eloquent, ready fighter against those who are in opposition. His restraint overlaps his heroine's, though not exerted to the same extreme as hers, but to a certain acceptable extent.

As a matter of fact, as stated by Muscatine, "(i)t is truly the tale of Chaucer's Clerk: sharing his threadbare leanness, he despises ordinary riches for the rarer, more educated pleasures of philosophical morality" (191). Chaucer's voice and image appears and disappears in the tale now and then. Though not a mouthpiece of Chaucer, the Clerk does in many places voice Chaucer's opinion. It is actually Chaucer's favorite device to impose himself in his texts as some kind of narrator figure. His self-identification in his texts is worked in different ways, from including himself in his text, like one of the pilgrims in Tales, to listing his work or focusing his place in the literary canon (Rudd 165). In this *Tale*, Chaucer makes the Clerk speak out his own homage to Petrarch. However, this is not the focus of my attention and it won't greatly matter if the overlapping of the two does not occur in respect of restraint. But the following questions are worth attention. Is Chaucer a man of restraint as the Clerk in his *Tale*? If so, how can his restraint be perceived in his *Tales*? What is behind his restraint? An examination of the form of the *Tale* might serve as a good starting point for the exploration of these questions.

The form of the *Tale* is in rhyme royal, which is also used in other religious or semi-religious tales of pathos, eg, the *Man of Law's Tale*. This indicates that it is a tale of high moral. Yet it is not simply a didactic sermon, which might come not often from Chaucer but from his contemporary, the "moral Gower." It is after all a story, and the final envoy adds special flavor of mockery. Judging from this point, Chaucer tends to appear as a man of moderation and balance. So is the style of the *Tale*. It is also "restrained, even ascetic" "in narrative development and circumstantial detail" (Cooper, *Guides* 200).① According to Muscatine, "In the *Clerk's Tale* Chaucer meters out scenes and speeches in stanzas and blocks of stanzas and this deliberateness

---

① Cooper has made a detailed analysis of the careful diction in the *Tale* to elaborate the restraint of style. See Cooper, 1989.

CHAPTER FOUR
WISDOM AND/OR WEAKNESS

supports the sense of self-containment and restraint felt in the whole poem's rhythm" (192). Obviously it will not be controversial to conclude that Chaucer tells this *Tale* in a style of restraint.

In addition, the *Tale*, if examined in the context of the *Tales*, tells more about Chaucer's attitude of moderation and balance. The contrast between Walter and the Knight in the *Wife of Bath's Tale* serves as a good example to illustrate this. In the *Clerk's Tale*, Walter demonstrates his restraint when he sees Griselda in his hunting:

> Ful ofte sithe this markys sette his ye
> As he on huntyng rood paraventure;
> And whan it fil that he myghte hire espye,
> He noghte with wantown lookyng of folye
> His eyen caste on hire, but in sad wyse
> Upon his chiere he wolde hym ofte avyse
> (ll. 233—238)

In the *Wife of Bath's Tale*, however, the knight acts directly, giving in to desire. Walter is presented as a real noble person, who can exercise "pruidence," a quality that implies exercise of control (Collette 71). Prudent restraint is the quality that Chaucer admires and approves. Yet the endings of both tales are better proof of Chaucer's advocating of moderation and balance, with the "Wife's knight's allowing his bride's 'soveraynetee,' at least the power to decide her own future, and Walter's honoring Griselda (he even gives houseroom to Janicular, l. 1133). So it is mutual obedience and 'blisse' that count" (Cooper, *Guides* 198).

The treatment of the sources and analogues also shows Chaucer's attitude towards restraint. Griselda's story can be traced back at least as far as Boccaccio's *Decameron*. But Chaucer's version is more closely connected to Petrarch's Latin adaptation of Boccaccio's tale (as Chaucer himself confesses in the *Tale*), and a close French translation of that, the anonymous *Livre Griseldis*. The alteration of and addition to these versions are telling in revealing Chaucer's attitude. For instance, the exclamations on the needlessness of Walter's testing are elaborated and sharpened, which shows the

Clerk's, or Chaucer's, disapproval of the excesses. The fact that Chaucer is alone in his suggestion of anguish in joy when Griselda embraces her children in her faint is also a kind of mild criticism of Walter's abuse of power. According to Aers's Marxist critique, "the poem is thus a powerful dramatization of the effects of absolutism on both the ruled and the ruler" (*Chaucer* 34). Aers links this directly with the political position in England in the late 1390s with its growing concern about despotism. Some critics even infer that Walter's tyranny can be read as a reflection of Bernobo Visconti's Milan, which is arguably true, because it is only on rare occasions that Chaucer refers to contemporary affairs (Rudd 126).

No matter how true the inference is, the style, the form and the inventive use of the sources, all stand to reflect Chaucer's character of restraint. The crux of the issue is what is behind Chaucer's restraint. Is there any analogy between his restraint and the "unnatural restraint" of Griselda, and the acceptable restraint of the Clerk? For the latter two, restraint has not only the implication of passivity, withdrawal, subordination. On the contrary, it indicates the possibility of insubordination. The temporary constraint is a preparation for later freedom, virtue or possible insubordination. The apparent quietness, meekness, and "pacience" may foretell the approach of something else, either absolute virtue or the inevitable contrary result. To put it in another way, it will bend or break. Yet the reason for the constraint is never just a matter of personality or character. For Griselda, her restraint can be understood as her pursuit of perfection. Meanwhile her "perfection" has become so powerful that the insubordination seems to derive from the subordination. For the Clerk, his restraint can be more overtly and literally interpreted as a strategy to battle against his counterpart, represented here by the Wife of Bath, though still in a relatively mild manner. For Chaucer, restraint is even part of his attitude toward life. This attitude is certainly reflected in his works on various levels and in various perspectives, from the form, the style, to the arrangement of the stories, the inventive rewriting of the sources. It is, in fact, pervasive throughout the *Tales*. In the *General Prologue*, Chaucer modestly puts himself at the end of his description of the pilgrims, and humbly admits that "My wit is short, ye may wel understonde" (l. 746). He pretends to be such a shabby story teller in telling *Sir Topas* that he is interrupted by the Host and has to start a new one—the *Tale of Melibee*. The pretence of incompetence is in fact an effective way of writing, with the purpose of attracting the readers' or audience's attention to the characters in the tales rather than the teller of the tales. This detached point of view is not only a helpful device employed for the sake of the plausibility of his tales, but also a deliberate choice in expressing his individualism, his dissent from the established system while shunning any possible harm in the context of the Middle Ages. Although he is of merchant origin and has royal connections, Chaucer is after all an intellectual. Like the Clerk, he is a scholar of philosophy and rhetoric, though not so "povre" because he has a profession as well. He has a sober mind and is alert to reality, blessed and cursed. However, he is not from the landed class and has no political power to take the world under his control. Thus restraint might be the best strategy in dealing with despotism. It is more effective in the long run than a hasty face-to-face confrontation.

It is my least intention to present Chaucer as a democratic fighter in the modern sense. As Aers points out, although Griselda's ability to rule well offers a radical alternative to monarchical rule, Chaucer does not endorse it.

> Here we meet one of the horizons of Chaucer's social imagination, for... it tends to abandon all ideas of fraternity, social justice and the social embodiment of charity, foreshadowing an ideological position that would become common-place with the triumph of bourgeois individualism in the later seventeenth and eighteenth centuries. (*Chaucer* 35—36)

It is not easy for him to transcend the limitations of his time and its social hierarchy. Yet it is not going too far to acknowledge his efforts in exploring the soundness of contemporary life, from the point of view of the social system, the church system and the gender system. Restraint, shared by Griselda, the Clerk and Chaucer himself, is after all an effective strategy in reaching their own goals. Chaucer was in fact playing the role of an intellectual by voicing out his ideas about gender, politics, or society, in a strategical way though.

The above analysis demonstrates that Chaucer's choice of literary devices, including genre, tone, style as well as variation on the source texts is also closely related with his social function as an intellectual. Chaucer is in fact either making social commentary or enlightening his audience by writing poems. His writing devices should not be considered as a mere literary matter. They are his commenting strategies as well.

Wisdom in Life: Chaucer and Chinese *Shi*

Chaucer's wisdom is not only manifested in his literary work, but also well recognized to be evident in his social life. He has shown good judgment and has dealt with thorny issues wisely in an age of turmoil, trying to avoid any political or partisan conflicts. He seems to know the art of balance, stepping forward or backward accordingly at appropriate moment. Such wisdom is, interestingly, shared with some ancient Chinese intellectuals, who are commonly named *Shi*. In fact, *Shi* and the intellectual are similar in many ways. A comparison between them will be made in the following aspects: their social position, their poetic composition and the interaction between their respective social life and literary career.

Shi *and Intellectuals*

Shi is a term usually used to refer to a social stratum between senior officials (*Dai Fu*) and the common people (*Shu Min*) in ancient China. In feudal China, they resembled closely another group termed *Shi Dai Fu*. This term is specifically used to refer to literati and officialdom. In most cases the two terms are interchangeable, especially when those who have sought official position through taking part in the imperial examinations are referred to. The following discussion will be confined to examining the group of *Shi*, who had been educated and trained, and at the same time held a royal or governmental position.

Though in China, the term "intellectual" applied to a person is

CHAPTER FOUR
WISDOM AND/OR WEAKNESS

rather broad and nonspecific, it is not impossible to examine it. ① By adopting French sociologist Edgar Morin's approaches, the famous Chinese scholar Yue Daiyun has keenly perceived the similarity of traditional Chinese intellectuals to those so designated in the Western conception. Following Morin, Yue holds that the term "intellectual" refers to one "who is professionally involved in some aspect of culture or learning, who answers a specific function in society and in political affairs, and who is conscious of principles of universality" (6). ② Thus it is valid to make a comparison between Chinese and Western intellectuals so long as the definition is applicable to both. *Shi*, a term traditionally taken as the Chinese equivalent of "intellectuals," may also share some features with intellectuals of the present day in the West.

Shi, an ancient term, and the intellectual, a modern notion, are two concepts that surely differ in many respects. As a social stratum, they appeared at different historical moments. *Shi* as a group has a long history in China and its implications are multi-faceted and complicated. It has been used continuously but the referents have undergone continuous changes over time. ③ On the other hand, the intellectual as a social stratum did not emerged until the eighteenth or even nineteenth century, closely associated with the Enlightenment Movement.

Despite differences between them, similarities are also evident. Both groups are educated and highly literate, both are deeply concerned with the common good, concerning the fate of nation and society rather than of their own, having the common goal of improving the present world. To be sure, these similarities originate

---

① As the famous Chinese scholar Yue Daiyun puts it: "Anyone who labors with his brain and is in possession of certain cultural or scientific knowledge, such as workers in science and technology, workers in literature and the arts, teachers, physicians, etc." may be called an intellectual, according to the 1979 edition of the encyclopedia *Ci Hai*. See Yue, 5.

② See note 4 in Yue, 6.

③ Yu Yingshi has made pioneering efforts in his historical and cultural study of Chinese *Shi*: Shi *and Chinese Culture*. I am firstly and greatly inspired by it. *Shi* has a long tradition in Chinese history, and it is developed and appears with different faces in different historical periods. See Yu, 7.

from different sources. In the West, intellectuals' taking the responsibility to reform and improve the world is inseparable from the Christian tradition. In the Middle Ages, the role of intellectuals as social conscience was taken by Christianity. Modern intellectuals are similar to priests in medieval times, who considered that everyone should do his best to contribute to a better world. It was a religious pursuit for everybody. Roughly equivalent to the intellectual in English, *Shi* played a similar role of medieval priests. They were also well-educated, faithful servants of state rather than of the church, feeling a responsibility for changing and improving the world. By way of contrast, in China, *Shi* considered themselves no ordinary beings but had the privileged obligation to accomplish their divine mission, that is, to "Set your heart upon the Way" (Confucius 81).① The "Way" here implies the value system. To establish and help maintain the value system became a responsibility peculiar to *Shi*. Nevertheless, the intellectual and *Shi* held the same belief that the world could be improved, and they would do it. But how?

For most Chinese *Shi*, the only way of realizing their political ideals was through an official career. So they took part in the imperial examinations to seek a position in the government. By writing the conventional eight-legged essays, they expressed their concern about and opinions on political and social issues. If they were admitted to the bureaucracy, they would seemingly have the opportunity to help cure the disease of the society or nation and help achieve their divine goal of improving the world.

In fact, the close relation between writing and holding a public position is characteristic of *Shi*, who are usually scholar-officials. Before Confucius' time, scholars were usually employees of the court or the government, dealing with governmental affairs. They were people who had the so-called "six skills": manners, music, shooting, riding, writing and counting, and held some public positions in the meantime. Confucius, the prototype of Chinese *Shi*, he himself acted as warehouse manager. Before the Spring and Autumn Period, they were not intellectuals in the strict sense. They

---

① See *The Analects*, "The Master said, Set your heart upon the Way, support yourself by its power, lean upon Goodness, seek distraction in the arts." Confucius, 81.

were the lowest in the aristocratic class. Thus, they were confined in three respects: socially they were confined in the aristocratic class; politically they were confined to their own position; and ideologically they were confined to the official schools. After the Spring and Autumn Period, the position of *Shi* was played down, the distance between *Shi* and common people became shorter than that between *Shi* and grand masters. It was until the Warring States Period, when *Shi* was put together with other three classes, the merchants, the peasants and the workers that they were liberated from the feudal system and became free in many aspects. The disintegration of the feudal system and the social mobility of *Shi* lead to the shaping of Chinese intellectual. ①

The history of *Shi* briefed above shows that *Shi*, with their literate background, seemed inescapably entangled with officialdom, especially when they hoped to realize their social or political ideals. It is at this point that Chaucer resembles a Chinese *Shi*. This resemblance naturally leads to a comparison between them, which will be significant in understanding their intellectuality.

Chaucer and Shi

The similarity between Chaucer and the traditional Chinese *Shi* can be manifested in several respects. Firstly, they both played a double role, as an official and a member of the literati. Secondly, they shared an inclination towards concern for certain universal issues, such as good governance, truth, fate etc. Thirdly, Chaucer's wisdom in "speaking to power" (a supposed typical feature of an intellectual in the modern sense), shown in his literary writing as has been elaborated earlier in this chapter, was also embodied in many

---

① *Shi* before the Spring and Autumn Period, and in Shang and Zhou Dynasty are those who are employed by the government to deal with governmental affairs. Above them are grand master (*dai fu*), duke, minister and king. They are socially identified with the feudal aristocracy, politically restricted within certain position and ideological restricted within the court culture, such as poetry, calligraphy, etiquette and music. Hence no criticism and reflection upon the reality. After the Spring and Autumn Period, the position of *Shi* was played down. The distance between *Shi* and common people was shorter than that between *Shi* and grand masters. See Yu, 597—620.

Chinese *Shi*, in their professional lives and their literary works.

Take Bai Juyi, a famous poet of the Tang dynasty for instance. It is not a randomly choice to pick Bai to be compared with Chaucer, because Bai shared many features of Chaucer. Both Bai and Chaucer had connections with aristocrats. Bai was from a high-ranking official family, while Chaucer, though the son of a well-to-do merchant, enjoyed royal patronage. Both were widely traveled and rich in experience, though for different reasons—in Bai's case, the result of being demoted, in Chaucer's, for diplomatic missions or commercial business. The traveling experiences provided them first-hand knowledge of all walks of life. Thus they had the opportunity to know lower-class people as well as had the access to the aristocratic way of life. This results in their breadth of vision and keenness of insight into human nature, which is essential for the composition of great works. Also, both lived in an age of transformation and turmoil, and had experienced personal ups and downs in their political careers, though to different degrees.

Despite these similarities, they differ in attitude to life, writing tone, and political gestures as an intellectual. Bai, like Chaucer's contemporary Langland, wrote about and for the common people. Chaucer, though he advocated writing in English, the language of the common people, rather than Latin or French, which were regarded then as aristocratic languages, wrote for multiple audiences. Among them were his immediate audience in the court, including royalty and those of equal status to himself, and possible readers outside the court. Bai directly criticized the emperor Tang Xuan Zong's licentious life in his famous poem *A Song of Unending Sorrow*. This, however, was impossible for Chaucer, who was cautious in political life and whose evasiveness in almost all his literary works was so characteristic and evident.

Nevertheless, Bai was not always a courageous fighter against misgovernment or corruption. He sometimes took an approach similar to Chaucer's when he was in unfavorable circumstances. Because of his submitting a statement to the then Prime Minister Li Jipu, pointing out the inappropriateness of his policy of dismissing officials at will, Bai fell prey to factional struggles. As a result, he experienced a series of demotions, though he had the talents and will

CHAPTER FOUR
WISDOM AND/OR WEAKNESS

to serve the state. Frustrated by these events, Bai started to change the focus of his life from political affairs in officialdom to traveling around and composing poems in praise of the beauty of mountains and streams, silencing himself to any worldly issues. This reminds us of Chaucer's retreat from London, the factional struggles centre, to Kent, where he could distance himself and avoid any possible troubles.

In dealing with factional matters, Chaucer was also different from some other intellectuals of his time, like Thomas Usk for instance. Under political pressure in 1380s, he dealt with matters of affiliation in his own way. Having assured access to the ranks of the gentry in court service which resulted from his birth in a prosperous family, Chaucer did not waste but actually marshaled his initial advantages effectively, "presenting a model of circumspection in pursuit of factional reward" (Strohm, *Politics and Poetics* 90). But he had a keen sense of the dangers of factional activity. Despite his connections with Richard II and John of Gaunt, Chaucer kept himself independent. During the difficult years of the 1380s, Chaucer tried wisely and systematically to curtail the extent of his factional visibility (Strohm, *Politics and Poetics* 91). His withdrawal to Kent, no matter how it is interpreted, did distance him from the court, the centre of factional struggles (Strohm, *Politics and Poetics* 92). His granting his Exchequer annuities to John Scalby on 1 May 1388 also helped him curtail his royal commitments and protected himself from condemnation by the Merciless Parliament. Though no general nullification or large-scale transfer of annuities seemed to have actually occurred, the step he took in response to the Merciless Parliament was cautious but correct. What he should do at the moment was to further "his apparent objective of leading a modestly restricted life in Kent until circumstances would permit a safe reentry into national affairs" (Strohm, *Politics and Poetics* 94).

Chaucer's way of dealing with difficult circumstances actually resembles that of *Shi* in China. When it is dangerous to act with justice, it is at least wise to do nothing, or to distance oneself from the vortex. Like Chaucer's absenting himself from London, taking the responsibility of a Justice officer in Kent during the period of turmoil, Bai volunteered to take the position of prefectural governor in Hang Zhou, a city far away from Chang An, the capital. Abhorring the cruel internal strife in the court, and influenced by the Buddhism, Bai seemed to stand aloof from worldly affairs, drinking wine to excess and visiting brothels frequently. Everything that once mattered paled into insignificance.①

However, thanks to their withdrawal from worldly affairs, both Chaucer and Bai had composed more literary works of excellence during that period. The greater part of Chaucer's masterpiece was composed when he was in Kent. Bai also composed many great poems after witnessing the life of the common people and experiencing his own ups and downs. The same was true of most men of letters in China. They achieved excellence in literature when they are frustrated with life.

Therefore, sharing similar concerns and confronting similar dilemmas, Chaucer and the Chinese *Shi* are similar as scholar-officials. Their life experience interacts with their literary writing.

On the other hand, in the respect of how to realize their political ideals, Chaucer and the Chinese *Shi* also have something in common. Wang Anshi, a highly placed servant of the Song dynasty, instances the relationship between *Shi* and their own conscience and ideals, and the society they serve. For Wang Anshi, it was his duty to serve the nation if it was reigned by a wise and moral king. So intellectuals like him would make efforts to consult or advise the king, to aid in his wise governance. However, if they were restrained by their political situation and had no opportunity to do that, they would be frustrated. Some of them might no longer care for the rebuilding of the right order, at least in practice, and would retreat from reality. More time and talents would be spared for the production of literary works. But without doubt, they never separated themselves absolutely from the worldly life. What they would and could do was to probe matters in another way.② As the famous Chinese scholar

---

① But it is not true that he did nothing but wasting his life. He has done many things for the common people. For example, he helped build "Bai Di," an embankment project for irrigation. It is so named to commemorate his contribution.

② For more details, see Yu, 3.

CHAPTER FOUR
WISDOM AND/OR WEAKNESS

Yue Daiyun analyzes it,

> (T) hey are men who lived lives of chaos and upset, who are dissatisfied with the realities of life around them, who hope, through their writing, to probe that life. Chapter 51 of the Song Shu (Documents of the Song) tells us that Liu Yiqing, "finding that the roads and ways of the world had become difficult and that he could no longer straddle a horse [i.e., pursue an official career], summoned the masters of literature, and without fail, from far and near, they came to him"—and A New Account of Tales of the World was compiled. (1)

What *Shi* could do in an age of chaos was to retreat from the official life and turned to their pen and wrote to probe the life, the truth, hoping and waiting for the birth of wise and moral kings.

Certainly, Chaucer had a different career path from Liu Yiqing. In general, he had been successful in both worlds, public and literary. However, he had also experienced his low ebb. Some of the tales in the *Canterbury Tales*, his most prestigious work, were composed when he distanced himself from the royal circle in London, acting as a Justice Officer in Kent. By then he had more time to focus on his literary career. The themes, genres and styles changed from the "court flavour" to reflections upon the society. Their withdrawal from the official life thus does not indicate their indifference to the society. On the contrary, it is a kind of wisdom. They know when to advance and when to withdraw.

Such wisdom can be explored further from the perspective of Taoism, the system of wise philosophy. Taoism is a deep, fundamental trait of Chinese thinking, and of the Chinese attitude toward life and society. Unlike Confucianism, which provides a practical sense of proportions, Daoism provides more freedom and release. It might be too absolute to conclude that when a Chinese succeeds, he is always a Confucian, and when he fails, he is always a Taoist. But this statement significantly indicates the different wisdom the two philosophies offer. Confucianism emphasizes involvement in the present world. A follower of Confucianism knows what cannot be done, but still does it. The Taoist knows what cannot be done, and does not do it.① Influenced by these two great thoughts, *Shi* would make their own choice as to when and how to attach themselves to or detach themselves from worldly affairs.

However, their detachment is always relative, because all human beings are social beings. The transcending of one's social attributes can only be by degree, to a certain extent or in a certain sense. Meanwhile individual *Shi* differs from each other in experience and personality. In *This Human World*, Chuang Tsu conveys his own choice by structuring the order in which the characters appear. Firstly Confucius and Yen Huei, then Ye Gongzi Gao, then Yan He, and finally Jie Yu. In fact, the presenting of these characters describes three relations: Yen Huei represents a kind of intellectual full of enthusiasm who wants to save the world; Ye Gongzi Gao and Yan He etc, are people who are already involved in political power and order; Jie Yu is a person who determines to keep a distance from the world and acts as a detached observer. Chuang Tsu adopts the last attitude.②

Like Chuang Tsu, some traditional Chinese intellectuals adopted the attitude of escapism. When they were frustrated with the present situation, they chose to withdraw from a world full of troubles. Having been too disappointed to involve themselves in the present world, they retained no interest in politics and held no illusions about the future of society. They lived in seclusion in the mountains and by the streams. Nature, as always, became a world outside the world, a refuge for disheartened intellectuals from society.

Shen Sanbo (Shen Fu) was a representative of such kind. Depicted in his autobiographical fiction *Six Chapters of a Floating Life*, he was leading an idyllic life with his wife Yun, who was praised by Lin Yutang the translator as "one of the loveliest of women in Chinese literature" (Lin, *Preface* 20)③ Shen is a characteristical traditional Chinese intellectual, or scholar-official, who was "aloof from world affairs and material pursuits," and

---

① See Wang, 2004.
② See Wang, 2004.
③ See Lin's Preface to *Six Chapters of a Floating Life*. Shen, 20.

CHAPTER FOUR
WISDOM AND/OR WEAKNESS

"'lived a straight life and ha[d] a free conscience'" (Yue 42). ① He sets a typical image of Chinese *Shi* who enjoyed free life with free souls.

Different from Shen Sanbo, Lin Yutang, the very translator of *Six Chapters of a Floating Life*, also a famous lexicographer and literary figure, acted in another way as an intellectual. Caught in a similar dilemma to that of those intellectuals mentioned above, he had to face "the age-old problem of how to serve without becoming corrupted and how to retain self-respect when out of office or favor" (Yue 143). But unlike Shen Sanbo, Lin seemed to have participated in many worldly activities, with a conscience but without the goal of earning fame or money. He was a keen observer of what was going on in the world. But at the same time, he was an actor, acting as an intellectual, *speaking* courageously to those in power.

China in 1930s witnessed turmoil, feudal warlords fighting one another incessantly. Lin wrote articles to criticize the corruption and ineffectiveness of the government. Offending the government, his name was on the list when Duan Qirui ordered the arrest of some fifty professors and newspaper men who were charged because of their criticizing the government. Under political pressure, in adverse circumstances, he still retained self-respect and continued to act as an intellectual, as a person of integrity. He started the publication of *Analects*, a bi-monthly magazine specializing in humor and satire, mocking the absurdity of life. He laid bare the troubles of the society in his book *My Country and My People*, holding hope for the future, for the improvement of China. Not surprisingly, the book was not welcomed by those who were politically motivated. In contrast to them, Lin's response was more typical of a modern intellectual. As he claims, "If a man must be a writer, he should have some courage and speak his mind" (Lin, *Forward* 10).

Some intellectuals may not behave as Lin did. They either choose to live a secluded life, being far away from the present world, or to live a worldly life, but wisely. For those who lead a life in seclusion, they also differ. Some decide to live the life, caring no

---

① For more detailed analysis, see Yue, 38—56.

longer for worldly issues. Some are in fact waiting for the right time to reenter the world, making contributions to better the world. They will return from their seclusion if a moral king appears. For example, Zhuge Liang is considered as this type of intellectual in Chinese literature. "He is the servant of the nation, the man whose talents are drawn upon to the benefit of all" (Yue 136). He finally agreed to aid Liu Bei when he took Liu as a wise and moral lord, after Liu's persistent visits to his shabby thatched cottage.

Similarly, Chaucer had kept a low profile after he successfully saved himself from indictments by making a series of prudent adjustments of his relation with the court party. But he returned to the court soon after Richard II's reassertion of his authority in 1389, and became one of the two "old courtiers" soon thereafter "cautiously given preferment" (Strohm, *Politics and Poetics* 97). Thus, to be away from the contemporary world does not necessarily mean to detach oneself from it totally. It is also a strategic measure, a kind of wisdom.

It is also true that both Chaucer and some Chinese *Shi* exhibit their wisdom in their artistic creation. Chaucer was obliged to make decisions about the uses of art in the service of faction. Unlike Usk who "embraced the politics of faction completely," "Chaucer sought ways of containing and moderating the impact of its all-or-nothing approach" (Strohm, *Politics and Poetics* 84). As Strohm states, "In his works, Chaucer mainly avoided direct personal and political commentary, finding a counterpart for his experience of faction on the literary plane of genre- and discourse-conflict" (*Politics and Poetics* 84). In fact, Chaucer has made many strategic comments on society and universal matters, by means of the dream vision form, juxtaposition, restraint, leaving voices silenced and leaving endings unresolved. In this way, he plays his role as an intellectual while exhibiting his wisdom in art and in life.

Weakness or Not?

As has been elaborated previously, Chaucer's artistic strategies are not irrelevant to the social scene of his age. Ideological pressures contribute to Chaucer's intention and changes of intention. It is equally important to examine what he has and has not written in his *Tales*. The absence and silence of any pilgrim and his tale may indicate the author's response to the contemporary scene. The immediate social and textual environment in which he wrote may inevitably have an impact upon his strategies of writing.

Certainly some may not agree with the idea that Chaucer is an intellectual of righteousness and integrity. For these people, only those who show their disregard of and contempt for the authority, those who are fearless in violating and challenging authority are honored as an intellectual. Chaucer was however not aloof from worldly affairs and material pursuits. On the contrary, he enjoyed material gain and access to high ranks mainly from his service for the court. Yet, surrounded by royalty and aristocrats, he was still alert to the problems of society. He composed poems not only to please kings and princes and the like, but to provide proper advice to them, in a unique way that was proper for his position. He challenged authority, though not openly, in his own way with wisdom. His poems explored many aspects of society from various angles. Thus he should not be regarded as a coward or a pure prince-pleaser, caring only for his own benefits, shunning possible blame. He was actually a worldly man with moral judgment, social conscience and wisdom. The strategies he adopted for his poems, at least as a side effect, may attract more attention and tease more reflection from different kinds of audience than pure blunt criticism may allow. He was in fact a wise man who understood the natural law, as the Cook in *Carving Up an Ox* by Chuang Tzu did, and therefore successfully connected the material world and the world of spirit (Wang 191).

Chaucer in some sense resembles the Cook in *Carving Up an Ox*. The Cook understands how to do things according to the natural laws, and the importance of concentration and caution. By his skill in carving up rather than cutting or hacking an ox, he succeeds in getting the job done without any damage to his blade. As Wang Bo interprets it, there are three factors in the tale: the Cook, the blade and the Ox, representing respectively humans, humans' lives and society in real life (Wang 191). Hence, his story inspires Duke Wen Hui to "learn a principle of life" (Wang 191). For me, the principle of life here is also an art of life: to achieve the goal with wisdom instead of through pure bravery. Thus brain rather than brawn is more highly prized. ① The Cook does his job well because firstly he knows exactly the structure of the openings and joints of an Ox, and secondly he does the work with great concentration and caution. Analogously, Chaucer is, in my opinion, also a wise man who perceives situations keenly and makes considered decisions with great care, trying to avoid having a brush with anyone. He resembles the image of Wei Yi which has the characteristics of being tender and amiable, adapting oneself to changing circumstances and acting accordingly. ② He observes established principles, rules and regulations, and follows the general tide.

It is not my intention here to imply that Chaucer is in any sense influenced by this Chinese tale or the philosophy of Taoism. But there is certainly no lack of evidence that Chaucer's response to world affairs is relevant to his access to Boethius' philosophical thought. Seeing how the wheel of Will works, he has understandably made efforts to avoid any face-to-face collision, especial with those in power. He is, generally speaking, a man who is "round outside and square inside," to borrow a Chinese idiom. He is free and unfettered spiritually when he is confined and constrained by his position, his occupation and his social conditions. He is an intelligent person who knows how to adapt himself to the changes in worldly conditions and currents, while staying clean and alert to social ills, making efforts to remedy them in his own unique way.

As Strohm comments, "Chaucer managed through his life to exhibit a more balanced assessment of possibilities, a less headlong plunge toward factional affiliation. So too does his poetry sidestep the temptation to make a direct case, offering instead a mediation of faction" (*Politics and Poetics* 112). Chaucer knows well the art of

---

① It is in fact also what is more favored by the traditional Chinese intellectuals and common people as well. Zhou Yu in *The Three Kingdoms* is one example of such fictional character whose intellect as brilliant strategist rather than his martial prowess impresses and appeals more to the audience.

② Wei Yi is a kind of animal that lives in swamp. It shapes similar to a loach. For detailed information about it, refer to Wang, 2004, 190.

balancing, which significantly demonstrates his wisdom in both his art and life. It becomes more evident and illuminating when it is viewed in the light of the above brief comparison with the traditional Chinese intellectuals, *Shi*, and in the light of Chinese philosophy Daoism. I believe Chaucer's intelligence, or wisdom in his worldly life should not be taken to be equivalent to his shrewdness resulting from cowardice. This wisdom is in fact a manifestation of his wide vision and sharp perception of the world, a character usually represented and employed by an intellectual. Chaucer's artistic devices or textual strategies are not a pure matter of literary art, but a way of playing his role of a social commentator, which is partly the main task of an intellectual.

Conclusion
Possibility of Transcending

Chaucer as an intellectual, so far as has been discussed, has become a more possible and persuasive idea than it first appears. He no longer stands in the background quietly, received and reverenced by his contemporaries and descendants merely as the Father of English Literature. Rather, we may tentatively regard him as on the one hand, a man of great wits, both in his literary world and social life, and on the other hand, a great contributor to the promotion of the common good, through his indirect counseling and indirect manner of social criticism. His more fundamental achievement lies in his role as an enlightener, arousing common people's awareness of subjectivity and stimulating their hidden capacity to make judgments rather than accept any authority blindly.

Certainly, the study of Chaucer as an intellectual is not born out of thin air. In fact, the Middle Ages never lacked intellectuals. Historians in the fifties of the last century displayed enthusiasm in studying this group. They took the first steps in the paths of intellectual history, though their studies focused exclusively on clerics. However, despite different jobs they did, these intellectuals shared some common characters with each other. As Le Goff summarizes,

> It appeared in the High Middle Ages, developed in the town schools of twelfth century, and flourished in the university at the beginning of the thirteen. It denotes those whose profession it was to think and to share their thoughts. This alliance between personal reflection and its

dissemination through instruction characterized the intellectual. (1)

Unlike the medieval intellectuals who first appeared in the twelfth century, who were translators, specialists who introduced Greek philosophy and science, Chaucer played a combined role as both royal servant and court poet. Yet, the tradition Chaucer inherited contributed to his being an intellectual in the special sense. Ancient Hellenism communicates with Western Latin heritage, bringing their curiosity, their reasoning to Christians. Therefore, Chaucer's poetry is remarkably filled with his curiosity about nature and science, as well as the theme of reason.

On the other hand, Chaucer's intellectuality also originates from another group of medieval intellectuals, "a strange group of intellectuals, the goliards" (Le Goff 22—23). They were sometimes seen as "agitators, those who held the established order in contempt," or "a sort of urban intelligentsia, a revolutionary milieu, open to all forms of opposition against feudalism" (Le Goff 25). The birth of such medieval intellectuals was never irrelevant to the social mobility characteristic of that age. They were "escapees from the established structures" (Le Goff 26). Attacking society constituted one of the themes of their poetry.

Like the twelfth century, the fourteenth century witnessed a more mobile social order. Chaucer, unlike the goliards in the twelfth century though, who had to worry about going hungry as the Parisian students did, could not fit himself neatly into the established social structure either. Thus his marginal position permits him to watch and wonder at the happenings in and out of his social circles. Hence in Chaucer there exists a certain kind of revolutionary, but not rebellious spirit. Therefore his reflection and criticism of social reality is naturally more stimulating, if not more irritating.

Certainly, he was not the only intellectual of his time in this sense. Gower, the man to whom Chaucer dedicated his *Troilus*, was also concerned with many social problems. Similar to Chaucer, he observed some social and royal problems against the historical scene too. But his interest and emphasis were different from Chaucer. He was rather a moral instructor, as his epithet "moral Gower" usually indicated. Another shining star of Chaucer's time is Langland.

Unlike Chaucer and Gower, Langland wrote for a wider audience, not only for Londoners and aristocrats, but also for the public. Yet, what he dealt with had more to do with religious issues, with the shepherds and the sheep.

Chaucer also resembles Peter Abelard, "the glory of the Parisian milieu". Peter was regarded as "the first great modern intellectual figure—within the limits of the term 'modernity' in the twelfth century" (Le Goff 35). Aside from his being a logician, a moralist, a theologian, Abelard was a humanist, who proclaimed more than any others the alliance of reason and faith (Le Goff 47). He acknowledged that "fides quaerens intellectum" (faith itself seeking understanding) (Le Goff 47). At this point, Chaucer seems to be an inheritor of Abelard. His writing in the vernacular has the effect of helping everybody to gain knowledge. He would agree willingly with Peter of Blois that "(o)ne does not go from the darkness of ignorance to the light of knowledge, without rereading with ever more ardent love the works of the Ancients" (qtd. in Le Goff 10).

Chaucer was never far from absorbing nourishment from the great ancients. However, it is also without doubt that he never really imitated with servility. The food of ancient thoughts laid the foundation of his rather modern ideas, the ideas that were more advanced than the ancients, and even those of his contemporaries, as illustrated above. Chaucer was modern rather than medieval in the logic of his thinking. He seemed to be more in the age of Renaissance, standing side by side with Shakespeare, sharing the comic spirit combined with a serious theme. He was not a mere man-of-letter, but a thinker, a philosopher.

Chaucer was, in a sense, an intellectual, if it is difficult to accept him as an intellectual in the modern sense, holding an oppositional gesture toward power. He was an intellectual because of his strong social conscience, his habits of reflection, and his enlightening endeavors. It is not proper in any case to emphasize modern intellectuality in him in the sense of being opposed to power. We should not expect him to go that far. Located in the toils of the royal circles, he was inevitably trapped to some extent by his position. Yet, his wide worldly experience both in England and Europe enabled him to achieve a wider vision. What he attempted have already transcended the border of his age.

A study on Chaucer as an intellectual attempts to provide a new perspective for reading Chaucer's canon, and hopefully for seeing something that has not yet been fully explored. Certainly Jones has praised directly Chaucer's intellectuality as in the following quote: "He was one of the most prominent members of his society—one might even say the intellectual superstar of his time. He was certainly celebrated by his contemporaries as their greatest living poet, rhetorician and scholar" (3). I have attempted to extend the understanding and significance of him as an intellectual. In fact, embodied in Chaucer are the features of both medieval and modern intellectuals. He speaks the truth to power, though in an indirect and wise way; he plays the role of enlightener and helps to arouse and cultivate the subjectivity of the public. Such a study allows us to see beyond Chaucer's poetic endeavor and achievement and get a fuller view of how his artistic choices are influenced by and interact with his social position and the social scene of his age.

Finally, I would cite the famous quotation by Bernard of Chartres to end this book, though it is such a familiar saying as to have become a cliché. "We are dwarfs perched on the shoulders of giants. We therefore see more and farther than they, not because we have keener vision or greater height, but because we are lifted up and born aloft on their gigantic stature" (qtd. in Le Goff 12). It is a fact that I owe so much to previous studies on Chaucer and on the intellectual. On the other hand, I do hope, humbly, that some new and different landscapes I have captured through this study contribute to the understanding of Chaucer and the notion of intellectual, and thus achieve, in a sense, some transcendence in this field for the new insights it provides.

Selected Bibliography

Primary Sources

Abrams, M. H., and Stephen Greenblatt, eds. *The Norton Anthology of English Literature*. 7th ed. Vol 1A: The Middle Ages. New York: Norton, 2000.

Bai, Juyi. "A Song of Unending Sorrow". ⟨http://academic.evergreen.edu/curricular/asiancultureart/sorrow.html⟩

Benson, L. D., ed. *The Riverside Chaucer*. 3rd ed. Oxford: Oxford University Press, 1988.

Boethius. *Consolation of Philosophy*. Trans. with Introduction and Notes by Richard H. Green. Mineola, NY: Dover Publications, 2002.

Brewer, D. S., ed. *The Parlement of Foulys*. Old & Middle English Texts. Manchester: Manchester University Press, 1972.

Chaucer, Geoffrey. *The Canterbury Tales*. Trans. Nevill Coghill. Harmondsworth: Penguin Books, 1960.

———. *The Works of Geoffrey Chaucer*. Ed. F. N. Robinson. 2nd ed. Oxford and New York: Oxford University Press, 1986.

———. *Troilus and Criseyde*. Trans. Nevill Coghill. London: Penguin Books, 1971.

Confucius. *The Analects*. Trans. Arthur Waley. Beijing: Foreign Languages Teaching and Research Publishing House, 1998.

De Lorris, Guillaume, and Jean de Meun. *The Romance of the Rose*. Trans. Charles Dahlberg. Hanover: University press of New England, 1983.

Phillips, Helen, and Nick Havely, eds. *Chaucer's Dream Poetry*. London and New York: Longman, 1997.

Shen, Fu. *Six Chapters of a Floating Life*. Trans. Lin Yutang. Beijing: Foreign Language Teaching and Research Press, 1999.

Secondary Sources

Aers, David. *Chaucer*. Brighton: Harvester, 1986.
——. *Chaucer, Langland and the Creative Imagination*. London: Routledge and Kegan Paul, 1980.
Alford, John A. "The Wife of Bath Versus the Clerk of Oxford: What Their Rivalry Means", *The Chaucer Review* 21 (1986): 108—132.
Allen, Mark, and John Fisher. *The Essential Chaucer: An Annotated Bibliography of Major Modern Studies*. London: Mansell Publishing Limited, 1987.
Allen, Valerie, and Ares Axiotis, eds. *New Casebooks: Chaucer*. Basingstoke: Macmillan, 1997.
Ashton, Gail. *Chaucer: The Canterbury Tales*. Basingstoke and London: Macmillan, 1998.
——. Feminisms. *Chaucer, an Oxford Guide*. Ed. Steve Ellis, Oxford: Oxford University Press, 2005. 369—383.
Askins, William. "The Tale of Melibee and the Crisis at Westminster, November, 1387", *Studies in the Age of Chaucer. Proceedings* 2 (1986): 103—112.
Astell, Ann. Introduction. *Political Allegory in Late Medieval England*. Ithaca: Cornell University Press, 1999. 1—22.
——. Chaucer's Ricardian Allegories. *Political Allegory in Late Medieval England*. Ithaca: Cornell University Press, 1999. 94—116.
Barr, Helen, ed. *The Piers Plowman Tradition*, Everyman. London: J. M. Dent, 1993.
——. *Socioliterary Practice in Late Medieval England*. Oxford: Oxford University Press, 2001.
——. "A Study of Mum and the Sothsegger in its Political and Literary Contexts". Diss. University of Oxford, 1989.
Behrman, M. D. "Chaucer, Gower and the vox populi: Interpretation and the common profit in the 'Canterbury Tales' and 'Confessio Amantis.'" Diss. Emory University, 2004.
Belsey, Catherine. *Critical Practice*. 2nd ed. London and New York: Routledge, 2002.
Benda, Julien. *The Treason of the Intellectuals*. Trans. Richard Aldington. London: Norton, 1980.
Benson, L. D., and Siegfried Wensel. *The Wisdom of Poetry: Essays in Early English Literature in Honor of Morton W. Bloomfield*. Kalamazoo: Medieval Institute Publications, 1982.

Besserman, Lawrence. "Ideology, Antisemitism, and Chaucer's Prioress's Tale", *The Chaucer Review* 36.1 (2001): 48—72.

Birney, Earle. *Essays on Chaucerian Irony*. Ed. and with an Essay on Irony by Beryl Rowland. Toronto: University of Toronto Press, 1985.

Bisson, L. M. *Chaucer and the Late Medieval World*. New York: St. Martin's Press, 1998.

Blamires, Alcuin. *The* Canterbury Tales: *An Introduction to the Variety of Criticism*. London: MacMillan, 1987.

Bloomfield, M. W., and Charles W. Dunn. *The Role of the Poet in Early Society*. Cambridge: D. S. Brewer, 1989.

Boitani, Piero, and Jill Mann, eds. *The Cambridge Companion to Chaucer*. Cambridge: Cambridge University Press, 1986.

Bowers, J. M. Chaucer's Canterbury Tales—Politically Corrected. *Rewriting Chaucer*. Ed. Thomas A. Prendergast and Barbara Kline. Columbus: Ohio State University Press, 1999. 13—44.

Brewer, Derek, ed. *Chaucer: The Critical Heritage*. The Critical Heritage Series, 2 vols. London, Henley and Boston: Routledge & Kegan Paul, 1978.

——. *A New Introduction to Chaucer*. 2nd ed. London and New York: Longman, 1998.

Brinton, Laurel J. "Chaucer's 'Tale of Melibee': A Reassessment", *English Studies in Canada* X. 3 (1984): 251—261.

Bronfman, Judith. *Chaucer's Clerk's Tale: the Griselda Story Received, Rewritten, Illustrated*. New York and London: Garland Publishing, 1994.

Brown, Andrew. *Church and Society in England*, 1000—1500. Social History in Perspective. Basingstoke: Palgrave Macmillan, 2003.

Brown, Peter, and Andrew Butcher. *The Age of Saturn: Literature and History in the* Canterbury Tales. Oxford: Blackwell, 1991.

Brown, Peter, ed. *A Companion to Chaucer*. Oxford: Blackwell, 2002.

Burrow, J. A. The Poet as Petitioner. *Essays on Medieval Literature*. Oxford: Oxford University Press, 1984. 161—176.

——. *Ricardian Poetry: Chaucer, Gower, Langland and the "Gawain" Poet*. London: Routledge and Kegan Paul, 1971.

——. *Medieval Writers and their Work: Middle English Literature* 1100—1500. Oxford and New York: Oxford University Press, 1982.

——. ed. *A Critical Anthology: Geoffrey Chaucer*. Harmondsworth: Penguin Books Ltd, 1969.

Carlson, David R. *Chaucer's Jobs*. New York: Palgrave Macmillan, 2004.

Chesterton, G. K. *Chaucer*. London: Faber & Faber, 1932.

Coghill, Nevill. *The Poet Chaucer*. London: Oxford University Press, 1949.

Coleman, Janet. The Literature of Social Unrest. *Medieval Readers and Writers* 1350—1400. New York: Columbia University Press, 1981. 58—156.

Colish, Marcia L. *Medieval Foundations of the Western Intellectual Tradition*, 400—1400. The Yale Intellectual History of the West. New Haven and London: Yale University Press, 1997.

Collette, Carolyn P. *Species, Phantasms, and Images: Vision and Medieval Psychology in the Canterbury Tales*. Ann Arbor: University of Michigan Press, 2001.

Cooper, Helen. *The Structure of The Canterbury Tales*. London: Duckworth, 1983.

———. *Oxford Guides to Chaucer: The Canterbury Tales*. Oxford: Clarendon Press, 1989.

Copeland, Rita. *Pedagogy, Intellectuals, and Dissent in the Later Middle Ages: Lollardy and Ideas of Learning*. Cambridge: Cambridge University Press, 2001.

Coulton, G. G. *Chaucer and His England*. London: Methuen, 1952.

Coser, Lewis. *Men of Ideas*. New York: Free Press, 1965.

Crow, Martin M., and Clair C. Olson, eds. *Chaucer Life—Records*. Oxford: Clarendon Press, 1966.

Curry, Walter Clyde. *Chaucer and the Medieval Sciences*, 2nd ed. New York: Barnes & Noble, 1960.

Dalrymple, Roger, ed. *Middle English Literature: A Guide to Criticism*. Blackwell Guides to Criticism. Oxford: Blackwell Publishing, 2004.

David, Alfred. *The Strumpet Muse: Art and Morals in Chaucer's Poetry*. Bloomington: Indiana University Press, 1976.

Davis, Norman, et al, eds. *A Chaucer Glossary*. Oxford: Oxford University Press, 1979.

Dean, James M. Introduction. *Richard the Redeless and Mum and the Sothsegger*, Kalamazoo: Western Michigan University, 2000. 7—15.

Delany, Sheila. *Chaucer's House of Fame: The Poetics of Skeptical Fideism*. Gainesville: University Press of Florida, 1994.

———. *The Naked Text: Chaucer's Legend of Good Women*. Berkeley: University of California Press, 1994.

———. *Medieval Literary Politics: Shapes of Ideology*. Manchester: Manchester University Press, 1990.

Dillon, Janette. *Geoffrey Chaucer*. Writers in Their Time. New York: St Martin's Press, 1993.

Dinshaw, Carolyn. *Chaucer's Sexual Poetics*. Madison: University of Wisconsin Press, 1989.

Donaldson, E. T. "The Ending of 'Troilus'", *Speaking of Chaucer*, London: The Athlone Press, 1970. 84—101.

Dupre, Louis. *The Enlightenment and the Intellectual Foundations of Modern Culture*. New Haven & London: Yale University Press, 2004.

Edwards, Robert R. *Chaucer and Boccaccio: Antiquity and Modernity*.

Basingstoke: Palgrave, 2002.
Ellis, Steve, ed. *Chaucer: The Canterbury Tales*, Longman Critical Readers. London and New York: Longman, 1998.
——. *Chaucer at Large: the Poet in the Modern Imagination*. Medieval Cultures 24. Minneapolis: University of Minnesota Press, 2000.
——. *Chaucer, an Oxford Guide*. Oxford: Oxford University Press, 2005.
Evan, Ruth. *Feminist Readings in Middle English Literature: the Wife of Bath and all her Sect*. London and New York: Routledge, 1994.
Eyerman, Ron. *Between Culture and Politics: Intellectuals in Modern Society*. Cambridge: Polity Press, 1994.
Fein, Susanna Greer, and David Raybin. *Rebels and Rivals: The Contestive Spirit in the Canterbury Tales*. Studies in Medieval Culture. Kalamazoo: Medieval Institute Publications, 1991.
Ferster, Judith. *Fiction of Advice: The Literature and Politics of Counsel in Late Medieval England*. Philadelphia: University of Pennsylvania Press, 1996.
Finke, Laurie A. *Women's Writing in English: Medieval England*. London and New York: Longman, 1999.
Fletcher, Alan "The Topical Hypocrisy of Chaucer's Pardoner", *The Chaucer Review* 25.2 (1990): 117—20.
Forster, Edward E. "Has Anyone Here Read Melibee?", *The Chaucer Review* 34.4 (2000): 398—409.
Foucault, Michel. What is an Author? *Foucault Reader*. Ed. Paul Rabinow. New York: Pantheon Books, 1984. 101—120.
——. Technologies of the Self. *Technologies of the Self: A Seminar with Michel Foucault*. Eds. Luther H. Martin, Huck Gutman, and Patrick H. Hutton. Amherst: University of Massachusetts Press, 1988. 16—49.
Fradenburg, Louise O. "Criticism, Anti-Semitism and *The Prioress's Tale*", *Exemplaria* 1 (1989): 69—115.
Fruedi, Frank. *Where Have All the Intellectuals Gone?* Trans. Dai Congrong. Nanjing: JSPPH, 2005.
Fung Yu-lan. *Chuang-Tzu: A Taoist Classic*. Beijing: Foreign Languages Press, 1991.
Goldie, Matthew Boyd, ed. *Middle English Literature: A Historical Sourcebook*. Oxford: Blackwell, 2003.
Grace, Dominick. "Telling Differences: Chaucer's *Tale of Melibee* and Renaud De Louens' *Livre De Mellibee et Prudence*", *Philological Quarterly* 82:4 (2003): 367—400.
Gramsci, Antonio. *The Prison Notebooks: Selections*. Trans. Quintin Hoare and Geoffrey Nowell-Smith. New York: International Publishers, 1971.
Green, Richard Firth. "Ricardian 'Trouthe': A Legal Perspective", *Essays on*

Ricardian Literature in Honour of J. A. Burrow. Eds. A. J. Minnis, Charlotte C. Morse and Thorlac Turville-Petre. Oxford: Clarendon Press, 1997. 179—202.

——. *Poets and Princepleasers: Literature and the English Court in the Late Middle Ages*. Toronto, Buffalo and London: University of Toronto Press, 1980.

——. *A Crisis of Truth: Literature and Law in Ricardian England*. Philadelphia: University of Pennsylvania Press, 1999.

Grudin, Michaela Paasche. *Chaucer and the Politics of Discourse*. Columbia: University of South Carolina Press, 1996.

Hansen, Elaine Tuttle. *Chaucer and the Fiction of Gender*. Berkeley and Los Angeles: University of California Press, 1992.

Hirshi, John C. *Chaucer and the Canterbury Tales: a Short Introduction*. Blackwell Introduction to Literature. Oxford: Blackwell, 2003.

Howard, Donald R. *The Idea of the Canterbury Tales*. Berkeley: University of California Press, 1976.

Hussey, S. S. *Chaucer: An Introduction*, 2nd ed. London: Methuen, 1971.

Jacoby, Russell. *The Last Intellectuals: American Culture in the Age of Academe*, Trans. Hong Jie. Nanjing: JSPPH, 2002.

Jameson, Fredric. *The Political Unconscious*. Ithaca: Cornell University Press, 1981.

Jeffrey, David Lyle, ed. *Chaucer and the Scriptural Tradition*. Ottawa: University of Ottawa Press, 1984.

Johnson, Lynn Staley. "Inverse Counsel: Contexts for the Melibee", *Studies in Philology* 87.2 (1990): 137—155.

Johnston, Andrew James. *Clerks and Courtiers: Chaucer, Late Middle English Literature and the State Formation Process*. Heidelberg: Winter, 2001.

Jones, Terry, et al. *Who Murdered Chaucer? A Medieval Mystery*. London: Methuen, 2004.

Justice, Steven. *Writing and Rebellion: England in 1381*. The New Historicism: Studies in Cultural Poetics 27. Berkeley, Los Angeles and London: University of California Press, 1994.

Keller, Douglas. "Intellectuals, the New Public Spheres, and Techno-Politics", *New Political Science* 41—42 (1997) 〈http://www. brooklynsoc. org/toulouse/cyberpol/ kellner. html〉

Kittredge, George Lyman. *Chaucer and His Poetry: Lectures Delivered in 1914 on the Percy Turnbull Memorial Foundation in the John Hopkins University*. Cambridge: Harvard University Press, 1915.

Klassen, Norman. "Two Chaucers", *Medium Aevum* 68.1 (1999): 96—104.

Knapp, Peggy. *Chaucer and the Social Contest*. New York and London: Routledge, 1990.

Knight, Stephen. "Ideology in 'The Franklin's Tale'", *Parergon* 28 (1980): 3—35.

——. *Geoffrey Chaucer*. Rereading Literature. Oxford: Blackwell, 1986.

Kuczynski, Michael P. "'Don't Blame Me': The Metaethics of a Chaucerian Apology", *The Chaucer Review* 37.4 (2003): 315—328.

Lawton, David. *Chaucer's Narrators*. Cambridge: D. S. Brewer, 1985.

Le Goff, Jacque. *Intellectuals in the Middle Ages*. Trans. Teresa Lavender Fagan. Cambridge MA & Oxford UK: Blackwell, 1993.

Lewis, C. S. *The Discarded Image: An Introduction to Medieval and Renaissance Literature*. Cambridge: Cambridge University Press, 1964.

Lin, Taiyi. Forward. *Six Chapters of a Floating Life*. By Shen Fu. Trans. Lin Yutang. Beijing: Foreign Language Teaching and Research Press, 1999. 5—16.

Lin, Yutang. Preface. *Six Chapters of a Floating Life*. By Shen Fu. Trans. Lin Yutang. Beijing: Foreign Language Teaching and Research Press, 1999. 20—23.

Liu, Naiyin. *Reading The Canterbury Tales: A Bakhtinian Approach*. Shanghai: East China Normal University Press, 1999.

Lipset, S. M. *Political Man*. New York: Doubleday, 1960.

Lynch, Andrew. "'Manly cowardyse': Thomas Hoccleve's peace strategy", *Medium Aevum* 73.2 (2004): 306—323.

Machan, Tim William. Textual Authority and the Works of Hoccleve, Lydgate, and Henryson. *Writing After Chaucer: Essential Reading in Chaucer and the Fifteenth Century*. Ed. Daniel J. Pinti. New York and London: Garland, 1998. 177—199.

Mann, Jill. *Chaucer and Medieval Estates Satire*. Cambridge: Cambridge University Press, 1976.

——. *Geoffrey Chaucer*. Feminist Reading. New York: Harvester Wheatsheaf, 1991.

Medcalf, Stephen. "On Reading Books from a Half-alien Culture", *The Later Middle Ages*. The Context of English Literature. London: Methuen, 1981. 1—55.

Mehl, Dieter. *English Literature in the Age of Chaucer*. Longman Literature in English Series. Harlow: Longman, 2001.

Middleton, Anne. "The Idea of Public Poetry in the Reign of Richard II", *Speculum* 53 (1978): 94—114.

Miller, Robert P, ed. *Chaucer: Sources and Backgrounds*. Oxford: Oxford University Press, 1977.

Minnis, Alastair. *Medieval Theory of Authorship: Scholastic Literary Attitudes in the Later Middle Ages*. 2nd ed. Aldershot: Wildwood House Ltd, 1988.

Minnis. A. J., et al. *Oxford Guides to Chaucer: The Shorter Poems*. Oxford: Clarendon Press, 1995.

Moore, Stephen G. "Apply Yourself: Learning while Reading the *Tale of*

Melibee", *The Chaucer Review* 38. 1 (2003): 83—97.
Morgan, Gerald. "Moral and Social Identity and the Idea of Pilgrimage in the General Prologue", *The Chaucer Review* 37. 4 (2003): 285—314.
Muscatine, Charles. *Chaucer and the French Tradition: a Study in Style and Meaning.* Berkeley, Los Angeles, London: University of California Press, 1957.
——. *Medieval Literature, Style, and Culture.* Columbia: University of South Carolina Press, 1999.
Olson, Gary and Lynn Worsham. *Critical Intellectuals on Writing.* Albany: State University of New York Press, 2003.
Olson, Glending. Chaucer. *The Cambridge History of Medieval English Literature.* Ed. by David Wallace. Cambridge: Cambridge University Press, 1999. 566—588.
Olsen, Paul A. *The Canterbury Tales and the Good Society.* Princeton: Princeton University Press, 1986.
Patterson, Lee. *Chaucer and the Subject of History.* Madison: University of Wisconsin Press, 1991.
——. "'No Man His Reson Herde': Peasant Consciousness, Chaucer's Miller, and the Structure of the Canterbury Tales", *Literary Practice and Social Change in Britain, 1380—1530.* Berkeley, Los Angeles and Oxford: University of California Press, 1990. 113—55.
——. *Negotiating the Past: The Historical Understanding of Medieval Literature.* Madison: University of Wisconsin Press, 1987.
Pearsall, Derek. "Hoccleve's Regement of Princes: The Poetics of Royal Self-Representation", *Speculum* 69. 2 (1994): 386—410.
——. *The Canterbury Tales.* London and New York: Routledge, 1985.
——. *The Life of Geoffrey Chaucer: A Critical Biography.* Blackwell Critical Biographies 1. Oxford: Blackwell, 1992.
Peck, Russell. A. "Social Conscience and the Poets", *Social Unrest in the Late Middle Ages: Papers of the Fifteenth Annual Conference of the Center for Medieval and Early Renaissance Studies.* Ed. Francis X. Newman. Binghamton: Medieval and Renaissance Texts and Studies, 1986. 113—148.
Phillips, Helen. "Register, Politics, and the *Legend of Good Women*", *The Chaucer Review.* 37. 2 (2002): 101—128.
——. *An Introduction to the Canterbury Tales: Reading, Fiction, Context.* Basingstoke and London: Macmillan, 2000.
——. Dream Poems. *A Companion to Medieval English Literature and Culture C. 1350—C. 1500.* Ed. Peter Brown. Oxford: Blackwell Publishing, 2007. 374—386.
Pope, Rob. *How to Study Chaucer.* Basingstoke: Macmillan Education, 1988.
Powell, Stephen D. "Game Over: Defragmenting the End of the *Canterbury Tales*", *The Chaucer Review* 37. 1 (2002): 40—58.

Prendergast, Thomas A., and Kline, Barbara. *Rewriting Chaucer: Culture, Authority, and the Idea of the Authentic Text, 1400—1602*. Columbus: Ohio State University Press, 1999.

Quintero, Ruben. *A Companion to Satire. Ancient and Modern*. Blackwell Companions to Literature and Culture. Oxford: Blackwell, 2007.

Rabinow, Paul. *Foucault Reader*. New York: Pantheon Books, 1984.

Rigby, S. H. *Chaucer in Context*. Manchester: Manchester University Press, 1996.

——. Society and Politics. *Chaucer: An Oxford Guide*. Ed. Steve Ellis. Oxford: Oxford University Press, 2005. 26—49.

Robertson, D. W. Jr. "The Historical Setting of Chaucer's Book of the Duchess", *Essays in Medieval Culture*. Princeton: Princeton University Press, 1980. 255—256.

Rooney, Anne. *Geoffrey Chaucer: A Guide through the Critical Maze*. Bristol: Bristol Classical Press, 1989.

Rowland, Beryl. *Companion to Chaucer Studies*. Oxford: Oxford University Press, 1979.

Rudd, Gillian. *The Complete Critical Guide to Geoffrey Chaucer*. London and New York: Routledge, 2001.

Said, Edward. *Representations of the Intellectual*. London: Vintage, 1994.

Salter, E. "Chaucer and Boccaccio: The Knight's Tale", *Fourteenth-Century English Poetry: Contexts and Reading*. Oxford: Oxford University Press, 1983. 141—181.

Saunders, Corrine, ed. *Chaucer*. Oxford: Blackwell, 2001.

Scala, Elizabeth. *Absent Narratives, Manuscript Textuality, and Literary Structures in Late Medieval England*. New York and Basingstoke: Palgrave Macmillan, 2002.

Scanlon, Larry. *Narrative, Authority and Power: The Medieval Exemplum and the Chaucerian Tradition*. Cambridge Studies in Medieval Literature 20. Cambridge: Cambridge University Press, 1994.

Scattergood, V. J. *Politics and Poetry in the Fifteenth Century*. London: Blandford, 1971.

Schoff, Rebecca Lynn. "Freedom from the Press: Reading and Writing in Later Medieval England". Diss. Harvard University, 2004.

Shepherd, Geoffrey. "Religion and Philosophy in Chaucer", *Geoffrey Chaucer. Writers and Their Background*. Ed. Derek Brewer. London: G. Bell & Sons, 1974.

Spearing, A. C. *Chaucer: Troilus and Criseyde*. Studies in English Literature 59. London: Edward Arnold Ltd, 1976.

Spiegel, Gabrielle M. "History, Historicism, and the Social Logic of the Text in the Middle Ages", *Speculum* 65.1 (1990): 59—86.

Starkey, David. "The Age of the Household: Politics, Society and the Arts c. 1350—c. 1550", *The Later Middle Ages*. The Context of English Literature. Ed. Stephen Medcalf. London: Methuen & Co Ltd, 1981. 225—290.

Stillwell, Gardiner. "The Political Meaning of Chaucer's *Tale of Melibee*", *Speculum* 19 (1944): 433—444.

Strohm, Paul. "The Social and Literary Scene in England", *The Cambridge Chaucer Companion*. Ed. Piero Boitani and Jill Mann. Cambridge: Cambridge University Press, 1986. 1—18.

——. *Hochon's Arrow: The Social Imagination of Fourteenth-Century Texts*. Princeton: Princeton University Press, 1992.

——. *Theory and the Premodern Text*. Medieval Cultures 26. Minneapolis and London: University of Minnesota Press, 2000.

——. "Politics and Poetics: Usk and Chaucer in the 1380s", *Literary Practice and Social Change in Britain, 1380—1530*. Ed. Lee Patterson, 1990. 83—112.

——. *Social Chaucer*. Cambridge: Harvard University Press, 1989.

Swanson, Robert. "Social Structure", *A Companion to Chaucer*. Ed. Peter Brown. Oxford: Blackwell, 2002. 397—413.

Tchalian, Houig. "Noble Counsel in the age of Chaucer and Langland: Authority, Dissent and the Political Community". Diss. University of California, 2005.

Wagenknecht, Edward, ed. *Chaucer: Modern Essays in Criticism*. New York: Oxford University Press, 1959.

Wallace, David. *Chaucerian Polity: Absolute Lineage and Associational Forms in England and Italy*. Stanford: Stanford University Press, 1997.

——. ed. *The Cambridge History of Medieval Literature*. Cambridge: Cambridge University Press, 1999.

Warren, M. L. "Griselda's 'Unnatural Restraint' as a Technology of the Self", *Middle English Literature: Chaucer*. 1998. ORB: The Online Reference Book for Medieval Studies. Ed. Kathryn M. Talarico. 2003. ⟨http://www.the-orb.net/encyclo.html⟩

Watt, Diane. *Amoral Gower: Language, Sex, and Politics*. Medieval Cultures 38. Minneapolis: University of Minnesota Press, 2003.

Wetherbee, Winthrop. "Some Intellectual Themes in Chaucer's Poetry", *Geoffrey Chaucer: A Collection of Original Articles*. Ed. George D Economou. New York: McGraw-Hill, 1975. 75—91.

Williams, Raymond. *Keywords: A Vocabulary of Culture and Society*. New York: Oxford University Press, 1983.

Wogan-Browne, Jocelyn, et al. *The Idea of the Vernacular: An Anthology of Middle English Literary Theory 1280—1520*. Exeter: University of Exeter Press, 1999.

Wood, Chauncey. *Chaucer and the Country of the Stars*. Princeton: Princeton

University Press, 1970.

Woolf, Virginia. *The Common Reader*. First Series. Ed. Andrew McNeillie. London: Hogarth Press, 1984.

Yue, Daiyun. *Intellectuals in Chinese Fiction*. China Research Monograph. Institute of East Asian Studies. Berkeley: University of California, 1988.

Zhang, Zhongzai. *Selected Readings in Classical Western Critical Theory*. Beijing: Foreign Language Teaching and Research Press, 2000.

葛荃.《权力宰制理性——士人、传统政治文化与中国政治》.天津:南开大学出版社,2004.

王博.《庄子哲学》.北京:北京大学出版社,2004.

王增进.《后现代与知识分子的社会位置》.北京:中国社会科学出版社,2003.

肖明翰.《乔叟:英国文学之父》.北京:中国社会科学出版社,2005.

余英时.《士与中国文化》.上海:上海人民出版社,2003.